THE LAST ROMAN

Hammer of God

B.K. GREENWOOD

COPYRIGHT

Hammer of God

A Last Roman Story

Copyright © **2023 B.K. Greenwood**

All rights reserved.

www.bkgreenwood.com

No part of this publication may be reproduced, distributed, or transmitted in any form or by any means, including photocopying, recording, or other electronic or mechanical methods, without the prior writtn permission of the publisher.

This is a work of fiction. Any similarity between the characters and situations within its pages and places or persons, living or dead, is unintentional and coincidental.

Cover Artist **Dusan Arsenic**

Edited by **Gareth Clegg**

Published by:

Bat City Press 2023 Austin, Texas, USA

www.batcitypress.com

DEDICATED TO:

To my daughter McKenna;
a constant source of motivation, joy, and pride.

CONTENTS

Prologue	1
Chapter 1	7
Chapter 2	13
Chapter 3	31
Chapter 4	46
Chapter 5	65
Chapter 6	85
Chapter 7	95
Chapter 8	103
Chapter 9	110
Chapter 10	125
Chapter 11	133
Chapter 12	143
Chapter 13	161
Chapter 14	174
Chapter 15	203
Chapter 16	224
Chapter 17	234
Epilogue	246
Dear Readers	253
Stay Connected!	255
Please leave a Review	257
About the Author	259
Also By B.K. Greenwood	261

PROLOGUE

Revenge... is like a rolling stone, which, when a man hath forced up a hill, will return upon him with a greater violence, and break those bones whose sinews gave it motion.
—Jeremy Taylor

42 A.D.
Antioch

Marcus stared down at his half-empty cup of wine. The nearby pitcher was empty, so he didn't bother reaching for it. The innkeeper made it clear that no more wine was coming unless Marcus provided more coins. Without more wine, he would be sober within the hour. That was the last thing he wanted.

Marcus looked up, his bleary eyes scanning the dimly lit chamber. The orange coals in the distant fireplace simmered in the darkness, a fading reminder of the once blazing fire. A few random candles did what they could to light the room. It was enough for Marcus to make out a few remaining patrons, drunk like himself. The innkeeper was nowhere to be seen.

Marcus drained the rest of the bitter wine and dropped the cup onto the table. It fell on its side, a thin bead of liquid spilling out onto the worn wooden surface. He leaned forward, one hand rubbing his forehead and squeezing his temples. *Five years,* he thought, *five years since that damn battle in Gaul.* He had found his wife, but not his son and daughter. Marcus had spent the last three years chasing down every lead, crisscrossing the Roman Empire. Wanted for murder in three provinces, Marcus was a suspect in half a dozen more. He had killed so many slave traders, the word had spread. Now they all traveled with gangs of armed men. Despite his abilities and conviction, even Marcus couldn't fight his way through a dozen men.

Not that it mattered. He was out of money and out of leads. He thought about giving up the search, but he was not sure he could face the giant pit in his soul. But then again, no amount of wine or dead bodies could fill that pit. But he would keep trying.

He reached for the pitcher, knocking it over with his clumsy grasp. A dark figure appeared beside the table and set the pitcher upright with a slender hand. The stranger sat opposite the Roman and pulled the cloak back from his face. His dark skin was clear of blemishes or scars. A beard, clean and trimmed, framed his slender, handsome face, and a pair of sparkling brown eyes studied Marcus in the failing light.

"Who are you?" Marcus's eyes narrowed to slits. One hand slid to the dagger on his belt.

"A friend, if you'll have me." His eyes shifted to the dagger.

"I don't need any friends."

"We all need friends. Friends buy us drinks when we run out of money." He motioned for the innkeeper. "Friends help us find the way when we are lost. And friends tell us when we are in danger."

"I'm not lost, and I'm not in danger."

"That's what someone with no friends would say."

"Who are you?" Marcus leaned forward.

"My name is Thomas. I'm from Judea."

Marcus curled his lips into a sneer and spat on the floor. "I hate that fucking place."

"I'm sure you do." Thomas watched the innkeeper set down another cup and full pitcher, then poured Marcus a cup. "I often feel that way myself."

"And what do you want?"

"Nothing." He handed Marcus the full mug. "I want nothing."

"You understand if I'm skeptical." Marcus took a long pull, his face pinching as he swallowed the sour wine. The innkeeper must have served them his cheapest stock.

"Of course." Thomas took a sip, his lips pursing. "This is awful."

"Yes, it is."

"Do you get used to it?"

"No, and I've drunk an awful lot of it."

Thomas looked down into the liquid and set the mug on the table. His gaze drifted back up to Marcus. "The authorities know you are here."

Marcus nodded, but did not reply. He rubbed the wooden tabletop with his thumb as he waited for Thomas to continue.

"I think it's too late for us to sneak you out of the city."

"Us?" Marcus raised an eyebrow and looked around the room.

"The others are not here."

"Others?" He leaned forward. "Who are these *others*?"

"I have a community of brothers and sisters. We practice a certain faith."

"The 'One-God' people." Marcus leaned back. "You're all troublemakers."

"It would seem so," Thomas exhaled. "But in this case, we are not causing the trouble. I would suspect a large group of legionaries are on their way to arrest you. Something tells me they won't be taking you alive."

Marcus drained his mug and licked his lips. "No, they won't."

"Do me one favor when you crawl from that grave."

Marcus clenched his jaw. The response was a whisper. "How do you know that?"

"You and I share the same fate."

Marcus studied the Judean for a few minutes. "What favor?"

"Join me in Jerusalem."

"And why would I do that?"

"Because your wife is dead, and your children are gone." Thomas leaned forward, his expression softening as he saw the pain his words inflicted. "You can kill a thousand slavers, but that won't bring them back."

"And what's in Jerusalem?" Marcus asked.

"Salvation."

The word had barely slipped from Thomas's lips when a loud bang, of the door slamming into the wall, drew their attention to the entrance. A massive legionary was standing in the opening, gladius drawn. Several others stood behind him.

Marcus rose, the adrenaline cursing through his veins and clearing the drunken fog from his mind. He pulled off his cloak and tossed it on the chair behind him, then drew his sword and dagger. He looked back at Thomas. "Salvation is overrated."

"You!" The legionary pointed at Marcus. "Drop your weapons."

"Now, why would I do that?"

"Because we're going to kill you if you don't."

"That's what I'm depending on."

He feigned an attack to get the soldiers to respond. He had no quarrel with them, and despite his reputation, he did not like to kill fellow legionaries. Two of the men landed what would normally be lethal blows, knocking Marcus to his knees. He dropped both of his weapons as the soldiers pulled the blades free.

Marcus looked up at the leader. "Do it quickly."

The man knew what he meant. He swung his blade around and placed the tip inside Marcus's collarbone, right above his heart. Marcus glanced back at Thomas, their eyes meeting as the legionary shoved the gladius home.

Marcus gasped from the sharp pain, then welcomed the darkness.

CHAPTER ONE

*Do not let spacious plans for a new world
divert your energies from saving what is left of the old.*
—WINSTON CHURCHILL

FALL, 710 A.D.
ROME

Marcus sat opposite Pope Constantine, staring at the dumbest looking hat he had ever seen. It was a sort of crown, with a conical tip that extended at least a foot above his head. The contraption nearly tumbled from his head each time he moved, forcing the pope to reach up and adjust the monstrosity.

The refectory was large enough to seat two-dozen people, but only three of them had stayed beyond dinner, at the request of the Holy Father. A pitcher of wine and three goblets were the only reminder of the meal. Thomas leaned forward and refilled all three cups.

The pope was a fidgety man. Born in Syria, he was familiar with the workings of the Byzantine court. Now in Rome, he was a fish out of water, and struggled with his independent minded clergy. But that was not his primary concern this evening. He ignored the cup Thomas tried to hand to him.

"This is a disaster!" Constantine looked up from the parchment. "Have you read this?"

"Yes, sire," Thomas said. "Wittiza has always struggled to maintain order in Hispania. I'm not surprised they killed him, and the Saracens will take advantage of this situation."

"Of course they will." Constantine held up the letter. "It says they've already made several incursions."

"Yes." Thomas nodded.

"What are you going to do about it?" The pope tossed the letter onto the table in front of them.

"Me?" Thomas stopped the cup halfway to his lips.

Marcus chuckled.

"You think this is funny?" Eyes bulging, the pope glared from Thomas to the Roman.

"No." Marcus shook his head. "The Saracens are anything but funny."

The pope studied him through narrowed eyes. "We cannot afford to let these barbarians capture Hispania, or heaven forbid, push into Gaul."

This time, Marcus suppressed his smile. The *barbarians*, as Constantine called them, were extremely civilized. He looked down at his goblet. If he were sitting in Damascus, it would be made from glass. And filled with ice, if he wanted. The building would have running water and sewers.

"What would you have us do?" Thomas's question snapped Marcus back to the present. "Shall we march an army over to Hispania?"

"Heavens, no. I can barely defend Rome from the

Lombards." Constantine exhaled and rubbed his forehead. "No, you must find another way."

"The Franks." Marcus glanced over at Thomas, trying to ignore the skeptical look on his face.

"The Franks?" the pope repeated. "Pfft, more barbarians. I hear they still practice their pagan rituals."

"Rumors," Thomas said, though he did not sound very convincing. "But I'm not sure they can stand against the Saracens. They are too busy fighting among themselves."

"What about Pepin?" Marcus asked.

"Yes, Pepin. I've heard good things about this man. He is Christian, correct?" The pope looked from Marcus to Thomas.

Thomas smirked. "Mostly."

"How can you be *mostly* Christian?"

"Let's say he doesn't try very hard," Thomas continued, "and he is growing old. I fear there will be a power struggle when he dies."

"Go make sure there isn't," the pope said.

"Excuse me?" Thomas, eyebrows raised, glared back at the pope.

"I will make you my emissary. Do anything to ensure a smooth transition. Use the local clergy if needed. Or any other means necessary. But," the pope's eyes narrowed to tiny slits, "you must find a Christian suitor willing and able to stand against the Saracens."

"We will need gold if we are to back a suitor," Thomas said.

"I will get you the gold." Constantine sat back in his chair. "You find me a Christian champion."

"That was lovely." Marcus opened the door of the refectory, allowing Thomas to go through ahead of him.

"He's a nervous fellow." Thomas grinned.

Marcus followed him into the church beyond, and the pair walked the length of the nave, passing several dozen rows of pews. They pushed open the double doors and stepped into the cool autumn evening. The facade of the Archbasilica towered above them. It was the oldest church in Rome, and home to the pope. But you would never know by looking at it. The surface of the building was faded and dingy, as if time had worn away its resolve.

Marcus looked up at the building and couldn't help but compare it to the current state of his birth city. How far the mighty had fallen. Driving the thought from his mind, he glanced over at Thomas.

"So, what now?"

"Let's talk to Nico." He looked back at Marcus. "He spent a long time in Gaul."

"I'm not sure he wants to go back." Marcus grinned. "I think he said something like *curse that damn land and its lack of sun*."

"That sounds about right."

"And winter is coming."

Thomas smiled, but did not reply.

Twenty minutes later, Thomas and Nico were sitting in the villa of the courtyard they shared. Marcus found a pitcher of wine and walked back into the courtyard.

"Nope. That place is cold and wet, ten months out of the year. I won't see the sun for another six months!" Nico looked up as Marcus arrived and handed him a cup. "Was this your idea?"

"No, I don't come up with the ideas." Marcus poured him some wine and tilted his head toward Thomas. "That's his job."

Nico glared at Thomas, the shadows of the candlelight dancing over his soft, wrinkled face.

"It's important." Thomas took his cup from Marcus and held it while the latter filled it. "I wouldn't ask if there was anyone else."

"What about him?" Nico lifted his goblet toward Marcus.

"You want me to send Marcus on a diplomatic mission?"

"Ah, good point." Nico's face lit up. "Lazarus?"

Thomas shook his head. "He left for Constantinople."

Nico cursed beneath his breath.

Marcus sat and smiled at Thomas, then filled his own cup and took a sip.

"Why aren't you going?" Nico asked.

"I'm going to get Rebecca and Isabella." Thomas sighed. "And I've never been to Gaul. I'm not sure I would know what to do. You, on the other hand, know Pepin."

Marcus watched the exchange, knowing the result. His old friend would do anything Thomas needed. He just needed to complain enough to get it out of his system. After a few cups of wine, he would be ready to pack his bags.

Nico drained his cup and refilled it as he nodded toward Marcus. "Is he going with me? I might need a bodyguard."

Marcus smiled. "You want me to suffer with you?"

"Why not? Somehow I feel like this is your doing."

"No, it's all my idea," Thomas said. "Marcus is going to Hispania. I need to know how bad the situation is."

"Not good, I can tell you." Nico smiled at Marcus. "You'll probably wake up in Gaul a week after you get there."

Marcus grinned back. "Yeah, but I won't have to cross the mountains in winter."

"Well, here's to a cold, damp, and dreary winter." Nico held out his cup.

"I won't be there until spring, but I can drink to that." Thomas tapped Nico's cup with his own.

Nico mumbled something they didn't want to hear, and the conversation drifted off to other things. Marcus sipped his wine, thinking back to what Thomas had said.

Isabella and Rebecca were going to join them. He was sure neither of the other men had noticed, but his heart had jumped into his throat when he heard Isabella's name. It had been ten years since he had seen her. He should not have had that reaction. He gulped the last of his wine and frowned when he picked up the empty pitcher. There never seemed to be enough wine.

CHAPTER TWO

He who fears being conquered is sure of defeat.
—NAPOLEON BONAPARTE

JULY 19ᵀᴴ, 711 A.D.
SOUTHERN HISPANIA (MODERN SPAIN)

Marcus shifted in the saddle and looked up at the blazing sun. Of course, these bastards had to invade in the middle of summer. The padding beneath his armor was soaked in sweat, and his throat was parched, but he did not dare drink any more water until he knew he could replenish his water skin. At least he was near the front of the army. The poor foot soldiers marched in the dust kicked up by the cavalry.

"You dislike our summers?" The man riding next to him smiled and squinted at the sun. "I suppose it is cooler in Rome?"

"It is." Marcus glanced over at his companion.

Though he marched in the Visigoth army, Ander was not a descendant of the Germanic tribes. He was Basque, and a large one at that. He stood at least six inches taller than Marcus. Short, jet-black hair and strong, prominent cheekbones, split by a rather large nose. Bright blue eyes sparkled beneath a pair of furry brows. And he smiled more than any man Marcus had ever met.

"Perhaps the Saracens should have waited for a more convenient time to invade?" Ander grinned.

"I'm sure the King would agree."

Marcus looked toward the retinue in front of them. Roderic sat atop a giant white stallion, the only one in the small group of nobles. He was a sturdy man, with a deep, throaty voice and dark, probing eyes.

"How long have you ridden with him?"

Ander shrugged. "Ten years or more. Since before that bastard Wittiza killed his father."

"Wittiza?"

"Come now, you have never heard of him?" Ander did not wait for a response. "Wittiza the Wicked. And he earned that name several times over. He was a terrible little man who never should have been king."

"The world seems full of them."

"Yes, it is."

"How did he earn this title?"

"Debauchery that would make a Roman blush." The Basque smiled at Marcus. "More wives than you can count on two hands, and twice as many mistresses."

"If that were it, several rulers would earn that title."

"True, but that was not all. He saw conspiracy in every corner. He ordered his own fortresses destroyed so usurpers could not use them to take the throne, and murdered a dozen nobles that showed no interest in the crown." Ander nodded toward the King. "Including Roderic's father."

"And now Roderic is king."

"Yes, he is." Ander pointed to the surrounding army. "But

now we face this Saracen invasion because of what Wittiza did to this land."

Marcus nodded, but he did not agree. It was only a matter of time before the Saracens continued their expansion. Islam had exploded from the Arabian Peninsula and swept across North Africa. The Roman had taken part in several battles to check their advance, but so far, the Jihad was unstoppable. For several years, the Saracens had raided Hispania from the North African coast, but this time, it appeared they planned to stay.

An army of Berbers, North Africans who had converted to Islam, had landed a few weeks back. Roderic was dealing with an uprising in the north when he received the news. Racing south, he recruited men along the march, hoping to meet the Saracens with an equal, if not larger, force.

But Marcus was worried. He looked around at the men riding beside him. His companion aside, they were not the Visigoths that had swept in from Germania, smashing through the defenses of the Roman empire and sacking Rome. No, these men, despite their fearsome legacy, had grown soft. They had become landowners and nobles, happy to subjugate the local peasants and live off the spoils of others. He doubted many had ever seen actual combat, and not the type of combat they were about to engage in.

He shrugged and wiped the sweat from his brow. It wasn't like this was the first time he faced terrible odds. He swiveled in his saddle and looked back at a pair of nobles. "Who are they?"

Ander followed his gaze and spat onto the ground. "They are Wittiza's two eldest sons."

"They ride with Roderic? Even after he deposed their father."

"Yes."

"Why?"

"They brought with them a thousand heavy cavalry."

"That seems risky."

"I agree." Ander grinned. "But what can we do? We live, we die. That is our fate."

If Marcus planned to reply, a short horn blast interrupted him, which brought the entire army to a halt. He took a moment to free the water skin from his saddle and took a long pull, his eyes scanning the nearby terrain.

They had passed through Cordoba, climbing up and over a rugged set of mountains, before descending into this vast, fertile plain, split into two halves by a wide, slow-moving river. They had crossed that same river a half-dozen times, as it meandered toward the sea. Wheat fields, the fluttering stalks turning yellow, extended as far as the eyes could see. A smattering of houses, little more than huts, was the only sign of life.

"The locals are gone," Marcus said.

"I'm sure they fled to Seville."

Marcus took another pull from his waterskin and sat taller in the saddle, trying to see why they had stopped. It appeared they had reached another river crossing, which would allow him to refill his skin. With that in mind, he sprayed his face and neck, enjoying a brief respite as the water slid down his shoulders and back.

He stuck the cork back into the opening and hung the skin back onto his saddle. Frowning, he looked up at the sun, which had reached its zenith and seemed intent on staying there.

"Why aren't we crossing?" Ander asked.

Marcus sat up in his saddle to see beyond the troops in front of him. "The King and his retinue are gone."

Ander smiled. "Maybe they went looking for lunch. That reminds me; I'm hungry."

"I prefer going into battle hungry, but if you must, I have some dates."

"No, I'll try your way."

Marcus stared over at his newfound friend. He had met the

Basque the day before, but was pretty sure he liked him. "Can I ask you something?" Marcus crossed both hands over the pommel of his horse.

"There is never a good answer to that question."

"Why are you fighting for Roderic? Didn't he come from suppressing a Basque rebellion?"

"Rebellion means you were conquered in the first place." He winked. "The Basque never consider themselves conquered."

"That does not answer my question."

"No, it does not." Ander ran one hand through his thick black hair, stopping to scratch the top of his head. "I have connections with both parties, hence I was a negotiator."

"How was that going?"

"Have you ever negotiated with a Basque?"

"No, I have not."

"Someday you will, and then you can answer that yourself." He looked back toward the river. "Roderic is a good man. He does not plan to subjugate the Basques, which is refreshing."

"How did your Basque brethren take that news?"

"They did not trust him, or me." He smiled. "Despite my persuasiveness."

"And while Roderic is away?"

"My kin will prepare to resist the winner of this coming battle." He shrugged. "That is the Basque way."

Marcus shook his head, looked back toward the front of the column, and spotted a pair of riders galloping back along the road. They skidded to a halt near one of the King's troops, where they sought the remaining commanders. Within minutes, a dozen riders galloped toward them. One stopped and addressed Marcus and Ander. He was a young man, no older than twenty, with sweat pouring down his dirt-covered face.

"Saracens blocked the way. We must cross the river and secure the other side."

Without waiting, he galloped away.

"That sounds dangerous." Ander reached back and unstrapped his shield from behind his saddle. "I wonder how deep the ford is?"

"I'm sure the water will be refreshing." Marcus had retrieved his helmet and put it on. Next, he slipped on a pair of gauntlets.

"Have you ever fought Saracens?" Ander asked.

"I have."

"And?"

"They win."

Ander frowned. "And I thought I liked you."

Marcus glanced over at him, one eyebrow raised. "And now?"

"Now, I am sure of it."

With that, he spurred his horse forward, forcing Marcus to catch up.

They reached a shallow rise in the dirt road, occupied by the King and his nobles. Ander was not lying when he said he knew Roderick and rode straight up to the monarch.

"Sire." Ander nodded at Roderick and looked to the river slithering across the valley below. "What is the problem?"

The King glanced over at Ander and shifted his gaze to Marcus, who nodded in return.

"The bastards have set up on the other side of the ford." He pointed to a mass of men deployed across the river.

"It's almost like they knew we were coming." Ander looked back at the giant dust cloud behind them and winked at Marcus.

The King glared at the Basque. "You have something to say?"

"No, sire." He lowered his head. "I'm your humble servant, willing to do whatever you desire."

"Cut the shit, Ander." He tilted his head toward Marcus. "Who is this?"

HAMMER OF GOD

"A Roman friend." Ander nodded. "We have the same sense of humor. You will like him."

"Lord knows I don't need two of you."

"You may need one hundred of us if you plan to cross that river," Ander replied.

"You read my mind." Roderick sat taller on his horse. "I need someone to push them back, so the rest of the army can get to the other side."

"You want me to drive back several thousand soldiers with a few hundred riders?"

"Not drive them back, keep them occupied."

"Sounds like a terrible plan." Ander looked over at Marcus, the latter shrugging. "But my Roman friend likes terrible plans, so we shall do it."

"Excellent." Roderick turned to a noble next to him. "Find two hundred volunteers among the heavy cavalry."

"Yes, sire." The man spun his horse around and disappeared.

Roderick shifted his attention to another noble. "March the men down to that field." He pointed to the flat ground near the riverbank. "We'll cross when these good men push the Saracens back."

Ander urged his horse forward, Marcus right beside him.

"You do this often?" Marcus asked.

"Suicide missions? Would I be here if I did?" Ander smiled. "You?"

Marcus grinned. "More often than you'd guess."

The two trotted along the dirt road, reining in their horses as they approached the river's edge. To their right, the surface of the water was smooth and inviting. No sign of the current that flowed toward the sea. In front of them, the river widened, the water rushing over a bed of gravel and sand. To their left, it narrowed again, this time tumbling over boulders, white foam clinging to the slick rocks.

"This is a damn fine place to cross." Ander looked beyond the river to the soldiers amassed on the far side.

The Saracens had set up camp about a hundred paces from the river. Most of the army was milling around their tents, while a small group of men on horses stared back at them.

"I doubt they think we will cross right away." Marcus squinted in the midday sun. "We may catch them by surprise."

"Aye." Ander grinned. "We'll probably still die."

Marcus looked up at the sun and back at the Basque. "At least we'll be out of the heat."

"Speak for yourself, Roman." He smiled. "I'm going to hell."

Marcus chuckled as the lead elements of the foot-soldiers marched past. They angled off the road and lumbered up the shallow rise to the field Roderick had pointed to.

Ander looked back to the Saracens. There was a heated discussion among the small group. "I think they are figuring out our plan." Ander glanced over his shoulder. "Here come our reinforcements."

Marcus spun to see a troop of riders galloping down the road. As they neared the river, the Roman smirked at his new best friend.

"Shall we?"

"Indeed."

Marcus spurred his horse forward, gripping the reins in both hands. He would have plenty of time to pull his sword once he crossed the river. He was near a full gallop when his mount plunged into the water, the cool spray a welcome respite for both horse and rider. Marcus heard the cries of alarm from the Saracens above the splashing of the hooves. He trusted his horse to find his way as he glanced up toward the enemy camp. The riders had scattered, calling the soldiers to form up.

Marcus reached the far side, Ander right beside him. He pulled his sword free and directed his steed toward a pack of riders who had gathered into a loose formation. Only half of the men wore their helmets, and most looked like they had hastily donned their armor.

The first Saracen stabbed his spear at Marcus, and the Roman battered it aside with his shield, then leaned forward to drive his blade into the man's exposed underarm. He pulled the sword free, moving on to the next soldier. Dozens of other riders joined Marcus. The nobleman had picked the more experienced of Roderick's troops, and within minutes, the camp defenders had fled the field.

"Hold up!" Ander called after the men pursuing the vanquished enemy.

Marcus saw what Ander had seen. The Saracens were gathering on an open field beyond the camp.

"This will allow the army to cross." Ander wiped the blood from his blade and slipped it back into his scabbard.

"How many men does Roderick have?" Marcus said as he studied the Muslim army.

"A thousand foot soldiers, six-hundred calvary."

"There are at least three thousand men over there." Marcus nodded toward the Saracens.

"Do you like giving people bad news?" Ander said while he watched the soldiers march across the ford.

"Do you think Roderick knows?" Marcus asked.

"I don't think it matters." Ander looked back at the Roman. "He either fights today or loses his kingdom tomorrow."

Marcus motioned toward the river. "Here he comes."

Roderick smiled as he reined in his horse, the other nobles in his group doing the same. "Very nice work!" He leaned forward and studied a cut on Ander's forehead. "Is that deep?"

Ander wiped away the blood flowing down his face with his forearm. "I'll live."

"Good." The King sat back, his hands holding his reins in his lap. His eyes shifted to the distant Saracen army. "How many do you think?"

The question was not aimed at anyone in particular. Marcus looked over at Ander, who nodded in return.

"At least three thousand men," Marcus said, meeting the King's gaze.

"Hmmm." Roderick looked around at the field and watched the foot soldiers deploy. They anchored their line on a bend in the river beyond the ford. The troop of heavy cavalry was further inland, anchored on a copse of trees that shielded a stream feeding the river. "The men will have their backs against the river. They will fight or die."

"Yes," Ander said, "but they will have no room to maneuver."

"Neither will the Saracen horsemen," the King countered.

"True." The Basque nodded. "Where would you like us?"

The King paused, and his steel-blue eyes focused on the Saracens. He looked back to Ander. "With the cavalry. I don't trust the brothers."

Ander nodded. "Neither do I."

A horn blast echoed across the field. Nodding at the King, Ander wheeled his mount around and bolted toward the mass of heavy cavalry, Marcus on his heels. The Basque angled toward a man with long blond hair who sat on a pure black stallion. His eyes narrowed as Ander and Marcus halted before him.

"Hello Sisberto," Ander said, as he tugged on the reins of his fidgety steed. "I assume your brother Oppo is leading the other wing?"

"Why are you here, Basque?"

"I'm pleased to see you as well. The King asked us to ride with you into battle."

"To watch me, you mean." The deep scar that ran down the side of his face hinted he was no stranger to combat. "You can tell the King I will fulfill our vow."

"You can tell him yourself. I have fighting to do." With that, Ander galloped toward the edge of the amassed riders.

Marcus followed, then stopped beside him and hopped down from the saddle.

Ander frowned. "Are you taking a piss?"

"No, I'm too damn thirsty to piss." Marcus untied a war hammer that hung near the back of his saddle and remounted his steed.

"What the hell is that?"

Marcus grinned. "A hammer. The Saracens don't wear heavy armor. I find the blunt end of this does a wonderful job of knocking them from their horses. Once on foot, they are not nearly as dangerous."

"I want one!"

"If we live, I shall give you mine."

"Deal!" Ander pulled his sword free. "I believe the odds of that are very slim."

"For you, perhaps." Marcus grinned. "But I will do my best to even them out."

Another horn blast from somewhere near the center of the Visigoth line cut short any planned response. The enemy was advancing across the empty camp, their line twice as wide as the defenders. It was Berber cavalry, with some light infantry support. The riders would strike and run, taking advantage of their mobility. As a result, it was critical that the Visigoth army maintained a compact formation. In theory, that would allow the wings of the army, made up of the heavy cavalry Marcus was riding with, to drive away the Berbers, but then return to protect the flank.

The enemy had closed to within a hundred paces when the first group of Berber riders burst forward. The dark-skinned warriors rode small horses, not much bigger than ponies. Most Berbers were shirtless, or wore togas, and carried round or oblong shields covered in animal hides. A spear and sword rounded out their weaponry.

The first group reined in their horses about twenty-five

paces in front of Marcus and hurled their spears toward the Visigoths. A few struck home, but most bounced off shields or missed their target. A couple of horses struck by the lances stumbled, tossing their riders to the ground. Marcus knocked one spear to the side with his shield.

"Are they going to sit there?" Ander asked.

"No, they will harass us until we chase them." Marcus looked for Sisberto. "I hope your friend knows we can't do that."

"He's not my friend, and I'm not sure he knows anything about Saracens."

Their answer came quickly. Another group of Berbers made a similar attack, this time wounding several men in Sisberto's entourage. The nobleman was enraged and ordered the surrounding riders to join in pursuing the Berbers. The rest of the cavalry took that as a signal to charge, and soon the entire right wing of the army was pursuing a few hundred Berber riders. Except for Marcus and Ander. They both watched in dismay as the mass of horsemen disappeared in a cloud of dust.

"Oh shit," Ander said.

"I couldn't have put it better." Marcus guided his horse toward the center formation of foot soldiers. "This is going to be over quickly."

As if on cue, the entire right side of the Berber army attacked, but not directly. They drifted farther away, then angled back toward the Visigoth formation, the line of riders forming a giant crescent. The infantry watched in dismay as the riders swept past and spun around to attack. This forced the rear elements to spin around and confront the new threat.

Before the rest of the Berber riders closed, Marcus peered across the line and saw the other wing, commanded by Sisberto's brother, chasing after another small group of riders. The center of the Visigoth line was vulnerable.

"I think the brothers planned this," Marcus said, glancing over at his companion.

"Probably," Ander agreed, and nodded toward the approaching horsemen. "We may never find out."

Marcus spurred his horse forward and split two attackers, swinging his hammer in a tight arc toward the closest. The man raised his shield to block the strike, but the blunt force knocked him off the back of his horse. Marcus smashed the second rider with his shield, nearly unseating him as well. A quick overhand strike with his hammer was followed by the crunch of metal against skull. As the man tumbled to the ground, Marcus looked for another victim. A few feet away, Ander dealt out his own lethal damage as he moved through the mass of horsemen.

For the infantry, the situation was more frustrating. Although they were not as armored as the Visigoth cavalry, they were encumbered enough to prevent them from engaging the speedy horsemen. The Berbers would ride in at an angle, launch a spear and veer away before the foot soldier could land a blow. Any attempt to chase down the rider was deadly, as a pack of Berbers would swarm the lone target and strike him down.

The Saracens suffered losses, usually from spears tossed back at them by the Visigoths. But without heavy cavalry, Roderick's men were doomed. Marcus and Ander fought their way toward the King as he continued to rally his troops.

"Those damn brothers!" Roderick bellowed when he recognized Ander. The King was covered in sweat, blood, and dirt. His fierce blue eyes sparkled with rage. "If I die today, I swear to God Almighty I will return to haunt their souls!"

"Let's try to avoid that," Ander yelled back. "We should try to get you back across the river!"

"And abandon my men?" Roderick dispatched a Berber rider with one blow of his sword and glared at Ander. "Never! I will not let these heathen bastards drive me from the field!"

"We have to at least retreat to the river so they cannot flank us." Marcus pointed his hammer toward the long, flat ground along the riverbank. "We may have a chance."

"Let's get them moving!" Roderick looked around to see if he could ride his horse through the packed formation. That would be impossible without trampling his men. "We ride around!" He yelled back over his shoulder as he led his entourage around the outside of the infantry.

Unfortunately, a large group of Berber riders spotted the King and intercepted them in the open ground between the army's flank and the river. Marcus smashed his larger horse into one of the smaller steeds, nearly knocking the animal to the ground. Spinning around, he brought his hammer down on the back of another man's skull and spurred his horse forward to join Ander, who was surrounded by three riders. As Marcus arrived, one of them bypassed the Basque guard and speared him in the side.

As Ander grunted in pain, Marcus caught the side of the attacker's face with the hammer, knocking him back into a second rider. The third rider tried to stab Marcus with his spear, but the Roman knocked the tip aside with his shield and rammed the top of his hammer into the Saracen's face. Blood exploded from his nose and mouth as he tumbled to the ground.

Marcus spun back to his friend, who was slumped over the neck of his horse. Marcus nudged his mount forward. "How bad is it?"

"Bad enough," Ander replied.

"The King!" The exclamation came from a pack of riders thirty paces from them.

Roderick was still atop his giant steed, but was surrounded by a dozen riders. He had a spear embedded in his back and was covered with blood. Marcus angled his horse toward the monarch when the King fell from his horse and disappeared. A victory cry erupted from the Berber cavalry, and the effect on the infantry was almost immediate. Within minutes, most of the Visigoths had thrown down their weapons and were sprinting for the river.

That is when the slaughter began. The Berbers were experts at cutting down fleeing men. And a dead man was a man you would never have to fight again.

Marcus tossed his shield to the ground and grabbed the reins of Ander's horse. Their only chance of survival was to get across the river and to the nearest town. Marcus urged his mount to a gallop, and the pair of riders made for the ford. They may have made it across, but Marcus's steed stumbled as it entered the river, throwing Marcus from his saddle. He still had the other horse's reins in his hand, which caused that mount to pivot, resulting in Ander tumbling into the water.

They were on the deeper side of the ford, deep enough for a man to disappear under the surface. Marcus fought against the heavy chain mail he wore and somehow stood. He lurched forward, found Ander near where he had fallen, and pulled him to the surface.

The Basque gasped for air, his face twisted in pain. Marcus looked around, but his horse was nowhere to be found. Instead, he spotted a dozen riders bearing down on them. He glanced at Ander's steed, but it would never outrun the faster Berber mounts, especially carrying two men.

He reached forward, unclasped Ander's chain mail and pulled it over his head, ignoring his painful gasp. He had just finished doing the same for himself when the riders hit the water. Pulling Ander with him, Marcus dove into the water and using one arm, swam as fast as he could toward the rapids. After three or four strokes, he came to the surface to take a breath and peered back towards the riders. There scanning the surface, and one man spotted the Roman. Pointing, he unleashed his spear.

Marcus watched it fly overhead, but was not so lucky when

the others launched their spears. One lance buried into his leg. Marcus twisted around and pulled it free, then lifted Ander up above the surface. The Basque's eyes were closed, his breath shallow or non-existent.

Marcus hoped for the best, positioned Ander on his back, and focused on guiding them both through the coming rapids.

The Berber cavalry lost interest and rejoined the slaughter taking place beside the river. Marcus let the water carry them away from the battle, using his free hand now and then to avoid smashing into a rock. Once clear of the rapids, he continued floating down the now calm river, putting as much distance between him and the Saracens. A short while later, he swam toward a flat area on the shoreline. Gaining his feet, he dragged Ander from the river, across a patch of sand and onto the grass beyond. He knelt beside the Basque and checked his wound.

Blood oozed from the gash, the skin puckered from the water. Marcus leaned forward to listen for any signs of breathing.

"I'm not dead."

Marcus sat back, hands on his thighs, and glared at Ander. "Were you awake the entire time I dragged your ass from the river?"

"Yes." Ander sat up on one elbow, wincing as he smiled. "Many thanks."

"I don't know what you're thanking me for. We are stuck in the middle of nowhere."

Marcus glanced around. There were more trees here than where they had fought the battle, but there seemed to be no farmland, and no sign of roads or towns.

"We are not nowhere." Ander pointed down the river. "There is a town a few miles away."

"But if we are closer to the coast..."

"Yes, it means the Saracens have already captured the town."

"Will they turn us in?"

"Probably not. If we were Visigoth, yes. But I'm a poor Basque, and you—"

"Me what?"

"Just a Roman, I guess."

Marcus stood and extended one hand down to pull Ander to his feet.

"Are you hurt?" Ander pointed to a cut in Marcus's bloody trousers.

"A scratch. You?"

"I don't think it hit anything important." He had one hand covering the wound. "We will find out for sure in the next day or so. For now, I will try to stop the bleeding."

They spent a few minutes preparing a makeshift bandage, which Marcus secured with his belt around the Basque's waist. He cinched it tight and smiled as Ander grunted in pain.

"That is for letting me drag your heavy ass."

Ander winced. "It was worth it."

Standing, they stepped into the underbrush, finding what looked like a deer path that ran beside the river. The warm afternoon breeze slowly dried their wet clothes. They had been walking for a while when Ander glanced over at the Roman. "Do you have a family?"

Surprised by the question, Marcus kept his gaze focused on the ground before him. "I did." He kept his head forward, but could still see his companion. "And you?"

The Basque looked up at the sun, eyes closed. "They were killed in a raid." Ander let a long sigh and opened his eyes again.

"Who?"

"Franks." Ander forced a smile. "My wife was beautiful, but not as beautiful as my daughter." The smile faded. "She was eight."

They walked on for a couple of minutes, and Marcus said, "I had a wife. And two children. A boy and a girl."

B. K. GREENWOOD

"What happened to them?"

A series of images passed through his mind. The brothel. The ship. Antioch. Chasing down rumor after rumor. The blood. He set his jaw and focused on the horizon. "They are dead."

Sensing that was the end of the conversation, Ander descended into silence.

A short time later, they spotted the edges of the town.

CHAPTER THREE

An investment in knowledge pays the best interest.
—Benjamin Franklin

Fall, 715 A.D.
Cologne, Duchy of Austrasia

Droplets of water dripped steadily from the low, arched ceiling, forming shallow pools on the floor of the dungeon. Based on the beam of light slicing across the dark chamber, Nicodemus judged it to be early afternoon. He stood and looked around his tiny cell. It contained a pile of straw, with a single blanket, a pissing pot in the corner, and a wooden plate for his daily meal. Or at least that is what they told him. He had yet to experience his first meal.

He walked to the metal bars that separated his cell from several others in the dungeon. Nicodemus wrapped his hands around the flat metal rungs and peered toward the other cells.

"Charles?"

After a long silence, Nicodemus called again, this time louder, "Charles!"

"What?" The reply came from the adjacent cell.

A tall figure moved to the bars and peered back at him. He was young, perhaps mid-twenties, with a thick, brown beard and long wavy hair, both matted with dirt. He glared at Nicodemus with intelligent brown eyes.

"My name is Nicodemus." The older man smiled at him. "I suppose the rumor is true."

His eyes narrowed to slits. "What rumor?"

"The son of Pepin was imprisoned by his stepmother."

"That bitch." Charles spat on the ground. "If I get my hands on her and that son of hers, Theudoald."

"Why the boy?"

Charles shifted along the bars, closer to Nicodemus. "Huh?"

"Did he put you in prison?"

"No, but if he lives, he can claim the throne."

"No." Nicodemus met his gaze. "He is an eight-year-old boy, thrust into this position by his mother. Much like the position you are in now. Except he is far younger." Nico lifted his chin. "You are his uncle, and you should protect and nurture him. And if you do, he will never pose a threat to you."

Charles did not reply, his eyes measuring the older man. They were filled with suspicion. "How do you know these things?"

"I am old."

For the first time, Charles smiled. "Why are you in here, old man?"

"I'm here to help you."

"Help me escape?"

"Not exactly."

"How will you help me?"

"You must become a man who can build a strong Frankish

HAMMER OF GOD

kingdom. One who can withstand the onslaught of the Saracens."

"The Saracens? Aren't they across the sea?"

"They were. Now they are in Hispania. And soon they will cross the Pyrenees."

"Why?"

Nicodemus smiled. "Because their prophet told them to."

Charles released the bars. "I have no time for riddles. I have more important things to deal with."

"Like what?" Nicodemus looked around the dungeon. "It is only you and me. We have nothing but time. And how you spend this time will determine the ruler you become."

"And what do you suggest?"

"Can you read?"

"No," his face twisted in disgust, "why would I waste time learning to read? That is for priests."

"Because books contain the greatest treasure in the world – knowledge." Nicodemus smiled. "And with that knowledge, you can conquer any enemy."

"You will teach me to read?"

"No, of course not. That would take years." Nicodemus held up one finger. "Wait one moment."

He moved to the pile of straw and pulled out a book from beneath the heap. Moving back to the bars, he held it up for Charles to see.

"How did you get that in here?"

"One of those priests you mentioned left it for me." He angled the cover toward the shallow light. "*Commentarii de Bello Gallico.*"

"What?"

"That is Latin. Commentaries on the Gallic War. By Julius Caesar."

"I know this man." Charles leaned forward. "He was a great general."

"Yes, he was. And perhaps a better politician. You will need to be both if you wish to lead the Franks."

"I do."

"Sit, and I will read to you."

Charles settled near the bars, while Nicodemus moved over to the beam of light. Lifting open the leather cover, he read, "*All Gaul is divided into three parts, one of which the Belgae inhabit, the Aquitani another, those who in their own language are called Celts, in our Gauls, the third.*"

For as long as there was light, Nicodemus read the book smuggled to him. When it was dark, or clouds prevented light from coming into the chamber, the two men discussed politics, warfare, religion, and a myriad of other topics. On the second day of a heavy thunderstorm, they encountered a long period of silence. Charles was at the far end of his cell, buried in darkness. Nicodemus heard scraping on the stone floor and looked up as Charles gripped the metal bars.

"Why are you here?"

"I told you already. To prepare you."

Charles peered at him. "Why me?"

Nicodemus studied the young man. "I met you once, when you were younger. I think you were ten."

"I don't remember."

"I visited your father, and he took me to watch your training with the other young men in the court."

"Yes, he liked to show us off."

"He was smart. You can learn a lot from watching young men play."

"I have scars that say it was more than play."

"I bet you do." Nico scratched his beard. "I remember watching you during the group sessions. You helped set up the defense by organizing the other boys. Even the older boys followed you."

Charles brushed it off. "It's always been that way."

"You're a natural leader." Nicodemus peered at him through the waning light. "Your father saw it. He wanted you to become the Mayor of the Palace when he died."

"That is what he said." Charles set his jaw. "Until that woman got into his head."

"Everyone makes mistakes."

"His landed me in here."

"Exactly." Nico smiled. "Right where I needed you to be. Speaking of which," Nico shifted his chair closer to the bars, "we need to talk about your power base."

"The nobles. I have to secure their support."

"Yes, the nobles are key. But they share power."

"The Church."

"Exactly. They control the messaging to the masses. They can rally the common folk to support you or rise against you. And this is where I can help."

The young man's eyes narrowed. "And how is that?"

"I have connections within the Vatican. We can influence the local clergy."

A long silence followed. Nico studied Charles through the waning light before asking, "Is there a problem?"

"I've learned a lot in the last month." He stood, pacing his small cell, then stopped and looked over at the older man. "Nothing comes for free – especially power."

Nico nodded. "That's true."

"What will the Vatican want?"

Nico stood and moved forward, placing both hands on the bars. "They want a powerful leader in Gaul when the Saracens attack."

"A powerful leader or a puppet?"

"Something tells me you will never be a puppet."

Charles set his jaw and nodded. "This will be my kingdom. I will take orders from no man, especially one in Rome. Is that clear?"

Nico grinned. "I would have it no other way."

They were interrupted by their evening meal. The storm broke that night, and the next day they resumed their studies. But the days grew shorter, the sunlight dimmer, and the nights colder.

They were finishing a chapter in *The Agricola and The Germania,* by Tacitus, when the main door leading into the dungeon creaked open. It was midday, so they were not expecting their meals. Nico closed the book and moved to the bed, slipping it under the straw. He returned to the bars and looked over at the puzzled expression on Charles's face.

A few moments later, two men emerged from the shadows. One was a dark-haired prisoner with an angry countenance. The second was a tall, hulking guard. The former had shackles on his wrists and ankles.

Nico glared at the prisoner. "You're early!"

The man held both his hands up, chains jingling. "Things have changed."

"Who is this?" Charles cut in.

The prisoner looked at Charles and shuffled forward. "My name is Marcus."

"So?"

Marcus glanced over at Nico. "He seems ungrateful."

"He doesn't know you are here to break him out." Nico tilted his head toward the guard. "Why did you get yourself arrested?"

"I didn't. This is Ander. I asked him to help me."

Ander glared at Marcus. "Help? It was my plan." He motioned to the tiny window. "You wanted to tie a bunch of horses to the bars and pull down the wall."

"It would've worked," Marcus said.

"No, it wouldn't," the other three men replied, almost in unison.

Marcus eyed the trio and held up his hands to Ander. "You can unlock me. And the ankle bracers were a bit much."

"We had to be convincing."

"There's only one other guard, and he's seventy years old." Marcus watched as Ander unclasped the shackles, the metal chains clanging to the stone floor.

"Trust me, he's a curious old bastard." The Basque moved to the anklets. When he was done, he stood and stepped toward Nico's cell. Pulling out a set of keys, he unlocked the door and pulled it open. He did the same for Charles's cell.

As Charles stepped through the opening, he glanced from Marcus to Ander.

"Did you bring weapons?"

Marcus shook his head. "I'd never pass as a prisoner if I was carrying a weapon."

Charles looked at Ander. "What do you have?"

"A sword and dagger."

"Give me the sword."

"Why would I do that?"

The two men, identical in height, glared at each other in the fading light.

Marcus chuckled.

Charles scowled at him. "What are you laughing at?"

"The two of you." Marcus reached forward and took the dagger from Ander and handed it to Charles. "It's an old man. We won't even need a weapon."

"How do we get out of the city?" Charles asked.

"We walk out."

"We walk out." Charles smiled at Nico.

"Oh Lord," Nicodemus shook his head.

Marcus looked from Nico to Charles. "I got us in, I can get us out."

Charles motioned to Ander. "I thought he came up with the plan to get you in?"

"He did, but—"

"I have a plan," Ander said.

"Good, what is it?" Nico pressed.

"We get weapons from the guardhouse," he stabbed his thumb over his shoulder, "and we fight our way out of the city."

Nico exhaled and glanced at Marcus. "That sounds like a plan you would come up with."

Charles cut them off. "We'll figure it out. For now, we leave this place."

They climbed the narrow, winding staircase leading up from the dungeon. Ander, sword free, led the small group. Charles, dagger in hand, went next. Marcus followed, glancing back now and then to ensure Nico was close behind.

Ander stopped at the door near the top and looked back at the others. "We do not kill the old man."

Charles glared back at him. "What if he sounds the alarm?"

Ander stared him down, his jaw twitching. "We do not kill him."

There was an awkward silence as the two men faced off in the dark confines. Charles exhaled and nodded. "That may get us all killed."

"So be it." Ander reached for the door and pulled it open.

The group stepped through the opening and into the small, dark chamber beyond. A narrow archway led to another room, light from the pale afternoon sun visible through the open window.

"Did you get him settled?" The old man looked up at Ander. "What is this?" he asked, rising to his feet, shoulders slumping forward. He glared at Ander with crisp, pale blue eyes.

"I'm sorry, but this man is coming with us." The Basque moved further into the room so Marcus and Nico could join them.

The guard pursed his lips, his eyes moving from the sword Ander held to the dagger Charles was twisting in his hand. He looked up and studied Charles, a look of recognition flashing across his face. "You are Pepin's son."

HAMMER OF GOD

"I am."

"He was a good man."

"Yes, he was."

"Not a great taste in women."

Charles frowned at him.

The guard shrugged. "I am sure your mother was the exception."

Charles's expression softened.

"I'll let you pass." The guard did not wait for a reply. "But you will need to hit me in the head."

Ander frowned. "What?"

"If you escape and I am unharmed, they will believe I helped you." He rubbed his chin. "Or I could go with you."

"I don't think that is a good idea," Marcus said.

"You don't?" the guard challenged. "How well do you know this city? Do you have an escape route planned?"

Marcus opened his mouth, but did not reply. He glanced at Ander.

The Basque shrugged.

Marcus motioned to the guard. "Lead the way."

"You'll need weapons." He pulled a set of keys from his belt and shuffled toward a door in the far wall. After unlocking it, he pulled it open and motioned them to go inside. Marcus and Charles did so, both men emerging a few moments later with swords.

"Now what?" Ander asked.

"You picked a terrible time to escape. It's midday. Everyone in the city is awake and about."

Charles glanced over at Marcus, the latter frowning.

"Do you have horses?" The guard looked around the group.

"Yes, we do." Marcus's smile faded. "But only four."

"I ride with one of you, I reckon." He squinted out the window and looked at Marcus. "Where are they?"

"A stable, a few hundred paces down the road. Past a tavern." The Roman's face scrunched. "The *One-eyed Duck?*"

"You mean the *Blind Pigeon.*" The old man wiped his forehead. "Good Lord, we will never make it from the city."

"One of us should go get the horses and bring them back here?" Nico looked from the guard to Marcus.

"Finally, someone with a bit of sense." The guard stabbed a finger at Ander. "You seem to have your wits about you. You go."

Ander smirked at Marcus. "Did you hear that? He thinks I'm the smart one."

"Shut up and get the horses." Marcus pointed to the door. "And hurry."

The Basque, a huge smile on his face, disappeared out the door. Marcus moved to the window, cracked open the shutter, and watched him cross the muddy intersection.

"How many guards at the main gate?" Charles asked.

"Four, maybe five. It might be more with the market tomorrow." The guard rubbed his chin again, this time his mouth splitting open to reveal his few remaining teeth. "They'll also have tax collectors there, which means more guards."

"Are there any other ways to leave the city?"

"Not today. Like I said, the market is tomorrow. They are very careful around that time." He grinned. "Your mother-in-law is keen to collect as many taxes as she can, so she can pay the army she raised."

"Army?" Charles raised his eyebrows. "What army?"

"Things have changed in the months you've been locked up, young man." He shuffled to a nearby chair and sat down. "Five thousand men, plus another three hundred knights."

A hiss escaped Charles's lips as he glared at Nico. "See what has happened while you read me books!"

Nico glared back at him. "And you didn't learn a damn thing."

Charles opened his mouth to reply, then paused. He tilted

his head to the side and bit his lip. "I need to learn more about this army."

"Yes, you do. What else?"

"I need men."

"And how will you get them?"

"Gold."

"Exactly. It took longer than I wanted, but we got there." Nico smiled. "We have gold. We need to get you out of the city."

Marcus stepped away from the window. "They are back." He looked at Nico and tilted his head toward the guard. "He needs to ride with you."

"Of course."

Marcus stepped to the door and cracked it open. Ander stopped the group of horses a few steps from the door. The nervous mounts pawed at the muddy ground with their hooves.

Marcus pushed the door open and motioned for Nico and the guard to exit. Charles was right behind. Nico moved to the closest horse and pulled himself up into the saddle. Charles and Marcus helped lift the guard, slipping him right behind Nico.

The other two men mounted their horses and looked over at the guard for direction. He pointed down a street crowded with vendors and their carts. Marcus nodded and led them forward. They slipped from the pale sunlight into the shadows of the tall wooden buildings that lined the street. Moving in single file, Marcus cleared the path for the others to follow. One farmer complained, but a snarl from the Roman cut him short.

As they rounded a corner, they exited the shadows and entered a large, open plaza. Hundreds of stalls lined the muddy field, and what seemed like a thousand people packed the square.

Marcus looked back at the guard. "I thought you said the market was tomorrow."

"I guess it started early."

"The gate?" the Roman asked.

The guard pointed to the far side of the market. "On that wall."

Marcus stood in the saddle and peered across the mass of booths. He sat back down and turned to the rest of the party.

"I think Charles should go first, with you." He nodded toward Nico. "If something goes wrong, we'll be right behind you."

The others nodded in agreement, so Charles led his mount forward. They made slow progress across the square, as the group stopped a dozen times to avoid running into patrons or hawkers. Marcus cursed beneath his breath as a farmer drove a pack of pigs across their path, several of his sons doing their best to keep the herd in one group.

They eventually reached the other side, where Marcus and Ander slowed and let Charles and Nico ride ahead. The pair were about twenty paces away when Marcus spurred his horse forward, one hand wrapped around his sword hilt.

Marcus watched Charles guide his horse into the line of people waiting to leave. It included several carts, which the guards inspected.

"I wonder why they are searching everything. Seems odd." Ander looked over at Marcus.

Marcus shook his head. "I don't know. I hear Charles's mother-in-law is ruthless. She is cautious as well. She has plenty of enemies."

The cart in front of Charles cleared the gate, so he nudged his steed forward. Marcus was out of earshot, so he could not hear the conversation between Charles and the guard holding his bridle. It seemed cordial, and after a brief exchange, the guard smiled and released the bridle.

"Stop!" another guard shouted and stepped from the shadows of the wall.

The guard retrieved the reins. Marcus inched his horse

HAMMER OF GOD

forward, and his gaze focused on what looked like the officer in charge of the guard post. To his right, Ander kept pace with him.

"I know you." The officer stopped ten paces from Charles, his face twisted. "I fought with you in Saxony, and with your father, Pepin." His hand dropped to his sword hilt. "You are supposed to be in our dungeon."

There was a long, awkward silence as Charles stared back at the officer. "Gerald of Hesbaye. You were younger," he motioned his hand around his chin, "without the beard."

"I was."

"That was a hard campaign."

"Indeed. If not for your father's wits, we would have surely perished." A grin creased his lips. "And you fought bravely as well."

Everyone had stopped and watched the exchange. The half dozen guards shifted their attention back and forth.

"I thank you for the kind words," Charles said. "Pepin was a great general and sometimes a good father."

"Though I respected him immensely," the grin faded, "I took an oath to support Lady Plectrude."

"I can respect that." Charles shifted in his saddle. "She claims something that is not hers."

"Yet, you are the one in prison."

"I was."

"And you shall be again." Gerald pointed at Charles. "Seize him!"

Marcus spurred his horse forward as the officer pulled his sword free.

Gerald took a step forward, sword ready, just in time to see Marcus and Ander bearing down on him. Several guards saw them coming and moved to block their path.

Those not involved in the skirmish scattered. Nico urged his mount forward, knocking aside a guard that reached for his reins. The guard holding Charles's horse pulled on the bridle, causing his horse to nearly stumble. Charles clung to the saddle, unable to draw his sword. Several other guards ran forward to grab him.

Marcus smashed his horse into a guard, sending him sprawling. Springing from the saddle, Marcus landed between two other guards, dodging one man's sword as he stabbed at the Roman. Marcus swung his blade around in a tight arc, severing the man's arm below the elbow. Stepping forward, he moved inside the next guard's attack and drove his elbow into the man's nose. It split in two, blood pouring from the wound. The man stumbled back, spat out a mouthful of blood, and raised his sword.

Marcus glanced back at Charles, just in time to see him being pulled from his mount. Cursing, Marcus set upon his foe with a ferocious series of blows, the swords clanking as the guard desperately tried to defend himself. But he was no match for the Roman, and seconds later, Marcus pulled his blade from the guard's sternum.

Ander appeared, covered in mud. Before Marcus could say anything, the Basque said, "I slipped when I jumped from my horse."

"You're out of practice."

"Perhaps." He smiled, his teeth shining through the caked mud. "Time to practice."

Without waiting for Marcus, he ran forward and smashed into the two guards holding Charles. The four men tumbled to the ground, arms and legs flailing in the mud. That left one guard and the officer for Marcus. The guard stepped forward, but Marcus dispatched him with three quick strikes of his sword.

The Roman glanced at the melee involving Charles and Ander. They disabled the guards and pulled themselves from the mud. Marcus looked back to the officer. There was no fear in his eyes.

Charles slipped his sword back into his scabbard, flung the mud from his hands, and walked over next to Marcus. But his gaze was on Gerald. "I need good battle lords."

"What kind of lord would I be if I betrayed my oath?" Gerald said.

"Men shift allegiances all the time." He stepped forward. "She will install an eight-year-old boy as Mayor of the Palace. The other lords will never stand for it. We will have years of war. I am the rightful heir, and you know it."

"My family. They will be in danger if I leave with you."

"Go get them and meet me in Metz."

"I will think about it."

"Very well." Charles nodded. "Do not think too long."

Ander had retrieved their horses, and the men quickly mounted up. A few seconds later, they were racing through the gate and toward Nico, who was waiting half a league down the road. As the trio pulled to a stop, Nico looked them up and down. "All in one piece, I see." He glared at the two muddied men. "But what the hell happened to you two?"

"Don't ask," Charles said.

"What now?" Nico studied the young man.

"I need that gold. We go South, to Metz." Charles redirected his steed. "That is where I have support."

CHAPTER FOUR

*The battle line between good and evil
runs through the heart of every man.*
—Aleksandr Solzhenitsyn

Spring, 716 A.D.
Off the coast of Nice, Gaul

The ship rolled with the angry sea, smashing into a giant swell that showered the deck with spray. Isabella clung to the railing with one hand, the other holding the edges of a cloak she had wrapped around her body. She studied the distant horizon and the spot the captain had identified as their destination. It seemed so far away.

For nearly ten days, the vessel had skirted the coast of Italia and Southern Gaul. Thomas had traveled to Gaul without them, promising to send word when it was safe. Once they had received his message, they had taken the next merchant ship bound for Gaul.

The captain was a gentle old soul, despite his harsh exterior. He forbade any of the crew to speak to the ladies and insisted on taking care of all their needs himself. They ate their meals with him and slept in the cabin next to his.

"We will not make it today, miss."

Isabella turned to find the captain standing next to her, somehow staying upright without holding on to the railing.

"I was hoping." She covered her mouth for a moment. "My sister is very ill."

"You should bring her out here and watch the horizon." He nodded toward the shoreline. "It helps the young sailors."

"I feel better when I'm out of the cabin."

The captain nodded and sighed.

"Is there something else, Captain?"

"Yes, there is." He scratched his weathered cheek. "Is there someone meeting you in Nice?" Before she could answer, he stepped forward, his voice a whisper. "Gaul is a pretty rough place for two ladies, traveling alone."

"Thank you for your concern, but my sister and I will be fine."

"I would still feel better if you were meeting someone."

She smiled and took his hand in hers. There was comfort in his firm, rough grip. "I appreciate all that you have done for us. We are in your debt." She released his hand and pulled her cloak closer. "But we are not as delicate as we seem."

"Of course." He stepped back and bowed. "I hope we can be in port by sunset tomorrow."

"Thank you, Captain."

As promised, the captain had them alongside the dock before the sun had disappeared behind the distant mountains. A pair of merchants were moored along the narrow wharf, one taking on cargo, the other offloading. Beyond the dock, a dozen tall, thin buildings faced the port, the wooden structures all leaning a bit to the right. Carts were parked in front of several of the buildings with contents, either moving into or out of the warehouses.

The captain recruited two sailors to carry their bags and led them down the gangway and onto the dock. After two weeks at sea, their legs wobbled, and Rebecca nearly fell into the water.

"Careful!" The captain caught her elbow. "Takes a bit of getting used to. I once fell flat on my face after a month at sea!"

"Thank you!" Rebecca said. "I'm a bit weak, that is all."

"The sea has a way of doing that. Where will you stay tonight?" The captain looked from Rebecca to Isabella.

"I'm not sure," Isabella said. "I plan to find an inn and secure passage north."

"I know just the place." He bowed his head. "If you would allow me, I'll take you there."

"You don't have to do that, Captain," Isabella protested.

"Of course, I don't! But I want to anyway." He picked up both of their bags and led them forward.

They stepped from the wooden dock onto the muddy street, encountering everything you would expect in a port town. Merchants and sailors of every race. Ox or donkey drawn carts. Cages with chickens, pigs, and other livestock. Large wagons laden with barrels, and others carrying bundles of wood or barley. They passed several men engaged in heated negotiations that seemed moments away from an open brawl.

The captain navigated the crowd, using his steely glare to thwart any potential hooligans.

Their destination was located three streets into the town, on the corner of a busy intersection. It was a three-story building that seemed to sag in two directions. The captain pulled open the door and motioned them inside. A fireplace lit most of the room, filled with tables and chairs, about half of them occupied. A man stood behind the bar, eyeing them suspiciously. After following them in, the captain set down the bags and made straight for the bar.

"Does Gertrude still run this establishment?" The captain peered at the bartender.

"Who is asking?" the man replied.

"I am, for God's sake." He leaned forward. "Is she here?"

"Of course I am you old sea pecker!" A woman, a foot taller and twice as wide as the captain, appeared from a doorway near the end of the bar. She rumbled toward him, arms wide open.

"Gertrude!" He welcomed her massive embrace and disappeared into her oversized breasts. When he reappeared, a smile covered his weathered face. "How long has it been?"

"Too long, too long." She leaned forward and kissed his forehead. She looked up at Isabella and Rebecca, then back down at the captain. "Who are they, Lagus?"

"Passengers that I brought from Rome." He leaned back. "They need a place to stay."

"Of course." She motioned toward the bartender. "Get yourself a cup of ale, and we will talk after."

"Only talk?" He grinned.

"Go away, you horny old man!" She looked at Isabella and winked. "Men are all the same."

Isabella watched the captain head to the bar. "He is a good man."

"Lagus? Oh yes, one of the best. But still a horny bastard." Rebecca blushed as Gertrude pushed on. "Two ladies traveling alone? Either brave or foolish."

"Perhaps a little of both," Isabella said. "I'm Isabella."

"And I'm Rebecca."

"Gertrude." She looked at their bags. "You need a room?"

"Yes, if you have any available."

"I do." She squinted, her eyes disappearing behind her chubby cheeks. "How long?"

"A few days? Only until we find passage north."

"Hmmm, north. Alone?" She pursed her lips. "Where are you going?"

"Lyon," Isabella replied.

Her eyes lit up. "I may have someone that can help you with that." She motioned to a nearby table. "Are you hungry?" Without waiting for a reply, she pulled out a chair for Rebecca. "I'll get you some stew."

The two sat down and waited. A few minutes later, Gertrude returned with two bowls of thick, brown stew and a half loaf of black bread. Isabella used a spoon to stir the contents, carrots and potatoes floating to the top. Gertrude returned and filled their cups from a tall wooden pitcher.

"Thank you," Rebecca said as she broke off a piece of black bread and dipped it into the broth.

"It looks like you're in excellent hands." The captain appeared at their table, a bit of ale spilling over the top of his large mug. "I knew Gertrude would take care of you."

"We cannot thank you enough," Isabella mumbled, her mouth full of stew.

Rebecca stood, leaned forward, and kissed his cheek. "Yes, thank you for your kindness."

He blushed, his ruddy cheeks growing even darker. "It was my pleasure ladies. Safe journeys." Embarrassed, he retreated to join other sailors at the bar.

They ate their meal and finished their cups of ale. Gertrude cleared their plates, and motioned for them to follow her up a narrow set of stairs. They looked back at their bags, but she waved her hand.

"I'll have them brought up." She continued up the stairs. "Let's get you settled."

She led them to a door at the end of the hallway, opened it and stepped inside.

"It is not much, but it will be plenty of room." She furrowed her brow. "No one would dare try anything in my inn, but still bolt the door when you sleep. I don't want some drunkard interrupting your sleep."

"Of course," Isabella said.

"Tomorrow we will discuss arrangements north. I know a merchant leading a caravan to Lyon." She grinned. "He owes me a few favors."

"We are forever in your debt," Rebecca said.

"Us ladies need to watch out for each other. The world is full of scoundrels with only one thing in mind." With that, she turned back toward the door. "See you in the morning."

It rained most of the next day, transforming the streets into shallow streams, which only a few brave souls navigated. One such individual burst through the door around noon, the rain dripping from his felt cap and leather coat. He was tall and wide, with thick black hair and a long, thin mustache.

"Gertrude?" he bellowed, shaking off his jacket and tossing it on a nearby chair. He peered toward the man behind the bar. "Where is she?"

The bartender flicked his thumb toward the nearby door, which flung open a moment later. Gertrude emerged, glaring at the newcomer.

"Pierre, why are you yelling? I have customers." She waved around at the nearly empty room.

"Ah, damn the customers." He took a few steps forward, grabbing both her hands. "You called for me?"

"Yes. I would like to call in one of my favors."

His expression collapsed. "That is not what I was hoping you would say."

"Now Pierre, you know that I love you." She lowered her chin and eyed him. "But not in that way."

"Damn it, woman, I'm a successful man! Any woman in Nice or Lyon would welcome my hand in marriage."

"I'm not any woman, Pierre." She released his hands. "Now, that favor."

He placed both hands on his hips. "What?"

Gertrude looked over at Isabella and Rebecca, the pair having watched the exchange from a table near the fireplace.

"They need passage to Lyon."

He shook his head, water flinging off his hair and beard. "No, no. I carry goods, that is all."

"Now Pierre." She smiled at him. "Do you remember how I helped you out of that cinnamon problem?"

"Of all the things, why do you bring up the cinnamon?"

Isabella stood and approached the pair. "I'm sorry to interrupt." She nodded to Pierre. "My name is Isabella. And we can pay a fair price for passage to Lyon. I assure you, my sister and I will cause you no trouble."

"You do not know my men." He chuckled.

"Pierre." Gertrude crossed her arms, the cleavage of her large breasts exposed.

"Damn you woman. You vex my heart." Pierre sighed and shook his head in resignation. "When the rain stops, we wait one day for it to dry a bit, and we leave."

"I knew you would come around." Gertrude leaned forward and kissed his cheek.

"You are such a tease," Pierre said.

"Of course, and that is why you love me," Gertrude replied.

The rain stopped the next afternoon, and they spent the following day preparing for the journey north. They were told it would take two weeks by wagon, so Gertrude helped them procure the provisions necessary for the trip.

She sat down and had dinner with them the night before they left.

"Now girls, Pierre is a good man. He will keep you safe, warm, and dry." She shoveled in a spoonful of mutton, then continued. "But I cannot speak for his men. You must assume every one of them is a horny little troll."

Rebecca choked on a piece of bread, covering her mouth with one hand.

"Good advice." Isabella glanced over at her sister.

"What happens when you reach Lyon?"

"We meet with my husband," Rebecca said.

"Is he in Lyon?"

"No, Austrasia."

"Oh, Austrasia." She scrunched her face. "Lots of trouble in that province. Ever since Pepin died. There are many people looking to take advantage of the chaos."

"Yes, my husband is in the middle of that."

"Well, don't tell anyone that." Gertrude pointed her empty spoon at her. "You don't know who supports who. And alliances change every day. Men are fickle, and power to them is like sex. They will do anything to get more."

Rebecca blushed again, while Isabella nodded in agreement.

Gertrude left them to attend to bar business, while Isabella and Rebecca finished dinner. When they were done, Isabella waited until Gertrude was alone, then stood up and walked over to her.

"How much do we owe you? The food, lodging, supplies." Isabella smiled. "And the favor you called in."

"I have more favors with Pierre than I could ever call in." She leaned forward on the counter. "What currency are you paying in?"

"Papal gold."

"Hmmm, I would say three gold pieces will cover it all." She paused. "If you can spare that."

Isabella produced a small pouch and slid it over to Gertrude. "I think five is fair."

"I cannot be taking all your gold." Gertrude pushed the pouch back toward her.

"You're not. I keep it split up and hidden in many places." She winked.

"Smart girl." Gertrude picked up the bag, and it disappeared into the folds of her dress. "Your sister. She is a sweet young lady. But I feel she is not as wise to the world as you are."

Isabella glanced back at Rebecca, then at Gertrude. "You're right. She is too trusting. Always has been."

"Aye, I had a brother like that. Kind soul." Her face hardened. "But this world does not favor kind souls. It chews them up and spits them out. Keep a close eye on her."

"I will." She reached out and took Gertrude's hand, squeezing it. "Thank you."

"It was my pleasure." Her smile beamed. "Stop and see me if you come back this way."

They were off at the crack of dawn. Two dozen wagons creaking north, with a half-dozen men on horseback moving up and down the line. Each wagon had a driver, and every other one had a second man as a guard. Isabella insisted on driving her wagon, after assuring Pierre she was up to the task.

He rode up and down the line on a giant black charger, wearing the same leather coat and felt hat he had worn the day they met. The only difference was the longsword strapped to his side.

The road north sliced through a deep forest of elm and birch, a thick canopy looming above them. The spring sunrays cut through the foliage, a welcome companion on the cool spring morning. They made it to another small town by mid-afternoon, but did not stop. Instead, Pierre set up a camp about three hours north of the village.

HAMMER OF GOD

Each day was the same. Up at the crack of dawn, the wagons on the road after a cold breakfast. They paused midday for a lunch of dried meat and bread. Dinner was a reheated soup after the animals were put away for the night. The men kept to themselves, with only Pierre directly interacting with the two women. He checked on them each morning, and throughout the day. He insisted his men take care of the ox pulling their wagon, despite Isabella pointing out she could handle it herself.

They slept in the wagon, the open sky above. The third night was moonless, and with no clouds, the stars took center stage. It was as if an ocean's worth of diamonds had been cast into the sky.

"I'm anxious to see Thomas," Rebecca stated.

"I'm sure you are. It has been several months."

There was a long silence.

"Do you think people change?" Rebecca asked.

Isabella glanced over at her sister. "I think people try to change. And sometimes it works. It is a hard thing to change who you are. Most people tend to slip back into who they were."

"Do you mean Marcus?"

Isabella flinched. She did not think it was that transparent. Then again, it was her sister. "Yes and no. I think it applies to everyone."

"I do not think Marcus has changed."

"Really?"

"No. He is the same man he was seven hundred years ago; stubborn and impulsive."

"That I agree with," Isabella cut in.

"And fiercely loyal, to a fault. I think the only thing that has changed is where that loyalty lies."

There was a long silence, and eventually Isabella said, "I had not thought about it that way. He is loyal to Thomas and Nico. And I guess the church."

Rebecca glared at her. "Are you daft?"

"What?"

"Of course he's loyal to Thomas and Nico, and the church because *they* ask him to be."

"Why am I daft?"

"And I'm supposed to be the naïve one." She rolled to her side. "Marcus would move heaven and earth for you."

"What?" Her eyebrows furrowed. "I mean, he would do that for any of us."

"Maybe. But for you, he would march straight into hell and stay there if he needed to."

Isabella stared up at the sky. "Perhaps. But there is one thing he cannot do."

"And what is that?"

"Stop dying." She sighed. "And when he dies, he returns a different man."

Rebecca shifted closer to her sister, laying her head on her shoulder.

"I know. Someday." She paused, and when she continued, her voice was lower. Almost like she shared a secret she did not want anyone else to hear. "I think Thomas has changed."

"How so?"

"In the beginning, his only focus was sharing the word. Teaching people about Christ. Now he is more concerned about the church. It is almost like he has forgotten about the individuals that make up the church."

"In his mind, protecting the church *is* protecting the people in the church."

"Perhaps. But I'm not convinced the men who lead the church think of it that way."

"Because they're men, and they focus on power first."

"Or sex," Rebecca added.

"Yes, that too," Isabella laughed.

After a long pause, Rebecca continued, "I don't know how to

talk to him about this." She looked up at her sister. "He sometimes looks at me like I'm a child."

"No, not a child. But he wants to protect you. And when he does that, he cannot see that you're as strong as any of us. Perhaps stronger."

"I doubt it."

"Listen to me." Isabella looked into her eyes. "Strength is not controlling people or forcing them to do what you want. Strength is standing up for the weak, and doing what is right, no matter the consequences. And you should never stop doing that."

Rebecca nodded and looked back up into the sky. "How much longer?"

"Three days, I think."

"I enjoy traveling with you to unknown places. It's exciting."

Isabella grinned and glanced over at Rebecca, but she had already closed her eyes. Taking a deep breath, she snuggled further under her blanket and drifted off as well.

It took four days to reach Metz. A rainstorm slowed their progress near the end, soaking everything they owned. The sight of a city was a welcome relief.

Pierre rode back toward their wagon, the black charger trampling through the muck. He came to a stop next to them, his boots and legs coated with mud.

"Ladies." He pulled off his hat and wiped his forehead.

"Pierre." Isabella nodded.

"Where shall I lead you?"

"The cathedral."

"Of course. I shall ride ahead to find the way."

They stayed with the train as it moved through the wide gate of the city and into a plaza on the other side. Soon after they pulled to a stop, Pierre reappeared and motioned for them to follow. Leading their oxen away from the group, Isabella guided their wagon down a narrow street, the gutters swollen from the recent rains. They made three turns, and the church appeared before them.

The main spire stabbed at the light blue sky like a dagger. A long set of steps led to a pair of massive oaken doors. Isabella pulled the wagon to a stop near the base of the steps.

"Shall I go in with you?" Pierre started to dismount.

"No, I think we will be fine," Isabella said.

"Very well." He bowed his head. "It has been my pleasure. I'll be at the Dancing Pony Inn if you should need anything."

"Thank you. I appreciate your help and watchful eye."

He winked and galloped away.

Isabella looked at her sister and down at their dirty clothes. "These will not get any cleaner. Shall we?"

Nodding, Rebecca climbed down from the wagon, Isabella close behind. The two made their way up the steps and pushed open the door.

The inside was dark, with only a bare minimum of light coming in from the various windows around the room. The walls were made of thick stone, with wooden beams in support. Several rows of benches lined each side of the room.

An individual standing near the front turned from the altar he attended and made his way to them. He was tall and thin, with a large nose that appeared even larger because of his shaven head. He wore a simple brown woolen gown that extended down to the ground. "Is something wrong?" he asked.

"No, why?" Isabella glanced over at Rebecca.

"We rarely have female visitors, especially during the middle of the week." He looked at her muddy dresses.

"I apologize. We are not properly dressed," Rebecca said. "We came from Nice."

"We are supposed to meet someone here," Isabella added. "His name is Thomas."

"Oh." He rubbed his bald head. "You are Isabella and Rebecca!"

"Yes!" Rebecca said.

"Come with me."

He headed toward the far end of the church, where he led them through a small door that opened into a wide room with a long table. Two men were seated at the table, and a third stood near a door on the far wall. The man looked back toward the two ladies and introduced them to the others.

"This is Rigobert, the Bishop of Rheims," the priest said. Motioning to the ladies, he continued. "This is Isabella and Rebecca."

"Of course." Rigobert stepped forward and bowed. He wore a long white robe with gold stitching. "Pleasure to make your acquaintance."

"And yours." Isabella bowed. "Rheims? Why are you so far south?"

Rigobert smiled, a twinkle in his eye. "My lady knows her geography."

"It's important to know the land you travel in," Isabella said.

"Of course. Lyon is without a bishop, so I will shepherd this flock."

"I'm sure they are lucky to have you."

"You are too kind." His head tilted to the side. "We were worried, as we expected you days ago."

"We encountered some bad weather along the journey." Isabella looked from the bishop to the other man. "Where is Thomas?"

"I'm afraid he is occupied," the other man at the table said. He walked around the table and took Rebecca's hand, placing a kiss on it as he looked into her eyes. "I am Lord Allard of Aquitaine. My father is the Duke Odo of Aquitaine and an ally of Charles. Thomas asked me to escort you to Metz."

"He did?" Isabella's brow furrowed.

"Yes." Allard stood tall, glancing at Isabella. "I was already traveling to Lyon to purchase supplies for the upcoming campaign." His eyes traveled back to Rebecca, eyes sparkling. "I'm more than happy to be of service."

Isabella studied him. He was tall, with wide shoulders and a slender waist. His black hair was long and wavy, hanging just past his shoulders. A scar ran along his left cheek, wide enough to interrupt his short, trimmed beard. Allard could sense her apprehension and seemed to remember something. "I forgot." He reached into his tunic and produced a small piece of parchment, which he handed to her.

Isabella unfolded the paper, Rebecca leaning close to get a glimpse.

"That is Thomas's handwriting," Rebecca said.

"Yes, it is." Isabella folded the parchment back up. "I'm sorry for my skepticism, my Lord. But one can never be too careful."

"Of course." He smiled and continued, "Do you have luggage?"

"Yes, several bags in the wagon in front of the church."

Allard addressed the man by the door. "Add them to our caravan." He looked back to the ladies. "I'm sure you are exhausted. You can go with Felix, and he will take you to the inn on his way to our caravan. They will draw you a bath. We leave first thing in the morning."

"Thank you." Rebecca bowed. "Bishop." She nodded to Rigobert, and the two ladies followed Felix out of the church.

It was late. They had both taken baths, washing away a week's worth of grime. Isabella looked down at her nearly empty bowl and the half-eaten loaf of bread. Rebecca was staring into the nearby fireplace. Most of the inn was empty, save for Allard and his men. They kept the server busy, regularly refilling pitchers of ale.

Isabella glanced over as Allard stood, grabbing his mug as

he stumbled towards them. She reached over and tugged on Rebecca's sleeve as he arrived.

"Good evening ladies." His slurred salutation was directed at them both, but his eyes were on Rebecca. "I trust your meal was adequate."

"Quite," Isabella responded. "We were heading to our room."

"Come now, the night is early." He slumped into a nearby chair. "At least share one cup of ale."

"We don't drink." Rebecca forced a grin.

"Just a sip?" He angled his cup toward her, the contents spilling over the lip and onto the table.

"No thank you." Rebecca nodded.

"We should be going." Isabella stood, Rebecca following suit. "We shall see you in the morning."

He sat back and waved one hand at them as they left.

The pair had reached the stairs when Rebecca whispered, "I don't like him."

"Neither do I."

Isabella had to use the bathroom. A single, slow burning lamp cast its dull light across the room. She pulled on her robe and picked up a dagger laying on the nightstand, slipping it into her pocket. She stepped out into the hallway and down a flight of steps to the empty inn below. An older lady, the innkeeper's wife, was behind the bar, drying a wooden mug. She smiled, several of her front teeth missing. "How can I help you, my lady?"

"I need to use the bathroom."

She nodded. "Through the back door."

Isabella looked back over at the tables where Allard and his men had been drinking.

"They finally went to bed?"

"We ran out of ale."

"Really?" Isabella frowned.

"Well," she winked, "that's what my husband told them."

"Understood." She grinned and headed toward the back door. Ten minutes later, she returned and headed back up the stairs. As she approached the door to her room, she saw it was cracked open. Her heart jumped into her throat as she rushed through the door. Despite the low light, she could see a man lying on top of Rebecca, his trousers pulled down to his knees.

Isabella sprung forward and grabbed the man by his tunic, yanking him away.

One of his hands was over Rebecca's mouth, the other groping her exposed breast. He twisted toward Isabella, and she immediately recognized Lord Allard.

"Get off of her!" Isabella tried to drag him from the bed.

"Let go of me, bitch!" Allard struck her with the back of his hand.

Isabella recoiled from the blow, her jaw exploding in pain as she fell to the ground. He stumbled off the bed, pulling up his trousers.

Ignoring the pain that shot through her jaw, she pulled the knife free, and standing swung the weapon towards his face.

Allard jerked away, the blade having sliced through his cheek. He raised one hand to the cut, then looked at the blood on his fingers. He glared at her, but Isabella had backed away, knife held in front of her.

"Have you ever used one of those before?" He sneered.

She ignored him, sliding to the side as he tried to circle her.

"I'm going to gut you with that knife, and finish with your sister."

He lunged forward, and she instinctively thrust the knife towards him. But that was what he wanted, and one hand shot out to catch her wrist. Despite her superior strength, he used his leverage to break her grip on the blade. His other hand shot forward, smashing into her nose.

Darkness crept into the corners of her vision as Isabella fell

HAMMER OF GOD

to the floor. Allard bent over and picked up the knife, twisting the blade in his hand.

"It's not very sharp. This may get messy."

"No!" Rebecca ran forward, grabbing the lord by his tunic.

He shoved her to the ground. "Wait your turn!"

Focusing his attention back to Isabella, he straddled her and pinned one of her hands beneath his leg, holding the other with his left hand. His other held the knife, which he used to slice through the top of her nightgown. She struggled, but could not free her arms.

He leaned forward, breath wreaking of stale wine. Isabella spat in his face and channeled her energy into breaking free. One hand escaped his grasp, and she struck his face, aiming for the cut. Her fingernails dug into his flesh, eliciting a painful scream.

He hit her again, almost knocking her unconscious. The coppery taste of blood filled her mouth as she continued to claw at his face. He raised his hand to strike again, but Rebecca smashed the water pitcher into his head. The ceramic pitcher shattered into a dozen pieces, water splattering all around the room.

Allard's eyes rolled back as he slumped to the floor. Isabella pushed his limp body off her and stood. The room spun as she tried to maintain her balance. Rebecca moved closer and helped steady her.

Isabella looked down at the knife Allard had dropped.

"No, you cannot," Rebecca said.

"Why not? He was raping you!"

"No, we cannot kill him in cold blood." She looked at him, then at Isabella. "And how would we explain it? He is a duke's son. No one would believe us." She started to cry. "I never should have let him in. I didn't realize he was drunk."

Isabella grabbed her shoulders. "No, this is not your fault."

B. K. GREENWOOD

She glared down at Allard, and back to Rebecca. "We must get out of here. You change and I will pack a bag."

Rebecca wiped her nose with the back of her hand and nodded, then dressed. Isabella shoved a bunch of things into a single sack, retrieving the rest of the coins she had hidden in a drawer. Lastly, she picked up the knife and slipped it back into the folds of her gown, before grabbing both of their cloaks from a nearby chair.

"Where will we go?" Rebecca asked.

"We only know one person in this town."

"Pierre?"

"Yes."

Rebecca looked over at her sister as they started down the hallway. "Will he help?"

"I hope so."

CHAPTER FIVE

Patience is the art of concealing your impatience.
—Guy Kawasaki

Spring, 716 A.D.
Metz, Duchy of Austrasia

Marcus could hear the lively discussion before he entered the church hall. It sounded like a dozen men were yelling. Nothing gets men riled up like church politics, Marcus thought. He pushed the door open and stepped inside, then leaned back against the wall and observed.

There were only ten men in the room, and two of them were sitting in silence. The other eight were hurling insults and accusations at the pair. Thomas looked up as Marcus entered the room and shrugged. Nico shifted his attention from one angry face to another. A man at the far end of the table attempted to calm down his companions.

"Hold on, this is getting out of control." He held up both hands.

"You're meddling in our politics!" one of the younger men said. He was not dressed like a priest, but in the clothing of a hunter or trapper. The others pounded the table in support.

"Bishop Hubertus, please," the man at the head of the table said. "Let us hear what they have to say."

Hubertus, a tall, thin man with sharp eyes and narrow features, held his tongue. He stroked his thin beard and nodded.

The apparent leader motioned to Thomas. "The floor is yours."

"Thank you, Bishop Willibrord." Thomas stood, placing two hands on the edge of the table. "I have come here on behalf of the Holy Father. His concern is for the welfare of the Church, not local politics."

"Then why did you free Charles?" Hubertus asked.

"Fair question." Thomas moved away from the table, his hands pinned behind his back. "Less than a hundred years ago, a new religion emerged from the holy land. It swept across the African continent and jumped the sea," he stopped and scanned the table, "securing a foothold in Hispania."

"We know this." Hubertus took a step toward Thomas. "What does that have to do with Charles?"

"For now, the mountains provide a natural barrier to their expansion. But they have crossed deserts and seas. The mountains will not stop them. But Charles can. He is the legitimate heir of Pepin. He has trained his entire life to lead men into battle."

"Pepin had my predecessor assassinated," Hubertus said. "Why should I trust Charles?"

"Plectrude would place an eight-year-old boy on the throne. Do you trust him to stand against the Saracens?"

Hubertus glared at him, then looked over at Willibrod.

"I don't care about your internal politics," Thomas continued. "You can support whichever local lords you wish. I only care about one thing; creating a unified Gaul strong enough to face a Muslim invasion. Charles is the only man who can do that."

"We make all our own local appointments?" Hubertus eyed him suspiciously.

"The Holy Father still appoints bishops, but below that, yes. We will validate with Charles." Thomas looked back at Nico.

The latter nodded. "I will speak with Charles."

Hubertus looked at the others, eventually stopping at Thomas. "Can we talk among ourselves?"

"Of course." Thomas walked around the table as Nico stood to join him. Together they made for the door, Marcus pushing it open for them.

As the door closed behind them, Marcus noticed the smirk on Thomas's face.

"Will they go for it?"

The smirk shifted to a grin. "They have no choice. We have far more gold, a legitimate contender for the throne, and a dozen lords gathered to meet that contender."

"Why meet with them?" Marcus asked.

It was Nico who replied, "They can make a lot of noise. Better in private and to us than during a sermon."

"And Charles?" Marcus asked.

Nico grinned. "His exact words; you are the churchman, you deal with the other churchmen."

"So, we don't expect any issues with them?" Marcus held the chapel door open, allowing the men to step outside.

"No, Willibrod is the most influential of the group, and Charles has agreed to be his benefactor."

"What does that mean?" Marcus looked from Nico to Thomas.

"The Frisian King sacked Willibrod's abbey." Thomas grinned. "Charles will need to take it back and rebuild it."

Marcus shook his head. "I don't know how you stomach all these things." He looked up at the cloudless night, then over at Nico. "Can we get something to eat? Or drink?"

"No, we have to meet with Charles," Nico said. "I'm sure you won't starve to death."

"Not funny." Marcus frowned and tried to ignore the hunger pangs in his stomach.

Thomas, Marcus, and Nico waited in the antechamber. Nico looked nervous. Thomas looked skeptical. Marcus was hungry, and thirsty.

Marcus had decided to find some wine when the door to the bedchamber flew open and Charles burst into the room. The young man was a commanding presence. Gone were the rags he had worn in the prison, replaced by a tailored tunic, embroidered with gold and purple. His hair and beard were freshly cut, the grime from months of confinement scrubbed away.

Charles looked around at the men, his eyes widening. "No wine?"

"That's what I said." Marcus glared at his companions.

"This is very serious, Charles," Nico cut in. "You need to be sharp."

"Believe me, with no wine, I'm dull." Without waiting for a response, he waved to a nearby servant. "A pitcher of wine and cups. And be quick about it."

The servant nodded and scrambled from the room.

Charles gave a smile, which faded when his eyes fell on Thomas. "Who are you?"

"Forgive me." Nico stepped forward. "Allow me to introduce

our friend and trusted companion, Thomas. He just arrived from Rome. He brings good tidings and support from the Holy Father."

"Good tidings are always welcome." Charles's eyes narrowed to slits. "But what type of support is the question?"

"Spiritual, of course." Thomas smiled. "But also the shiny kind."

Charles's face split into a massive grin as the servant arrived with the pitcher of wine. "That is something I can drink to."

"It's about damn time." Marcus took the cup and waited as the servant filled them.

"To the pope," Charles said, raising his cup, "and to his shiny support."

Thomas shot Marcus a sharp glance and sipped his wine. Marcus ignored him and took a long pull himself, nearly draining the goblet. The liquid was bitter and lacked the complexity he was used to in his native wine. But then again, he had grown accustomed to terrible libations across the globe. The taste was not the reason he drank.

"What now?" Charles held out his cup to be refilled.

Nico set his down. "Dinner with local nobles. They don't think your mother-in-law can resist the Neustrians."

"Believe me, she can do more than resist," Charles said.

"Don't tell them that. They were loyal to your father and are looking for a reason to be loyal to you."

He drained his second cup and grinned. "I shall give them one."

Without waiting for a response, Charles disappeared down the hallway leading to the great hall.

"I like him." Marcus grabbed the pitcher from the nearby servant and followed Charles before the others could reply.

The great hall occupied the center of the castle. The ceiling was thirty feet above, lost in darkness. A dozen torches spaced around the room did an adequate job of lighting the chamber. A giant hearth occupied the far wall, with several pots hanging above the roaring fire. A long table filled most of the room, around which a dozen men sat talking and drinking.

Marcus had caught up with Charles, and they entered the chamber together. The crowd grew quiet as the confident young man strode into the room, his gaze sliding across the faces until it stopped on someone he knew.

"Frederic!" Charles darted around the end of the table and marched toward a noble who appeared to be of similar age.

Frederic stood as Charles approached and returned his embrace. "Charles!"

Charles leaned back, his head tilted to the side. "How long has it been?"

"Four years," Frederic said. "Maybe five?"

"I think five." Charles grinned. "Do you still have the limp?" He looked for Marcus before Frederic could reply. "This crazy fellow jumped from a horse, full speed, in armor, knocking a half-dozen men to the ground." He glanced back at Frederic. "Do you still have the limp?"

"I do, but it doesn't slow me down."

"Good to hear!" Charles slapped him on the shoulder, then looked around the table, and ignoring the empty chair near the end, pointed to a spot next to Frederic. "Can I sit here?"

"Of course." Frederic motioned for a servant, who brought a plate and cup.

The others slid down the bench, creating enough space for Charles to sit. As the young man stepped over the bench, he motioned to Marcus. "Sit at the end of the table." Charles grabbed a cup someone had filled and tilted it toward Marcus. "I would like to toast the man who set me free."

The other men raised their cups. "Here, here!"

Marcus bowed, sat and reached for the cup of mead in front of him. He looked over the chalice's edge as he took a sip and saw that Nico and Thomas had entered the room, but were staying back in the shadows of the torchlight.

Marcus reached for a piece of roasted meat on a nearby platter. He tore into the juicy flesh and watched Charles go to work. It did not take Marcus long to realize he was a natural.

Within minutes, he had all the nobles around him laughing, and those outside earshot eagerly leaned forward to hear what was said. Charles realized that was the case, and sitting back, projected his voice with more authority. "I will dispense with the pleasantries. We all know why we are gathered here today." He looked around at the faces staring at him. Most of them were at least twice his age. "My father was a fair and just ruler. Many of you stood with him as he fought to build a strong, unified kingdom." They all nodded in agreement. Charles looked at his friend, Frederic. "Some of you, I fought beside. It was always my father's wish that I succeed him as Mayor of the Palace. We talked about it many times. Unfortunately, he was convinced otherwise by my mother-in-law. Now, Theobald holds that title."

A low murmur swept around the table.

"Hold on," Charles said, raising both hands. "I have no ill-will towards my nephew. He is only eight years old."

That is Nico speaking, thought Marcus as he grinned and took a sip of mead.

"But," Charles continued, "I cannot in good conscience betray the honest intentions of my father, and leave you, my fellow nobleman, at the mercy of that wretched woman. Even now, she cowers in Cologne while the Frisians and Neustrians pillage the land. Is that who you want as your leader?"

"No!" several men, including Frederic, yelled.

"With you at my side, I will build an army and drive these invaders from our lands. Then, I will take my rightful place as the Mayor of the Palace and deliver stability and prosperity to our kingdom."

The nobles exploded in applause. I'll be damned, Marcus thought. He didn't ask for their help, he offered to save them. Genius. Marcus looked at Nico, and despite the shadows, he could sense his old friend smiling. The Roman's gaze drifted to Charles, who sipped his mead and winked back at him.

The dinner went on for another hour, and one by one, the nobles came and knelt beside Charles, pledging their fealty, and most importantly, troops and supplies. By the night's end, everyone was drunk, the raging fire was a pile of smoldering embers, and Charles had an army.

As the last noble left, Thomas and Nico stepped from the shadows and joined Marcus and Charles. The latter had stood and was draining yet another glass. He set it on the table, but too close to the edge. As it fell, Marcus snatched it from midair. Charles appeared stunned at the speed at which Marcus moved, but Nico distracted him.

"That seemed to go well."

"Well?" Charles scrunched his face. "It went how I planned." He yawned. "I'm going to bed. Tomorrow, we figure out how to take back my kingdom."

Without another word, Charles disappeared down the hallway towards his chamber. The trio left behind stared at one another before Thomas broke the silence.

"I'm stunned." Thomas scratched the stubble on his chin. "He might be the most natural leader I've ever seen." He glanced over at Marcus. "No offense."

"No need to apologize. You're right. I'd follow that man anywhere." Marcus looked from Thomas to Nico. "What do we do now?"

"I trust you and Ander can help Charles build an army?" Nico asked.

"We can."

"Who is Ander?" Thomas looked from Nico to Marcus.

HAMMER OF GOD

"He helped us free Charles," Nico said. "You'll like him. He's a more charming version of Marcus."

"Wait—" Marcus angled the empty chalice towards Nico.

"Marcus," Nico tilted his head, "trust me, he is."

Marcus frowned, but it was Thomas who spoke. "I'm looking forward to meeting him." His face twisted in thought as he turned to Nico. "How many spies do you have?"

"Enough," Nico replied.

"If you need gold for more, let me know."

"I will."

"Isabella and Rebecca will be here soon." Thomas looked from Nico to Marcus. "I assume we are safe at this location?"

Marcus maintained a stoic expression, despite his stomach doing flips. "Of course."

"Good." He glanced at the table. "Shall we eat?"

"I was hoping you would get to that." Nico moved to the chair near the end of the table.

As the two sat, Marcus grabbed a pitcher of mead and waved to his companions. "I'll see you tomorrow."

"You have better company?"

"I'm going to eat with a more charming fellow... he was not allowed into the dinner."

"Tell Ander I said hello," Nico said.

"I will." Marcus headed for the main door and exited into the courtyard. He crossed to a set of barracks running the length of one of the fortress walls. He could hear the ruckus before he pushed open the door.

A dozen men were gathered around a toppled table, some standing, some kneeling. Ander was on one knee, opposite the table, shaking his right hand. It flew forward, and a pair of wooden dice tumbled to the hard-packed floor. The yelling stopped as the dice careened off the table and came to rest next to a pile of coins. A symphony of moans shattered the silence, several men raising their hands to their heads.

Ander grinned and shrugged as he leaned forward to retrieve the coins.

"Wait a minute!" one of them said.

"Yes?" Ander said.

The man rose, towering over the Basque. "No one can be that lucky."

Marcus watched, trying to figure out where he was going to set the pitcher down when the brawl began.

Ander stood. "Would you feel the same way if I was that unlucky?"

The man's face twisted in thought. He was drunk, and the logic, or lack thereof, was stunningly confusing to him.

His reply was uncertain. "No?"

"Then maybe I am that lucky."

The man looked around at his friends, but none of them were sober enough to provide the mental support he required. "I guess so."

"Good." Ander leaned over and scooped up the pile of coins. When he stood, he spotted Marcus by the door, holding the pitcher. He clapped the man who had challenged him on the shoulder. "See, now you're the lucky one. My friend is going to pour you a cup of nobleman's mead." He poked the man in the chest. "That is worth more than these coins."

Marcus closed the distance between them and poured the man a cup. The group dispersed, leaving Marcus and Ander alone.

"I'm afraid this is ordinary mead." Marcus filled both their cups.

"He's drunk." Ander took a long pull. "To him, it is the best cup of mead he's ever had, and perhaps someday he will save our lives."

"Probably not."

"You're too skeptical."

"And you're too optimistic."

"And that," Ander held up his cup, "is why we make such a great team."

Marcus tapped his cup and drank. Ander did the same, then wiped his mouth with the back of his hand. "How did the meeting go?"

"We have an army."

"Good." Ander crinkled his brows. "What are we going to do with it?"

"That," Marcus smiled, "is an excellent question. And one we will answer tomorrow."

"Sounds like a wonderful plan." He drained his cup and held it out for Marcus to fill.

Over the next several days, Marcus helped Charles establish a general staff, and map out the plan to assemble his army. The nobles had been quick to swear their allegiance to Charles, but specific details around their contributions to the war effort were not as forthcoming. A week after the first meeting, Charles had two-thousand men at his disposal, including twenty-five knights.

They converted the great hall into a war room, and Charles and his staff were standing around the large table, a map of the surrounding region spread across its surface. Several pitchers of mead, some empty, occupied the rest of the tabletop.

"Cologne is the key," one of the older knights said. "As long as your mother-in-law—"

Charles glared at him.

"I mean, Plectrude. If Plectrude holds the city, she will prevent many nobles from backing your claim."

"Not to mention, she controls the treasury," a second knight added.

Charles nodded, but did not respond. He took another sip

of mead when the door flew open, a figure rushing into the room. Marcus's hand slipped to the hilt of his sword until he recognized the face that emerged from beneath the cloak.

Nico stopped nearby and looked straight at Charles. "Chilperic has marched a Neustrian army into Austrasia."

"Who the fuck is Chilperic?" Marcus asked, several of the knights chuckling.

"The King of Neustria." Nico placed both hands on the table and leaned forward. "And that is not all. The Frisian King, Radbod, plans to meet with them. They will march on Cologne together."

"Shit," Charles muttered. "How many men?"

"Between them?" Nico exhaled. "At least five thousand."

The only response was the soft crackle of the fireplace.

"Why all the long faces?"

They all turned to find Thomas standing behind Nico. He removed a pair of gloves, which he set on the table, and poured himself a glass of mead.

"A combined Neustrian and Frisian army is marching on Cologne," Marcus said. "Five-thousand strong."

"And how many men have we raised?" Thomas asked.

"Two thousand," Charles said.

"Add a thousand more." Thomas took a drink and smiled. "I am back from Strasburg, where I hired a group of Alemanni. Or a pack of Alemanni. I'm not sure what they call themselves. They hate Neustrians."

"That is wonderful news!" Charles beamed. "We should march immediately!"

The others nodded in agreement.

"Should we?" They all stopped and stared at Marcus, but he continued before they could respond. "We just formed the army. They've barely begun to drill together. Now we add a thousand mercenaries." He looked from Thomas to Charles.

"We would be marching against a superior force, one that has had months to prepare and train."

"They do not know Charles has this army," Thomas countered. "We will catch them by surprise."

"You don't think they have spies? And even if they don't know about the army, what do you think surprise will gain us?" Marcus pointed to the map. "We will have to meet them between the Neustrian border and Cologne. That puts Plectrude and her army behind us. What is to stop her from marching out and attacking us as well? Or perhaps she waits until we beat the hell out of each other and attacks what's left."

"We must act boldly." Thomas glanced at Charles, then back at Marcus.

"There is a fine line between bold and foolish," Marcus said. "I think this crosses that line."

"I agree with Marcus." Nico leaned forward and pointed to the area near Metz. "We can consolidate our base here, gather more men and strike after Chilperic attacks Cologne. Preferably while he lays siege to the city."

Some knights nodded in agreement. Charles, so far quiet, stared at the map. He was cradling his cup in one hand, his thumb rubbing the smooth wooden surface. The tense lines on his face softened, then he drained the cup and set it down on the table.

"We march tomorrow." He looked at Marcus. "I understand your concerns, and I share them. But I am my father's son, and he was foolishly bold."

Marcus nodded. "Of course. I will notify the men." The Roman nodded at the others and headed for the door. He needed to find Ander to make the preparations. Marcus exited into the night beyond, the chill cutting through his thin tunic. He was halfway across the courtyard when Thomas caught up with him.

"What the hell was that?"

Marcus turned back toward him. "What do you mean?"

"Why did you disagree with me?"

"Because I think you're wrong." He could see the frustration on Thomas's face in the pale moonlight. "Why are you so adamant about marching now?"

"We need Charles to consolidate these provinces. Divided, they will never stand against the Saracens."

"And we do that in due time, but rushing into battle will not improve our chances." Marcus motioned around the barracks. "I don't want to risk the lives of these men. I would think you, above everyone else, would understand that."

"I'm not worried about a single man, or even a thousand men."

"Do you hear yourself? What happened to the man who preached compassion and acceptance?"

"I've seen the way the real world works. The only way to stop violence is with violence." Despite the shadows, Marcus could see Thomas's jaw tighten. "I would think you, above everyone else, would understand that."

Marcus's heart dropped, an awkward silence settling between them. "You're right. I'm a killer. Some would say a murderer." Marcus swallowed back the emotions welling inside. "I'd like to say every man I killed either deserved it or was trying to kill me. But that's not true. There is a darkness inside me... a darkness that can't wait to escape. And when it does, people get hurt." Marcus paused, his eyes watering. "Sometimes innocent people, but that is why I have you." He pressed his lips together. "You have always been the light that keeps that darkness at bay. Without you, I'm afraid it may consume me."

Thomas studied Marcus, tears filling his eyes as well. "You, my friend, are strong enough to control that darkness. You don't need me for that. There is a goodness in your soul. You only need to accept that." He took a deep breath. "I'm sorry. I know you're doing what you thought was best. And so am I." Before the Roman could reply, he changed the subject. "Let's eat."

Marcus grinned. "I'll be there as soon as I can. I need to prepare the men for tomorrow."

Thomas turned away, calling back over his shoulder, "Don't be too long, I'm famished."

"I won't."

It was dark, but still they rode on. Pierre had assured Isabella that the city was less than an hour away. Rebecca rode beside her, cloak wrapped around her petite frame. Pierre was several horse lengths in front of them, his tall frame a silhouette in the darkness.

Isabella pulled back on the reins, slowing her horse. Rebecca noticed what she was doing and did the same. When they had dropped another dozen paces back, Isabella looked over at her sister.

"We're almost there."

"I know." Rebecca met her gaze. "We can't tell Thomas the truth."

Isabella sighed.

"Promise me?"

"Why? Why are you protecting him?"

"Protecting him? I'm not protecting him. I'm protecting Thomas. And everything he is working on."

"How so?"

"Thomas may believe us, but nobody else would."

"Marcus would."

"Of course. And he will kill Allard, without hesitation." She looked up at the sliver of a moon and back at Isabella. "What good would that do? Marcus would get himself killed, the duke would abandon Charles, and march against him."

They rode in silence for a few minutes before Isabella said, "You're right. I won't say anything."

"Good."

"What do we tell Thomas?"

"I'll tell him that Allard was delayed in securing supplies, and we wanted to reach Metz as quickly as possible. Pierre offered to bring us."

"Alright."

They rounded a corner and found Pierre stopped in the trail, looking back at them.

"I thought I had lost you, and so close to the end of our journey!"

"Of course not." Isabella looked down at one of her horses' legs. "He started limping, so I slowed down."

Pierre watched the horse's gait as they approached.

"He seems fine now. Perhaps he stepped on a rock. No matter." He pointed to a break in the trees covering the trail. "The city is beyond the open field."

"Wonderful!" Rebecca pulled her horse to a stop next to Pierre's. "We can't thank you enough for your kindness."

"How can I resist such charming ladies?" His smile was the only part of his face they could see in the night.

"I hope this will not damage your standing with Allard, or his father," Isabella said.

He shrugged. "Pierre always finds a way."

He nudged his horse forward, and the three of them emerged from the forest, following the trail across an open field. The city walls shone in the pale light, taller buildings visible above the battlements.

They rode up to the gate and waited. A few moments later, a single guard emerged from a small door. "The city is closed. We'll open the gates again at sunrise."

HAMMER OF GOD

Pierre urged his mount forward. "These young ladies are relatives to a man in Charles's entourage. They will not wait until morning."

"Who?"

"Thomas the Syrian," Isabella replied. "He's an advisor to Charles."

"Wait here." He disappeared back through the door.

Isabella looked over at Pierre. "Where else would we go?"

He chuckled. "Guards are simple men."

Ten minutes later, the main gate swung open. A pair of men, one of them the guard, emerged. Isabella recognized Thomas and slid off her horse. Rebecca did the same.

Thomas hurried forward and embraced Rebecca, then wrapped one arm around Isabella, kissing her cheek.

"Where is Allard?" He looked back along the trail, before glaring at Pierre. "And who is this?"

"This is Pierre." Rebecca moved between the two men as Pierre dismounted. "He was kind enough to escort us from Lyon."

"Escort you?" Thomas looked from Rebecca to Isabella. "That's what Allard was supposed to do?"

Isabella said, "Allard was delayed. Something about securing supplies. So, we hired Pierre to escort us."

"That was not wise. These are dangerous times."

Before he could continue, Rebecca took his arm. "I know, but I couldn't wait to see you. And Pierre is very familiar with this route."

He smiled at her. "Of course, I'm glad you made it safely." He stepped forward and reached out his hand. "I thank you for bringing my wife and her sister to me."

"My pleasure." Pierre returned his grip.

Isabella stepped forward, handing Pierre a bag of coins. "As we agreed."

He accepted the coins, removed his hat, and bowed. "It was my pleasure."

Thomas walked away, but stopped and said, "We could use good men in our cause."

"I am a trader, not a fighter." Pierre smiled. "When the war is over, I will return and help rebuild what has been destroyed."

"Fair enough. Good luck!" Thomas led the two women through the gate.

"You as well." Pierre called after them as he grabbed the reins of the three horses.

"Where to?" Rebecca asked.

"I'm sure you are hungry! I'll get you something to eat, then you can sleep. We have a very large manor that I'm sharing with Nico and Marcus."

"Great, I'm starving!" Rebecca said. She glanced at Isabella, but her sister avoided joining the conversation by looking away.

"I've missed the two of you." Thomas held Rebecca's hand. "Nico and Marcus are fine company, but..."

"But they're not as refined as we are." Rebecca grinned. "You can say it."

"I thought I did."

Isabella kept pace, but did not engage in conversation. She studied each building they passed, and the shadows they cast, thinking the Roman might appear from them at any moment. But he did not. And soon they reached the main keep's kitchen.

The reunion would have to wait.

Several hours later, Marcus slipped into the house, the door creaking as he pushed it closed. The only light in the large chamber came from a candle on a shelf by the door. The fireplace was nothing but a black hole in the far wall.

He moved to a nearby cupboard and pulled out a loaf of

bread wrapped in cloth. Ripping off a piece, he shoved it into his mouth as he searched for some wine or mead.

"Not much of a dinner."

Marcus nearly jumped out of his boots and spat out a piece of bread. "What the—"

Isabella stood in the middle of the room, the candle illuminating her slender form.

"There is some salted meat and cheese in the other cupboard." She stepped past him to grab the candle and moved it to a nearby table. "I'll get you a cup of wine."

He met her at the table with a knife and an armful of food. She took the knife from him and sliced off a piece of meat, then cheese. She sat, slid the plate with the food over to him, and poured them each a cup.

"Are they ready to march?"

"Word travels fast." He took a bite of meat, followed by a smaller bite of cheese. He continued with a mouthful of food. "Yes."

She poured herself a glass. "And you march with them?"

"Yes." He met her gaze for a moment, before taking a sip of wine.

She nodded and held the cup with both hands. "How long?"

"It is hard to say. If the weather holds, it's a week's march. A few days to maneuver for battle. If we win, we will march on Cologne. If we lose..."

Her eyes narrowed. "You think you might lose?"

"I said if we lose."

"It was the way you said it." She sipped her wine. "Thomas said he upset you."

"No." Marcus shook his head. "We had a disagreement. That happens. I'm not upset."

"You wouldn't tell me if you were." She eyed him over the cup, eyes sparkling.

"Probably not." He grinned. "I'm not much on sharing."

"That is the most accurate thing you've said in seven hundred years."

He chuckled and pushed his plate away. "I have my moments."

"I'll clean up." She set her cup down and stood. "You get some sleep. I'll see you in the morning."

He stood and watched her walk away.

"Good night," he said as he moved to the bedroom he shared with Nico.

CHAPTER SIX

You have to know when to strike and when to retreat.
—JOHN OATES

SUMMER, 716 A.D.
AACHEN, DUCHY OF AUSTRASIA

Charles shifted on his horse and studied the distant army. "What do you think?"

"I think that's over five thousand men," Marcus said, as he gripped the reins of his horse loosely in gloved hands.

They had ridden to a hillock overlooking the wide valley below. A wall of foot soldiers lined the opposite end of the vale, a thick forest behind them. A small cluster of knights waited behind the line, under the shadows of the leafless trees.

"Should I retreat?" The last word barely escaped Charles's lips, and it seemed like he wanted it back.

"No, that would be worse than a loss." Marcus exhaled. "But

we cannot withstand a long, pitched battle. Our only chance is to win a quick, decisive victory."

"And how would you suggest we achieve that?"

Marcus pointed to the forest. "It looks thin. Perhaps I can lead our knights through the forest and attack their flank. But I need time."

"How long?"

"I think it will take us three or four hours to get around."

"I will delay deploying the men." He smirked. "Then I can parley and ask for time to consider whatever offer they make."

"That could work."

"How will I know you are in a position to attack?"

"That's a good question."

"You can fire a flaming arrow into the sky," a third voice suggested.

They both spun around to find Thomas and Nico behind them.

"What the hell?" Charles twisted in his saddle. "How did you approach so quietly?"

"We have an excellent instructor." Nico winked at Marcus. "We wondered where you two had drifted off to. The sentry pointed the way."

"Sounds like you have a plan." Thomas urged his horse forward, his eyes on the distant army.

"Will it work?" Charles said to no one in particular.

"Perhaps, but it gives us options," Marcus said.

"What do you mean?" Charles leaned forward.

"One of two things will happen when we attack their flank." Marcus pointed along the tree line. "They will panic and flee to the east, which will allow your men to cut them down."

"Or?" Nico asked.

"If they're disciplined, which they are, and have good leadership, which they probably do, they will commit their knights and pivot part of their infantry to engage us. But that will allow you to disengage."

"Retreat? I thought you said that was a terrible idea," Charles said.

"It would be if you did not fight at all. But in this case, you have shown a willingness to fight." Marcus shrugged. "And we'll engage the knights, so you should not have to worry about them chasing you down."

Thomas eyed the Roman. "What about you?"

Marcus grinned. "That will go poorly."

"I'll go with you," Thomas stated.

"No." Marcus shook his head. "We'll need a couple of strong leaders here to rally the men during the retreat. You should support Charles."

Thomas met his gaze and nodded in agreement. "If you think that's best."

"Yes." Marcus glanced back at Charles. "No use getting both of us killed."

"What's the plan?" Ander was in full armor, which comprised chain mail, and a few select plates of iron. Like Marcus, he had decided not to use a shield.

"We sneak around." Marcus curved his hand toward the distant forest. "Ride through the trees and attack them really fast."

Ander looked back at the small band of knights. "How many?"

"Seventy-three."

"I think we're going to die."

"You said that last time."

"This time, I mean it." He adjusted the strap on his helmet. "It is important?"

"I think it is the only chance Charles has at surviving this battle."

"Then we do it." Ander grinned. "But you should go first."

They continued down the narrow dirt road and turned into the forest when they were sure they had passed the enemy line. The birch trees were spaced so perfectly, it looked like someone had planted them on purpose. Marcus looked up at the pale blue sky through the naked branches. Small green sprouts that promised to be leaves graced the tips of the branches.

Flat and unbroken ground allowed them to make good progress. Half an hour later, Marcus could see the trees opening in the distance. Motioning for the group to stop, he unslung the bow across his back and pulled an arrow from the quiver on his saddle. He retrieved a piece of damp cloth from a leather pouch and wrapped it around the tip.

"Can you light this please?" Marcus held it out for Ander.

The Basque retrieved a flint, and after a few times striking the stone, a spark ignited the cloth. Marcus knocked the arrow and guided his horse to the right with his legs to position himself under a clear spot in the branches. He pulled back the string and let the arrow fly. It zipped through the trees and into the sky beyond, leaving a thin black trail of smoke in its wake.

Tossing the bow to the ground, he motioned for the knights to gather around him. "The plan is to break their formation. Try to keep moving and drive them back." Marcus unhooked a mace hanging over the horn of his saddle. "If they don't break before reinforcements arrive, we need to keep them occupied long enough for Charles to retreat. On my signal, you disengage and head back to the camp." He looked around at the battle-hardened veterans. They all nodded. "Good luck."

They angled back toward the distant valley and prepared to move forward. Marcus held them back until he heard distant drums, along with several horns. He waited another few minutes and led the knights forward.

HAMMER OF GOD

They made it to the forest's edge without being sighted. The two armies were locked in combat, less than a hundred yards away from the tree line. Charles's men were outnumbered and giving ground. Wasting no more time, Marcus lowered his mace, and the tiny group sprang from the trees and galloped across the open ground.

They smashed into the formation of infantry near the back of the right flank. Marcus knocked one man down with the shoulder of his horse and crushed the helmet of another to his right. The cry of alarm rose from the infantry as the knights hacked and smashed their way into the line. At first, the plan seemed to work. Several of the infantry stumbled over their companions to avoid being trampled.

But a few seasoned soldiers spun and met the new threat, encouraging their comrades to do the same. By then, the initial momentum enjoyed by the knights was almost spent, and the scene devolved into a desperate melee, foot soldiers stabbing and clawing at the horsemen, while the knights tried to remain mounted and keep moving.

But the attack managed to distract the main line, which allowed Charles to disengage. Marcus heard the three short blasts that marked the retreat, as did the other knights.

"Keep them occupied!" Marcus yelled at Ander, who was hacking his way through a pair of soldiers.

"I am, you crazy man!" Ander spurred his horse on, knocking several more to the ground.

The screams of horse and man punctuated the clank of metal on metal. Marcus cleared enough space to spin his horse around, and could see Charles had disengaged his men. He also noted that a fresh set of enemy knights was on the way from the center of the battlefield, near the tree line.

"Time to go!" Marcus leaned forward in his saddle and urged his horse forward.

Ander wheeled his mount and followed suit. A couple

dozen other knights still in their saddle did the same. They pushed through the front of the enemy line and toward Charles's retreating infantry. The enemy knights had the advantage of fresh horses, but they had to ride around the edge of the line to pursue.

Marcus slowed, allowing the other knights to pass him. It was going to be tight. The last man was in front of him, with two enemy knights only a few strides behind.

He pulled his reins with one hand and swung his mace at chest level toward one pursuer. He caught the man by surprise, the bulk of the weapon smashing into his chest. The man flew from his saddle and thudded into the ground. The force of the blow knocked the mace from his hand, leaving Marcus without a weapon. The other knight flew by, but spun around and charged at Marcus, sword leveled.

Marcus spurred his horse forward, closed the gap, and at the last minute leaned toward the other knight and smashed the palm of his hand into the man's face. His head snapped back, and he nearly fell from his horse. Pain shot up through Marcus's hand and wrist, which meant he had probably broken several bones. The tip of the knight's sword slid along Marcus's thigh armor and pierced his hip. The blade slipped from the wound and to the ground when the knight dropped it to regain his balance.

Ignoring the sharp pain, Marcus spurred his horse forward and a few moments later, entered the safety of the infantry formation.

Marcus slowed his mount and guided it toward the other knights, who had been joined by Thomas and Charles.

Charles looked down at the blood seeping from his armor. "Are you alright?"

"Yes, just a nick." Marcus looked over at Ander, who was bleeding from a gash on his cheek. "Another memento?"

The Basque winked at him. "The girls like scars."

"So I'm told." He looked around the group. "How many made it out?"

The grin faded from Ander's face. "Twenty-three."

Marcus glanced at Thomas, who had yet to say anything. The latter looked away. The Roman shifted his gaze to Charles.

"You have shown them you will fight." Marcus grinned. "Now, let us build you a proper army."

"Indeed."

They spent the night in their fortified encampment. Chilperic did not pursue, and it was clear his goal was to march on Cologne and depose Plectrude. Cologne had formidable defenses, so they assumed it could hold out for at least a month or more.

The next morning, the army marched south into the Eifel mountains. It was a shallow mountain range, dotted with tiny villages and small, round lakes. They passed several farms shaking free of the winter snap, the rich brown soil ready for planting. On the third day, they stopped and made camp in the shadows of a giant granite monolith.

Charles sent couriers to all regions of Austrasia, requesting support. The nobles, having moved slowly to fulfill their vows, finally arrived with reinforcements. Gold, much of it provided by Thomas, allowed Charles to purchase supplies he needed. Within two weeks, several wagon trains laden with weapons and armor arrived from the neighboring Duchy of Allemani.

It had been a month since the initial battle, and Charles stood on the edge of a clearing, watching Ander lead the men through drills. The Basque relished his new role, and he used his stature and experience to hone the young men into a lethal fighting force. The angry red scar only added to his reputation.

Marcus was making his way to Charles, biting into a crisp

apple as he walked. Charles glanced at him, a puzzled look on his face. Marcus, reaching into his pocket, revealed another apple and tossed it to the young man. Charles caught it, wiped it on his tunic, and took a bite.

"I have an idea," Marcus said between bites.

"I sometimes like your ideas."

"The men did a great job when retreating in the last battle. They maintained their ranks. They trusted you." Marcus took another bite, continuing as he chewed. "That's rare."

"What are you saying? Should we retreat ourselves to victory?" Charles frowned.

"Perhaps." Marcus tossed the apple core over his shoulder. "Walk with me, and I'll fill you in."

As the sun set, Marcus headed back to camp, planning to meet Thomas and Nico for dinner. Nico had returned from a two-week trip visiting the nobles, and Marcus hoped that included commitments for more troops.

Marcus was lost in thought, trying to determine if Charles had enough troops to face Chilperic again. He started when someone called his name.

"Marcus!"

He turned to see a woman approaching from the shadows. He recognized Isabella immediately. "Stop doing that."

"What?"

"Surprising me."

"How else am I supposed to get your attention?"

"Make some noise when you walk up."

"That is stupid." She looked him up and down. "Thomas said you were wounded?"

"Just a scratch." He smirked. "You know how that goes."

"I do, and I doubt it was just a scratch."

"Why are you here?"

"Changing the subject, are we?" She smiled. "Thomas thought it was safe for us to join. He says Charles is

HAMMER OF GOD

gaining more followers every day. He says the Neustrians are awful and pillaging the countryside as they siege Cologne."

"All true. We are six-thousand strong now."

"You'll march soon?" It was more a statement than a question.

"I suspect we will."

"I have a request."

His eyes narrowed to slits. "What's that?"

"You must keep this between you and me."

He eyed her suspiciously.

"Promise Marcus."

"I promise."

She walked down the path as he settled in beside her. "I want you to teach me how to defend myself."

"What?" He stopped, and gripping her arm spun her towards him. "Why?"

"I think I should be able to protect myself. Is that wrong?"

He studied her for a long while. Her green eyes sparkled in the fading light, but there was a sadness in them.

"What happened?"

"Nothing *happened*," she looked down, "to me."

"Rebecca?" His voice was almost a growl.

She looked up at Marcus, trying to ignore the fury in his eyes. "Will you teach me?"

"Who was it?"

"Why would I tell you? So you can go kill someone? Or a bunch of people?"

"Yes—"

"That's not what I'm asking for!" She glared back at him. "I don't need you to be my protector. You won't always be there; we both know that. And we also know that I'm strong enough to protect myself. I need training."

He looked down and realized both his hands were clenched

into fists. He swallowed and unclenched them, nodding silently.

"Good. We will start when you get back." She smiled. "Are you hungry?"

"Yes," he whispered. Despite his calm demeanor, a rage filled his soul.

CHAPTER SEVEN

The backbone of surprise is fusing speed with secrecy.
—Carl von Clausewitz

Summer, 716 A.D.
Amel, Duchy of Austrasia

It was a beautiful spring day, about to be ruined by death and carnage.

Marcus, atop his coal-black charger, rode next to Ander at the head of a column of soldiers. The small valley they marched across was covered in yellow, ankle-deep grass. A thick, green forest encircled the shallow dale.

"Do you think this is going to work?" The Basque leaned over and rubbed his chocolate brown mare's neck.

"You tell me." Marcus glanced back at the men marching behind them. "You trained them."

"I trained them to fight and listen to commands."

Marcus grinned. "Then it should work."

B. K. GREENWOOD

"I have a good feeling about this."

Marcus frowned. "You do?"

"Yes." Ander looked up at the sky. "Blue skies, a cool breeze, and a well-trained army. What else could be in our favor?" Before Marcus could reply, Ander nodded across the open field.

Marcus squinted against the morning sun. A dozen large tents and hundreds of smaller ones marked the location of Chilperic's camp. A few short horn blasts confirmed someone had spotted Marcus and his tiny army.

"Now what?" Ander asked.

"We line up and fight."

"Where?"

Marcus scanned the edges of the forest, checking for the boulder he had seen the night before. When he found the marker, he pointed to it. "Line up even with that rock."

"Consider it done." Ander pulled on his reins, angling his horse back to the column where he barked orders to his leaders. Marcus moved his horse off to the side and let the column lumber past. Compared to the previous army, these men were well-trained, well-supplied, and in high spirits. They joked as they marched forward, several of them nodding at him and smiling.

They liked Charles. He had met with each unit, explained the plan, and asked for volunteers. These men knew what was expected of them and had taken an oath to follow the orders given.

About a hundred paces away, the column split in two and formed a line across the valley, four men deep. Marcus scanned the formation, a knot in the pit of his stomach. Neither flank was anchored on the forest's edge. The exposed formation violated every military axiom he had ever learned or practiced. His tiny force was primed and ready to be annihilated.

Ander guided his horse back to Marcus, coming to a halt beside the Roman. The Basque nodded behind Marcus, where

HAMMER OF GOD

a trio of riders galloped toward him. One carried the red and gold banner of the House Martel. Charles, in the lead, skidded to a stop next to Marcus. The banner man and Thomas joined soon after.

Charles looked past Marcus to the line of soldiers. "Are we ready?"

"We are," Ander said.

"Are they coming out?" Charles gazed across the field.

"They will, once they see your banner," Marcus said.

"Are you sure?"

It was Thomas who replied, "Yes. Chilperic knows how popular you are here. He must take the chance to eliminate you."

"Eliminate me. You didn't say that when we were planning this."

"We rarely tell the bait the entire plan," Marcus said.

"Bait? Is that what I am now?"

"Important bait." Marcus grinned and nodded to Ander. "We should join the men."

"I should be with you," Charles said.

"Absolutely not." Marcus shook his head. "We talked about this... you must stay out of danger. Everything falls apart if you are captured or killed."

"I don't like others fighting my fight."

"Get used to it." Marcus spun his horse around. "That is what great leaders do."

Without waiting for a reply, the pair spurred their horses forward. Within a few minutes, they had reached the back of the formation. As they came to a halt, a mass of infantry men marched out into the valley. Just behind was a large contingent of heavy cavalry. The latter was the most concerning.

Marcus slid off his horse, retrieved a shield tied to the saddle, and angling the steed back toward the way they had come, slapped its rump. The beast reared up on two legs and sped off down the valley. Ander did the same.

Marcus moved forward, making his way through the ranks until he was near the front, took a few more steps forward and turned toward the men. "For Charles!" he yelled, raising his sword into the air.

"Hurrah!" the men yelled.

Marcus raised his sword again, and this time the men banged their weapons against their shields. He did that several more times and turned around to track the enemy's advance.

They had formed up about five-hundred paces away. Twice as wide, and three times as deep. Several banners fluttered above a large group of mounted men. The cavalry was still lined up behind the infantry.

That is a good sign. Chilperic does not want to waste cavalry on such a small force. The thought had barely entered his mind when the entire enemy line advanced. About two-hundred paces away, they stopped, and a group of archers emerged from within the ranks.

Marcus took a few steps back and rejoined the formation, kneeling with his shield angled toward the sky. The others followed suit, forming an effective barrier. A few moments later, they heard a chorus of thuds as the arrows plunked into the shields, punctuated by a scream as a missile found its mark.

Marcus groaned in pain as an arrow burst through the gap between him and his neighbor, piercing his leg. It had entered above his knee, on the outside of his thigh. Looking down, he saw the tip protruding out the back of his leg. Shaking his head, he waited for the arrow shower to stop. A few moments later, the last of the projectiles had finished crashing into the wall.

Marcus peeked through the gap and spotted the enemy infantry advancing past the archers. He stood, wincing as pain shot through his leg. He lowered his shield and pulled his sword free.

HAMMER OF GOD

"One minute boys!" Marcus yelled to those around him. "I only ask for one minute."

Marcus looked at the lad next to him. The lad nodded back at Marcus, a steady resolve in his eyes. He looked down at the arrow sticking from Marcus's leg. "Does it hurt?"

"Only when I think about it."

The young man smiled, but it faded when he glanced toward the approaching enemy.

It was an imposing sight. Chilperic's men had won a series of battles, including the defeat Charles had suffered. They were experienced, eager, and confident.

That would be their demise.

The swaying grass between the armies disappeared as Chilperic's men closed the gap. Marcus could feel the apprehension from the surrounding men. At ten paces, Marcus spied one of the enemy soldiers moving ahead of his compadres.

Marcus took a few steps forward and smashed his shield into the man. As the man stumbled back, Marcus dropped the tip of his sword through his neck. He pulled out the blade, blood gushing from the wound.

"Remember your oath!" he yelled.

The other men in his line cheered the tiny victory and lunged forward to meet the advance.

The lines crashed together in a violent, twisted mass. Marcus was beset by a pair of soldiers, one wielding a massive two-handed axe. It was a splendid weapon for smashing into an enemy formation, but Marcus was too quick to be caught by such an unwieldy weapon. The Roman stepped into the wide, swinging arc, using his shield to pin the man's arms, and smashed him in the face with the pommel of his sword.

As the man fell backward, Marcus swung his sword back to parry the second man's attack. The latter screamed as the tip of a sword emerged from his chest. The soldier fell to the ground, and Ander pulled his weapon free.

"That was reckless!" Ander yelled, blocking another sword thrust with his shield.

"It worked." Marcus stabbed a portly fellow who carried a far too small shield.

His men had absorbed the initial impact, but could sense the momentum would be shifting. If they waited too long, it would be impossible to execute the plan with any precision.

"It's time!" Marcus screamed as he kicked the man in front of him in the chest, ignoring the sharp pain shooting up and down his leg. The man fell back into several of his companions, and Marcus used the brief respite to blow his whistle.

The hours of drilling paid off. On cue, the men who were not engaging a soldier bolted from the line. Those engaged used their shields to knock their opponent backwards, then joined the others in flight.

Marcus watched in awe as a gap appeared between the two lines. One in mass retreat, the other in shock at the sudden cowardice of their opponents.

"Marcus!" Ander grabbed the Roman's arm and pulled him toward the retreating soldiers.

Marcus groaned in pain as he ran alongside the Basque.

A loud cheer erupted behind him, and Marcus glanced back to see Chilperic's men bearing down on them. His eyes shifted to the forest edge, and his heart sank—they must have been delayed. Thoughts of the impending massacre filled his head as he struggled to keep up with his retreating men. Glancing to the forest one more time, his sense of doom turned to elation as a dozen heavy calvary emerged from the trees and galloped toward the flank of the enemy formation. Right behind, a mass of infantrymen poured into the valley.

None of Chilperic's men saw the new threat. They were focused on the retreating army, their once tight formation now spread thin across the valley. An alarm sounded among the enemy as the cavalry smashed into their flank, tearing through scattered ranks.

Marcus could not see, but assumed the same thing was happening on the other flank. A few minutes later, the infantrymen joined the melee, cutting down the confused and winded enemy.

Marcus stopped and blew the whistle again. The retreating soldiers stopped and rejoined the fight. Surrounded on all four sides, Chilperic's men were doomed. Those who understood their predicament dropped their weapons and surrendered. Once again, discipline and training won the day. Charles had been very clear that any soldier who surrendered would be spared.

Within minutes, the last of the enemy had surrendered or died. It was a stunning result, but the battle was not over. Out of nowhere, Charles appeared with a dozen other heavily armed men. Two of them pulled empty horses, which Marcus and Ander climbed onto, the former a bit gingerly.

"The camp!" Charles pointed to where Chilperic had been watching the battle with his heavy cavalry. They were gone, fleeing back to his camp. Charles rushed forward, his retainers close behind.

The mass of horses thundered across the valley and into the camp, cutting down anyone in their path. Marcus saw dozens of knights exiting the other end of the camp. They set out in pursuit, but a small group of soldiers blocked their advance. Outnumbered and outmatched, the rearguard was overrun. But its sacrifice was not in vain, as Chilperic escaped.

That was the only blemish in the otherwise flawless victory.

Charles shifted his attention to Chilperic's abandoned pavilion. He slipped from his horse and burst into the tent, his companions close behind. What they found was nothing short of astonishing. A dozen wooden chests, each stuffed with gold, silver, and jewels.

Charles strode to the closest chest and ran his fingers over the seal in the wood.

"This is from my father's treasury." He looked from Marcus to Thomas. "Plectrude must have paid Chilperic to abandon his siege."

"And now it is yours," Thomas said.

Charles lifted the lid and picked up a handful of gold coins. Dropping them back into the pile, he closed the lid. "Time to pay the men, and offer those who surrendered a place in our army." He pointed to the chest. "With a small reward to convince them."

"The same as your men?" Thomas failed to hide the skeptical look on his face.

"No, half. With a promise of equal share in future battles."

Thomas nodded.

Marcus scanned the chests and looked back at Charles. "What next? Do we march on Cologne?"

"I am tempted." He paused, deep in thought. "But Chilperic is still my most dangerous opponent. We must ensure he leaves Austrasia and does not hook up with the Frisian bastard."

"And Plectrude?" Thomas asked.

"In time. She is weak and no longer a threat." Charles turned to Nico, who had entered the pavilion. "For now, we go home. We celebrate this victory and I baptize my son."

Marcus looked from Thomas to Nico, a surprised look on his face. "You have a son?"

"Yes, Roman." Charles grinned. "You should pay attention to things other than war."

"Apparently I should." Taking a step forward, he extended one hand toward Charles. "Well, congratulations are in order." He looked around at the others. "And a feast, I believe."

CHAPTER EIGHT

If the path be beautiful, let us not ask where it leads.
—Anatole France

Summer, 716 A.D.
Metz, Duchy of Austrasia

"Feet spread, shoulder width apart." Marcus leaned forward. "Your weight should be just front of center. I don't want you on the balls of your feet, but your weight should not be set in your heels."

Isabella nodded as she watched Marcus intently. They practiced in a small private garden Marcus had secured with Charles's permission. He did not know why Marcus requested the garden, and it would stay that way.

"Remember, you are stronger and faster than any man. And more importantly, they won't expect that. Use that to your advantage." He raised one finger. "Don't overextend, that will put you off balance. Do everything with purpose."

B. K. GREENWOOD

He handed her a wooden sword and walked through the various defensive positions. During the first session, they worked only on parries. After an hour, Isabella stepped back and placed one hand on her hip.

"When do I get to attack?"

Marcus grinned. "When you can no longer be attacked."

"That's boring."

"Being defensive isn't boring."

"I've heard Thomas describe you in battle. Defensive does not come up in that discussion."

"Because that's not my personality." Marcus spun his wooden sword around and buried the tip into the garden soil. "A fighting style should reflect your personality. It doesn't mean you always use that style, but that should be who you are as a warrior. Some are methodical, defensive..."

"Thomas."

"Yes. That suits him." Marcus shrugged. "Others are not. Take Ander. He is one of the greatest warriors I have ever met."

"Better than you?"

"No," he grinned, "but not because I'm more skilled. I'm faster and stronger than him. That gives me an unfair advantage."

"Does he know?"

Marcus raised his eyebrows. "About?"

She cocked her head to the side, eyes probing.

"Yes, he knows."

"What did you tell him?"

"The truth."

"Why?"

"I don't know. We connected almost immediately. Almost like we were brothers."

She raised her eyebrow. "I thought you had that with Thomas?"

"I do." His gaze drifted. "But Thomas is like that serious,

older brother. We come from such different backgrounds... it's nearly impossible for us to connect on many levels."

"And you do with Ander."

"Yes. And that is why I told him the truth."

"I'm impressed you have that level of trust."

"With him or anyone?" Marcus eyed her.

"Both." She grinned. "Does he fight like you?"

"No." Marcus shook his head. "He is more carefree and fluid. It is almost like he is dancing. Much different from me."

She squinted at him. "You fight angry."

"Usually."

"Did you always?"

"No." He sighed. "That is something I learned along the way."

"And me?"

"You—"

"Be very careful," she warned.

He pulled the sword from the ground. "You will master whichever style you choose."

"Very good answer." She retrieved her sword and looked up at the noonday sun. "Let's get ready for the baptism."

It was the largest church in Austrasia, and it was bursting at the seams. Most of the nobles in the room had abandoned Plectrude after the latest victory, and now they came to the baptism to pay homage to Charles.

Their small band sat five rows back, allowing the nobles to sit closer to Charles. It took Nico and Thomas a week to arrange the visitors, ensuring rivals were placed far enough apart to avoid trouble, yet close enough to the front to represent their influence.

Charles was standing with his wife, whom they had met

that week. She was taller than the average woman, with coal black hair and a bronze complexion. She was from Iberia, the daughter of a lesser noble. Their son was born while Charles was in prison.

Bishop Willibrord conducted the ceremony in Latin, which meant the entire audience did not understand what he was saying. When it was over, they waited for Charles to greet and thank his visitors. Most of the church was empty when they approached the young couple.

"Beautiful ceremony," Thomas said, bowing.

"It was." Charles grinned, his son nestled in one arm. "I wish I understood what the hell they were saying."

"Charles," his bride said, pinching his arm, "language."

"Ouch!" He pulled away from her and nodded at Nico and Thomas, then the ladies. "Pardon me."

"Of course," Isabella smiled, "we all have our vices."

"I think she's talking about me," Marcus added.

"I assumed that." Charles handed his son to his wife. "I have some business to discuss. I will join you later for dinner."

"Yes, my lord." She took her son and joined a small group of women waiting a few feet away.

Charles looked back at them. "I've been so busy with the baptism. Are we ready to march?"

"We are very close," Marcus said. "Nico has secured the supply routes. Ander and I have been training the new recruits. Thomas purchased a thousand more war horses, plus wagons and oxen for the baggage train."

"How many men?" Charles looked from Marcus to Ander.

The latter responded. "Fifteen-thousand foot soldiers, and another two-thousand calvary."

"You will double anything Chilperic can muster," Marcus said.

"Excellent! When can we leave?"

"The roads should be dry in two weeks," Nico replied.

"Perfect. We march as soon as they clear." He rubbed his two hands together and looked at Rebecca and Isabella. "Pardon me, ladies. I'm sorry for such talk."

"Understood, my lord." Isabella smiled. "We are accustomed to these discussions."

"I should refrain from them in your presence. I know it is difficult to hear about your husbands going off to war."

"Husband," Isabella corrected with a smile.

Charles glanced from Isabella to Marcus, the latter uncomfortable. "Of course. My mistake."

There was an awkward silence, which Nico eventually broke. "Shall we go eat?"

A single lantern provided barely enough light to see the edges of the room. The front and back door of the stable were open, allowing a cool breeze to blow through. He was sitting on a short wooden stool, sharpening his sword with a piece of jasper. The steady grind of stone on steel, joined by the soft neighing of a horse.

He was lost in thought, mechanically running the stone along the edge. *Was splitting the army in two the right decision? Did we choose the correct routes? Will the weather hold?*

"I think it's sharp enough."

Marcus snapped back to reality and looked up to find Nico standing beside him. The older man grabbed a nearby stool and pulled it next to the Roman. Sitting, he nodded toward the sword.

"How long have you been sharpening that?"

Marcus looked down at the shiny edge and back up at Nico. "At least an hour."

"If you keep going, there won't be any sword left."

"That would take a long time."

Nico chuckled. "And we have plenty of that."

Marcus scrunched his face and returned his gaze to his sword.

Nico frowned and studied Marcus's face. "Something wrong?"

"Time. I've lost my sense of it. I've even come to despise it." He exhaled. "It's so precious to everyone else. To me, it's a curse. I know what it does to mortals, and what it will never do to me." He looked over at Nico. "Do you ever feel that way?"

"Sometimes. But I'm not the same as you. This could all end for me, like it has for other immortals. We can die. You and Thomas cannot. It must be a terrible burden to bear."

"Why would he do that to us?" Marcus's voice held a rare vulnerability.

Nico stared back at him, tears welling in his eyes. "I don't know, my son. I wish I did. I wish I could help make it go away. But I can't. All I can do is help guide you and be there for you when you need me. And perhaps, together, we can find a path."

"My path seems pretty clear." Marcus looked down at his sword, stood and slid it into its scabbard. He slipped the stone into a small pouch and looked back at Nico. "And I think most of the time, I take that path alone."

Nico stood as well. "You may feel alone, but that is never the case."

"I know." Marcus leaned forward and placed one hand on his friend's shoulder. "I do."

"Good." Nico joined Marcus as the Roman walked toward the nearest stable. "How long do you think the campaign will last?"

"Through summer." He pulled over the door and moved to put a bridle on his horse. "But all our spies say Chilperic has no money left in his treasury. I doubt he will field an army that can face us. So, we should be home by fall."

HAMMER OF GOD

"Good. We will continue to pry support from Plectrude." Nico smiled. "Hopefully, we can convince her to surrender."

Marcus smiled and led the horse toward the gate. "I like your optimism, but things never go that easy."

"Sure they do," Nico called back over his shoulder as he headed for the exit. "And someone in this group has to be hopeful."

CHAPTER NINE

Some may never live, but the crazy never die.
—Hunter S. Thompson

Fall, 716 A.D.
Cologne, Duchy of Austrasia

The walls of Cologne glared down at them like the enemy they were. Somewhere inside, Charles's mother-in-law was probably glaring at them as well.

A dozen men stood on a small hillock; a massive army spread out before them. They had spent the early days of summer marching across Austrasia and into Neustria. Chilperic had gathered an army of conscripts and mercenaries, meeting them next to the River Escaut in Northern Neustria.

This time, no elaborate plans or ruses were required. The armies met on an open field, and Charles crushed his opponent in less than an hour. Chilperic fled back to Paris, with Charles close behind. Unable to withstand a siege, the broken king abdicated, allowing Charles to appoint a successor of his choosing.

Soon after, the victorious army marched back to Austrasia and focused on dealing with Plectrude. Charles's army was fifteen-thousand strong. A cohesive, battle-tested force, hearkening back to the Roman legions. They now camped outside Cologne's walls.

Beyond the encampment, clear ground led up to the thick base of the city battlements. The walls cast long, dark shadows across the barren landscape. Towers protruded out and above the walls at regular intervals.

Marcus stroked the beard he had grown. "Strong defenses."

"My father believed a powerful kingdom began with a strong home."

"He succeeded." Marcus glanced over at Nico. "Are they ready for a siege?"

"Unfortunately, yes." Nico grimaced at Charles. "I agree with your decision to pursue and defeat Chilperic, but that gave her time to prepare."

"She is a smart woman; I will give her that." Charles scanned the walls. "Can we assault it?"

All the men standing around looked at one another. No one wanted to answer. Marcus finally said, "No. You do not have the siege engines. You need to batter the walls or break down the gates."

"Can we build them?"

"I cannot." He shrugged. "I'm a soldier, not an engineer. We can send for someone, but it would take weeks for them to join us. And another month to build the machines."

"Ladders?" Charles pointed to the lower sections of the wall. "I was with my father when we took a city with them."

"Perhaps," Marcus sighed. "I think most of the walls are too high, which means we will have to concentrate on a small section. It will be easier for the defenders to concentrate as well." He shook his head. "It'll be costly."

Charles studied the soldiers setting up camp. He didn't spend a year equipping and training an army to have it massacred in a frontal assault. He nodded. "We don't have to decide today. Nico, send messengers for an engineer. The best you can find. I won't be without one again."

"Yes sir," Nico responded.

Charles said to Ander, "Have the men build ladders. We may need them."

"Of course."

"I have an idea." Marcus grimaced. "It's unorthodox."

"They usually are." Charles crossed his arms on his chest. "But we should hear it, anyway."

"We need a sturdy horse and a very long rope."

Marcus knelt on the ground and drew out his plan in the dark soil. When he was finished, he stood and wiped the dirt from his knees.

"You're right," Nico said. "It's unorthodox... and a terrible idea."

Ander scratched his chin. "It might work."

"Of course, *you* would say that." Nico jabbed a thumb at Marcus. "You like all his stupid ideas."

"Not all of them." Ander held up both hands. "I was not in favor of the fire wagon idea."

"Doesn't count," Nico said. "Even Marcus knew that was stupid."

"Hey, I'm standing right here." Marcus glared at Nico, before looking at Charles. "What do you think?"

"I think it's too dangerous." He shook his head. "I can't risk losing you."

"Honestly, I could die storming the city." Marcus looked toward the army below. "And if I succeed, none of them will die."

"Fair." Charles studied the walls of the distant city. The others waited as he deliberated. He finally nodded his head. "When?"

Marcus looked at Nico. "When do we have the next new moon?"

The older man thought for a moment. "Three nights from now."

Marcus grinned. "Plenty of time to practice."

Three nights later, a small group of men waited in a grove of trees, a few hundred yards from the city walls. Marcus, dressed in all black, looked over at Ander and grinned. Thomas looked from the Basque to the Roman.

"Charles agreed to this?"

"Yes." Marcus smiled.

"Was he drunk?"

"No more than usual."

"And Nico?"

"Thought it was a terrible idea."

"I'm with him." Thomas looked back at the city. "Will it even work?"

Marcus nodded at the fourth man in the group, who was also dressed in black. "Berchar won the accuracy and distance contest. I think he is up for the task."

"What is this line made of?" Thomas pointed to a spool.

"Horsehair, I think." Marcus looked up at Ander. "That's what the fisherman said, right?"

"Yes, horsehair. It takes a very long time to make a line this long." He grinned. "It cost Charles two gold pieces."

"Is that strong enough?"

"To pull the rope? Yes." Marcus nodded.

"Why not shoot the rope?"

Ander shook his head. "We tried that. The arrow only went about twenty paces."

"You're crazy if you think this will work," Thomas said.

"Oh, it'll work." Marcus grinned. "Trust me."

"Trust has nothing to do with it." Thomas smiled. "But I'll pay for dinner if it does work."

Ander frowned. "Our dinners are free."

"Exactly." Thomas turned away. "I'll make sure the men are ready."

As he disappeared into the trees, the three remaining men waited for the signal. Right after midnight, Charles would feign an attack on the far side of the city. They hoped that would distract any guards on duty.

A few moments later, a horn blast marked the assault. Marcus nodded to Berchar, and the two men slunk toward the city walls, moving along a narrow ditch they had scouted the night before. As they moved forward, Ander moved farther back into the woods.

The two men reached their destination, about thirty paces from a corner tower of the city defenses. Marcus helped Berchar unravel the line and lay it neatly on the ground. When that was done, the archer pulled out the arrow the line was attached to. He knocked the arrow onto the outside of his bow and looked at Marcus.

"Like we practice, high over the wall. We do not have time to chase this for three hundred yards."

"I'll try." He aimed the bow so the arrow would fly over the inside of the tower and, hopefully, over the far wall.

Marcus pulled a coil of rope from the bag he carried and tied the end of the horsehair line to the rope. Looking up, he nodded at Berchar.

The archer pulled back the arrow, and after making one more adjustment, let it fly. The familiar twang filled the air, along with the soft zipping of the line as it disappeared into the

HAMMER OF GOD

night. Marcus lost track of the arrow, but was relieved when he did not hear it strike the stone wall.

Berchar set down his bow and started toward the city wall. When he reached it, he followed the base around the tower and along the wall on the other side.

This was the part Marcus was most worried about. Finding the arrow, in the dead of night, without moonlight, would not be easy. As the night crept on, Marcus found himself agreeing with Thomas. This was a stupid plan. To keep himself occupied, the Roman pulled a leather harness from his bag and wrapped it around his waist. He found the end of the rope, slipped it into the metal loop, and tied it in place.

He was about to give up and return to the forest when he heard, then saw, the line move. Eventually, the line pulled the rope up and over the wall. Marcus pulled on a pair of gloves and waited.

A single, sharp whistle punctuated the night. A few moments later, a man riding a giant workhorse burst from the trees and galloped toward the city. Ander guided the beast past the tower and out of view, though Marcus could still hear its thundering hooves.

He reached forward to grasp the rope with both hands. His eyes focused on the remaining coil of rope, which had not moved since the whistle. A minute after the hoofbeats stopped, they began again, and the roped moved. He watched as the coil dwindled away, then stood and moved forward as the rope stiffened and tugged on his harness.

They had practiced the correct pace, and so far, it was working. When Marcus was within three paces of the fortress, he jumped and swung his feet toward the stones. His boots landed as he planned, but the rope pulled his upper body forward. He struggled to stay perpendicular as he tried to walk, jog, or stumble upward.

He glanced up and realized the top of the wall was less than twenty feet away. Marcus reached for his knife with his right hand as he struggled to maintain his balance. He freed his blade, but his feet slipped from the wall and his upper body smashed into the stone. He grunted against the pain that shot through his elbows, but held on to the knife.

Marcus was trying to swing his legs back against the wall when he reached the top of the battlement. The rope no longer wanted to pull him up, instead pulling him forward and smashing his chest against the stone. The harness tightened around his chest, crushing the air from his lungs. He used his arms to pull himself up, his legs flailing below.

He felt one rib crack and found it nearly impossible to breathe. With one last attempt, he cleared the wall, the rope dragging him forward and onto the pathway beyond. But it did not stop there. It dragged him along the cold stone.

Marcus reached forward with his blade, desperately slicing at the rope. He twisted as the momentum carried him up against the far wall, again tightening the harness around his chest. With one last slash, the line was severed, and Marcus crumpled to the ground.

Panting, Marcus sat up, shrugged off the harness, and tried to catch his breath.

"Who the fuck are you?"

Marcus looked up at the guard standing over him, sword drawn. The Roman coughed and chuckled.

"What are you laughing at?" He took a step forward and shoved the tip of his blade at Marcus.

Marcus knocked the sword to the side with his hand and stabbed his knife into the top of the man's foot. The guard dropped the sword and cried out in pain. The Roman rose and grabbed the man by his leather armor, and flung him over the wall. The scream disappeared into the night.

He bent over, wincing as a sharp pain shot through his side. He picked up the sword and stepped to the nearby tower. A few moments later, the door burst open. Marcus shoved his sword into the guard who emerged, driving him back through the opening. A second man was close behind, but stumbled as the guard in front of him fell to the ground.

Marcus freed his blade and pounced on the second guard, dispatching him. Moving to the nearby staircase, he moved down the steps and exited the tower. He walked along the base of the wall, making sure he stayed in the shadows, until he came to a large set of metal and wooden doors.

A single guard stood on the far side of the opening, holding a spear as he leaned against the wall. He was asleep, or close to it. Marcus waited a few minutes to see if any others were around and crept along the wall and into the alcove. He inched forward until he was a few steps from the man. He wore the same leather armor as his companions, and a small metal helmet.

Marcus looked down at the blade and up at the sleeping man. He gave in to the pang of guilt and stepped forward, smashed his hilt into the guard's helmet. As the man slumped to the ground, Marcus grabbed the back of his armor and dragged him into the shadows.

The Roman shifted his attention to the door and soon found the heavy beam securing it shut. His heart sank as he realized it took two to three men to put the beam in place. Shaking his head, Marcus set the sword down and moved to where the beam sat in the door bracket. Squatting, Marcus placed his shoulder under the timber, and ignoring the throbbing in his ribcage, drove upward.

It slowly lifted from the brace as Marcus grunted and strained against the weight. When it was clear of the bracket, he angled it away from the door and shrugged it off his shoulder. The beam thudded to the ground. He wiped the sweat from his forehead and moved to the other side, repeating the process.

The beam was close to the door, preventing him from

opening it completely. But it opened enough for a man to slip through. Or a normal sized man. Ander was waiting outside and tried to squeeze through. He braced his weight against the door as Marcus pulled. The beam slid enough to let the Basque in. Several others followed, enough to secure the gate.

"Move that beam," said Ander, directing several of the men.

Four of them grunted as they lifted it up and out of the alcove. When they returned, one of them looked at Marcus. "How did you get that off the door?"

Marcus grinned. "Never underestimate the power of the Lord."

The soldier frowned.

"Secure the street." Ander pointed to the tower. "I want men in there as well."

"Yes, sir."

Fifteen minutes later, five hundred armored knights thundered through the gate, Charles in the lead. He stopped next to Marcus and Ander, a big grin on his face.

"I see you lived."

"Yes, I did." Marcus rubbed his ribcage. "A few bruises."

"Take the rest of the night off." He nudged his horse away from the men. "I think we can take the citadel before they even know we are in the city."

"Good luck."

"Who needs luck when you have crazy men with terrible ideas?" Charles said, then galloped after his men.

It was the largest feast Marcus had ever seen. It comprised a hundred nobles, their wives, and several dozen soldiers who had served key roles during the campaigns. Steaming platters of beef, lamb, venison, and boar flowed from the kitchen, along with baskets of cheese and bread. Pitchers of mead were emptied as quickly as they could be replaced.

Charles sat at a slightly raised table, with a handful of nobles and his young nephew. The latter barely touched his food as he looked around the crowded room. Plectrude took her meal in her heavily guarded, private room.

Marcus, Thomas, Rebecca, Isabella, Nico, and Ander sat at an adjacent table. Marcus leaned over to Nico and pointed to the man to the left of Charles.

"Who is that?"

"Duke Odo of Aquitaine." Nico took a sip of mead. "A powerful man."

"Whose idea was it to invite him?" Marcus popped a piece of cheese into his mouth.

"A smart advisor." Nico winked.

"I thought Charles had his eyes on Aquitaine."

"He does. That's why I invited Udo."

Any further conversation was interrupted as Charles stood and pounded his empty chalice on the table. The room grew silent as he held out his cup to be refilled, took a long swig, and looked out over the guests. "We have gathered tonight to celebrate my official ascension to the Mayor of the Palace, the same title my father held."

The room erupted in cheers. Charles held up one hand to quiet them.

"I owe my good fortune to many of you." He glanced at the table where Marcus sat. "You have provided strong counsel, fought beside me and, on more than one occasion, saved my life. For that, I am grateful. Here's to a long and prosperous reign. May it bring peace and prosperity to all!"

"Here, here!" The others raised their glasses and drank with Charles.

"Now, let the festivities begin!"

With that, music filled the room, as did a dozen young ladies dancing around and refilling cups.

Marcus took a sip from his cup and looked down at his table. Nico and Thomas were engaged in what appeared to be a far too serious conversation. *Probably planning to invade Hispania*, Marcus thought. His gaze shifted across the room to where Ander sat. A young lady with long black braided hair sat in his lap, a pitcher ready to refill his cup. They had spent a good amount of time together over the last few months, and the way the Basque looked at her, Marcus thought he was smitten.

It would be good for him to settle down, while he still could. Marcus took another long pull from his cup and leaned forward to refill it. His eyes drifted to the end of the table, where Rebecca sat, Isabella to her right. Rebecca was sullen, her eyes staring into her cup of wine. Isabella reached out and took her hand. Rebecca forced a smile.

Out of the corner of his eyes, Marcus saw a tall figure pass by. It appeared to be a noble who had made his way from the head table. He wore a cloak, one that very few of the men in the room could afford. He continued forward, stopping next to the two ladies. Isabella looked up, and the color drained from her face. Rebecca followed her gaze, and when seeing the man, stared down at the table.

Isabella glared at him, her jaw clenched. A knot formed in the pit of his stomach when Marcus saw the emotion in her eyes. The noble placed his hand on Rebecca's shoulder, and she flinched.

Marcus set down his cup and stood. Isabella saw him and shook her head, but he ignored her and took several steps forward. When he stopped next to the man, Thomas realized a group was gathering nearby. He looked up and smiled at the nobleman.

"Lord Allard!" He stood and reached his hand out to the young man.

HAMMER OF GOD

"Thomas." Allard returned his grip.

He was in his mid-twenties, with thick black hair and piercing blue eyes. A scar ran across his left cheek. Allard turned to Marcus as Thomas introduced them.

"Marcus, this is Lord Allard, Duke Udo's youngest son."

"Nice to meet you." Allard extended his hand.

Marcus ignored it. "How do you know Rebecca?"

Out of the corner of his eyes, he could feel Isabella glaring at him.

Allard met his gaze and lowered his hand as something short of a grin crept onto his lips. "We met in Lyon. I was to escort them to Metz." He smiled at Thomas. "But, alas, I was delayed."

"Delayed?"

"Yes, delayed." Isabella stood. "We found someone else to escort us to Metz."

"Oh yes, the trader. I believe his name was Pierre." Allard shook his head. "A shame what happened to him on the way back to Lyon. The bandits in that region are sometimes out of control."

"Bandits?" Rebecca asked.

"Yes, he was found a few days after he dropped you off. A pity." He shrugged. "I'm sure he knew the dangers of his profession."

"A trader? Dangerous?" Isabella replied.

"Depends on what he is transporting."

Marcus took a step forward, his face close to Allard's. The two men were nearly the same height.

"I think we should go outside."

Allard leaned back and smiled. "And why would I do that?"

"Your choice."

Marcus shot his right hand forward and closed it around Allard's throat. The nobleman struggled, his feet kicking as Marcus lifted him off the ground.

"Marcus!" Thomas and Isabella yelled at the same time.

The Roman ignored them, his eyes fixed on the reddening face of the noble. The music had stopped, and everyone's attention shifted to the struggle. Several men who wore the same color cloaks emerged from the shadows and ran toward Marcus. Ander appeared from nowhere, a table knife in his hand.

He wiped the mead from his lips with his free hand. "Are we killing these men?"

"Perhaps." Marcus grunted.

"Marcus!" Charles slammed his cup on the table, wine spilling over the top. "Put him down!"

The Roman looked over at Charles, and back at Allard, who was clawing at the hand around his throat. Marcus tossed him to the ground and nodded at Ander. The Basque set his knife down. The two men who had come to Allard's aid stood by with short swords in hand. They were not sure what to do, attack Marcus or help their Lord as he struggled to get to his feet.

"What the hell is this?" The question came from a noble standing next to Charles. "I came here as a sign of respect between our kingdoms. And my son is assaulted?" He glared at Marcus, and back at Charles. "I demand you arrest this man."

The only sound was the crackling of the fireplace. Charles looked from Udo to Marcus, then to several guards who witnessed the struggle.

"Take him into custody."

The men stepped forward and took Marcus by the arms. Allard stood and grabbed the knife from the table, rushing toward the Roman. But Ander stepped between them, tackling Allard to the ground. More guards arrived and separated the men, pulling Allard to his feet. Ander remained on the ground, one hand covering the knife wound in his side.

Marcus broke free from the guards and rushed to his friend. The Basque was sitting up when he arrived.

"That bastard stuck me," the Basque mumbled.

"You should have let him stick me."

Ander forced a grin. "What fun would that be?" He looked down. Blood was seeping from the wound. "It's not that bad."

Marcus ignored the guards trying to pull him away. "Let Nico take a look at it."

"Come with us." The guard pulled at Marcus's tunic.

Marcus clenched his jaw, but it was Ander who said, "Go, I'll be fine. I've been stabbed by worse."

Marcus stood and faced Allard. The Lord had a smug look on his face. "Your friend saved your life."

"No one can save yours." The Roman continued to glare at him as they pulled him away.

Nico knelt beside Ander, glanced at the wound, and looked up at Thomas. "Let's get him to my room."

That was the last thing Marcus heard as they led him from the chamber.

"Give me more light!" Nico was leaning over, two fingers inside the stab wound.

The Basque was doing his best not to squirm, as he drank down a mixture of alcohol and herbs. Thomas was holding down his legs, and Rebecca held a lantern above his torso, trying to get Nico the light he required.

Blood covered the long table and formed a pool on the floor at Nico's feet.

Ander groaned as Nico moved his fingers in the wound. "The blade nicked something. I can't stop the bleeding! I need to get inside." He glanced at the table and the sharp blade on it, then over at Ander.

Ander's face was pale, almost waxen, and his breath labored. The Basque looked over at the blade and nodded.

Nico grabbed the knife with his bloody fingers and sliced open the wound. Tossing the knife to the ground, he grabbed a nearby cloth and tried to soak up the blood. He went through several rags, knelt down and peered into the wound.

"Got it." He pinched the artery, stemming the flow of blood. "I need to stitch it."

"Nico," Thomas said.

The older man ignored him and reached out with this free hand. "Give me the needle."

"Nico!"

Nicodemus looked up at Thomas. The latter shifted his gaze to Ander's face. He was staring at the ceiling, his mouth slightly open.

"Damn it!" Nico pulled his hand from the wound and leaned forward to close the Basque's eyes. He wiped the sweat from his forehead with the back of his hand, which left a long, bloody smear. "I couldn't stop the bleeding."

"I know. You tried." Rebecca put one hand on his shoulder.

"Marcus will not take this well." Isabella set down the cup of alcohol she had been giving to Ander and scanned the group. "Should I tell him?"

Thomas used a cloth to wipe the blood from his hands. "No, I will."

CHAPTER TEN

When one burns one's bridges, what a very nice fire it makes.
—Dylan Thomas

Fall, 716 A.D.
Metz, Duchy of Austrasia

Marcus sat in the same cell Nico had occupied when he first met Charles. It was damp and cold, but those were the least of his concerns. He looked down at his hands, lowered his head, and rubbed his temples with his thumbs.

"Headache?"

Marcus looked up to find Thomas standing in front of the cell door.

"Not really."

"Well, you're the only one." Thomas exhaled and continued, "Do you have any idea the mess you have created?"

"I can imagine."

"Oh, you don't need to imagine. I'll tell you. We have a

dozen nobles wondering why they should back Charles. Udo stormed off, and Lord knows what he might do. Even the local clergy are pestering me." He took a step toward the bars. "What were you thinking?"

Marcus stood and approached Thomas. "I didn't know he was the duke's son."

"Why did you attack him?"

The Roman paused. If he shared his suspicions, Thomas would kill Allard. "I can't tell you."

"Why not?"

Marcus did not reply.

"Udo wants you executed."

Marcus shrugged. "That would solve the problem."

"I'm going to ignore that." Thomas placed his hands on the bar. "Marcus, there is something else."

"What?

Thomas started to speak, but stopped and looked down at the cell floor. He took a deep breath and said, "Ander. He didn't make it."

Marcus stared at him. "What?"

"Ander is dead."

Marcus stepped towards the bars. "What do you mean?" He looked at nothing in particular, then back up at Thomas. "It was a minor wound. A table knife."

"It nicked an artery. Nico did everything he could, but he could not stop the bleeding." His voice trembled. "I'm sorry."

Thomas watched the life drain from his friend's eyes, replaced by immeasurable sadness. Marcus stumbled a few steps back, bumping into the cot. He sat down, shoulder slumped, both hands resting in his lap. A single tear ran down his cheek.

"Marcus."

The Roman ignored him.

"Marcus!"

This time, the Roman looked up.

"Don't do anything stupid." Thomas lowered his voice. "I mean it, Marcus."

His response was a blank stare.

"I'll send food and a blanket." Thomas turned away from his friend, ignoring the sick feeling in his stomach.

The guards escorted Marcus into the massive chamber. It was early evening, and he had spent twenty-four hours in the cell. It reminded him how much he hated confinement. If possible, he might have done something about it. But there was no way to kill himself fast enough to avoid healing.

Charles sat at a desk at the far end of the room. He waved the guards away. "Wait outside."

The guard had arrested Marcus the day before. He studied the Roman and glanced back at Charles. "Are you sure?"

"Leave us," Charles growled.

As the door shut, Charles stood and walked around the desk, stopping in front of Marcus. "I'm sorry about Ander. He was a good man."

Marcus swallowed hard. "Thank you. He was."

Charles crossed his arms. "Why?"

Marcus squinted and went with his gut.

"Allard is a rapist."

Charles studied him for a moment. "I'm sure he is. He's also a spoiled brat and an arrogant bastard. He might even kill puppies for sport." He took a step closer. "But he is the son of the most powerful duke in Gaul. Choking him to death at my celebration dinner is not an option."

"Can I choke him to death in private?"

Charles glared at him and chuckled. "Good luck. He's on his way back to Toulouse, with two dozen of Odo's personal guard."

"Only two dozen?"

"Marcus!"

The Roman raised both hands. "I understand."

"The duke wants me to have you executed."

"That's what Thomas said."

"And that doesn't bother you?"

"If my death solves the problem with the duke, then so be it."

"That is very noble of you. Unfortunately, it won't solve the problem." He walked to the desk and retrieved his cup. "If I kill one of my close advisors, because Udo told me to... well, that creates a different dilemma." He took a long pull. "But I have another solution."

"And what is that?"

"Stockfish."

"What the hell is stockfish?"

Charles motioned for Marcus to follow him to a large table. On it was a map of Gaul and the surrounding kingdoms. Charles picked up a package sitting on the table and unwrapped the parchment. Inside was a block of white, flaky fish. He held it out to Marcus. "Try it."

Marcus broke off a piece and popped it into his mouth. It was salty, but otherwise bland. Nothing spectacular. "It's fish."

"Yes, fish that will last for years on a shelf." Charles set down the package and moved over to the map. He pointed to Hispania. "The Saracens have control of the entire peninsula. The Pyrenees protect them from invasion, and within, they have one kingdom. No internal strife. They can focus their efforts on expansion." He shifted to Austrasia. "Here is Cologne. We have at least a half dozen kingdoms surrounding us. Saxons and Lombards to the East. Burgundy and Neustria to the West. Frisians to the North."

"This map has changed a dozen times in the last decade," Marcus added.

"Exactly. And I'm going to change it again."

HAMMER OF GOD

"How?"

"I'm taking all of this." He pointed to the Pyrenees and the Alps. "I'll have mountains on these borders." He motioned to the top and bottom of the map. "And oceans to the north and south."

"How far east?"

"The Rhine. If the Romans couldn't push beyond that, I certainly won't try."

"What does this have to do with stockfish?"

"I need a large, mobile army." He spread his hand over the map. "And armies eat a lot of food. I'm going to put a two-year supply of stockfish in various strongholds across my realm. Then, I can march anywhere I need to."

"Sounds reasonable. What does this have to do with me?"

"I don't know where to buy it."

"Where did you get this?" Marcus held up the tiny piece of fish.

"A Frisian merchant had a dozen packs. One of my men confiscated one as a tax." Charles shrugged. "I saw him eating it and asked what it was."

"Why not ask the Frisian where he got it?"

"I did."

"And what did he say?"

"Northmen."

"Northmen." Marcus shook his head. They were a dangerous bunch. Savage warriors and shrewd traders. "Now I see the problem."

"Good, because you are going to solve it."

"What? Me?"

"Yes. I'm officially banning you from my kingdom." He walked over and filled an empty cup with wine, handing it to Marcus. "But unofficially, I'm asking you to do this for me."

"I'm not a merchant, or a trader." Marcus angled his cup toward the fish package. "Or a fisherman."

129

"But you're resourceful," Charles took a sip, "or lucky. I don't care which. Find someone who can provide me with a steady supply of stockfish."

"And what do I offer?"

"Iron. The Northmen always need iron."

Marcus sniggered. "You want to give them iron to make better weapons? What could go wrong?"

"We'll worry about that later." Charles eyed Marcus. "So, you accept?"

"Do I have a choice?"

"I could banish you." He took a sip of wine and smiled. "But something tells me you're up for the challenge."

Marcus thought about it and extended one hand. "Deal."

Charles returned his grasp. But before Marcus let go, he said, "I'm still going to kill Allard."

"I don't want to know."

Marcus released his grip and nodded in return.

"Banished?" Isabella said. "For how long?"

"I don't know." Marcus shoved a tunic into his bag. "I'm going to head north. He has something he wants me to investigate."

Isabella put her hand on his. "What does that mean?"

"It means, if I do this for him, everything should be fine."

"Where north?" Thomas was standing in the doorway, watching Marcus pack.

"Way north." He pulled the string tight on the bag. "Beyond the sea."

"Britannia?" Thomas squinted.

Marcus smiled. "No, the home of the Northmen."

"Who are the Northmen?" Isabella looked at Marcus, then Thomas. It was the latter who replied.

"Savages. The land is inhospitable, and the mountains run into the sea."

"Why?" Isabella glanced at Marcus.

"Charles asked me to."

She met his gaze, but could tell there was more he could not say. She nodded. "Stay safe."

A few minutes later, she found Marcus alone outside. He was leaning against the wall, looking up at the full moon.

"You didn't tell Thomas." It was a statement, not a question.

He glanced at her and back into the night. "No. It would kill him."

"That's what Rebecca said." She leaned next to him.

"How is she?"

"Not good." She paused. "Allard took something from her. Something no one can ever give her back. Now she needs to learn to live with that."

"I thought it was you," he whispered. "I thought that was why you wanted me to train you. Then I saw her face," he looked at her, tears filling his eyes, "that's when I knew."

"It was my fault. I never should have left her alone."

"No, no. It's not your fault that Allard is a despicable human." He turned, his shoulder against the wall as he looked into her eyes. "Do you understand me?"

"Yes." She looked into his eyes and nodded. "I know."

"Good."

She changed the subject. "I'm going with you."

"No, absolutely not."

She glared back at him. "I'm going, whether you like it or not. I'll either travel with you, or I will follow close behind."

He measured the resolve in her eyes. "Why?"

"I can't stay in this city." She looked around, her gaze drifting beyond the walls. "I need to get away."

He exhaled, his face twisted in thought before nodding. "You can go with me to the coast, but you're not going north with me."

"You say that now." She grinned. "We will see later."

He shook his head. "You better pack."

"I already have." She beamed. "What time do we leave?"

"Dawn." He squinted at her. "And don't tell Thomas. Have Rebecca tell him after we leave."

CHAPTER ELEVEN

Revenge is an act of passion; vengeance of justice.
—Samuel Johnson

Fall, 716 A.D.
Duchy of Austrasia

Isabella looked over at Marcus. "Aren't the Northmen north?"
"Yes." Marcus stared into the distance.
"Yet we are riding in the opposite direction."
"We have unfinished business."
Isabella exhaled. "You're going after Allard."
"Yes."
"Where is he?"
"The duke's entourage rode south once he heard I wouldn't be executed."
"Entourage?"
"Yeah, I can use big words when I want to." Marcus glanced over at her. "We'll need to ride all night to catch up with them."

Isabella paused. "I want him dead. I know that's not very Christ-like of me. Is that terrible?"

He grimaced. "I'm the last person to ask. Killing him won't undo what he did, but it will stop him from doing it again. And that always makes me feel better."

"Always?"

He looked up at the rising sun. "Not always."

They rode all morning maintaining a steady pace, faster than a wagon train would ride. They continued through several mountain passes and into the wide, green valleys below. Tiny farms, crops sprouting, were scattered across the open dales. They slept the first night under a giant oak, and the second night in a farmer's barn.

On the third day, the pair stopped in a small village for lunch and asked about the duke's wagon train. They were told it had left that morning. Smiling, Marcus left the proprietor with a gold coin and stepped out into the midday sun.

"We should catch them tonight."

"Then what?" Isabella took a long pull from her waterskin.

"I kill Allard."

"I thought you said the duke has an *entourage*. How do we get through them?"

"Not we." Marcus pulled himself up into the saddle. "I do this alone."

Isabella climbed up onto her mount. "What do I do?"

"You're my distraction." He grinned.

"So you have a plan?"

"I'm forming one as we go." He angled his horse away from the inn.

"Of course you are." She started after him.

They left the village and entered a dense forest, the trees blocking most of the light as they continued down the trail. It went on for miles, and by late afternoon, Marcus's belly was beginning to growl. He pulled a piece of dried meat from his pouch and bit off a chunk, slowly chewing on the tough morsel. He was about to take another bite when his horse reached a sharp bend in the trail. As they followed the path, the trees gave way to an open field beyond.

The two slowed their steeds and pulled off to the side. Marcus dismounted, Isabella close behind. Securing the reins to a tree, they snuck through the trees until they could see into the pasture. Marcus knelt and motioned for her to do the same.

The wagon train had stopped and was making camp for the night. Fifty or more horses were contained in a makeshift rope corral near the forest edge. The wagons were spaced around the camp, and dozens of men worked to set up several large pavilions. Another group was building a fire in the middle of the camp, while others were cutting vegetables on a long wooden table.

There was no sign of the duke or Allard.

Marcus rotated so his back was to the field and sat down, leaning against the tree. "We wait until dark to see if we can figure out what tent Allard is staying in." He picked up a piece of grass and stuck it into his mouth.

"How are you going to get in there?" Isabella had also settled against a tree.

"Getting in is never the problem."

"And how will you get out?"

Marcus glanced over at her, then down at the grass. "I won't." Before she could reply, the Roman continued, "You'll ride back to Cologne."

"That wasn't the deal."

"There was no deal." He looked into her deep green eyes. "I got you out of the city, and you get to help me kill Allard. That's as far as it goes."

"I want to go north."

"No." He held up one hand to cut off any additional protest. "Listen, I've never been north, but I've heard stories. Stories that

B. K. GREENWOOD

give me pause. I won't... I can't... risk you." He shook his head and looked down at his hands. "Not after losing Ander. I won't lose you too."

She was going to argue further, but the emotion in his voice held her tongue.

They sat in silence, bees buzzing around them. A few birds chirped in the distance, and leaves fluttered down from the treetops.

"What's it like?" Isabella looked over at Marcus.

"Dying?"

"Yes."

"Depends on how you go." He bit off a piece of grass and spit it out. "Burning is the worst. The pain and suffocation. The air was so hot, my lungs burned from the inside." He sat back and thought for a moment. "I don't enjoy falling. Several times I haven't died on impact, and that has been messy."

"That's terrible." Isabella's face twisted in pain.

"Being stabbed is hit or miss. If done correctly, it can be over quickly." Marcus pointed down through his clavicle. "Severing the heart is best."

"Drowning?"

"The first time, no. The second time it was more peaceful, once I got past the choking. I saw some very interesting things under the sea."

"Beheading?"

"It is never clean. It's much harder than it sounds."

"Are you ever scared?"

"No, death is not what I dread." He pulled the piece of grass from his mouth and tossed it aside. "It's what comes after."

She nodded. "I'm sorry that happens to you."

He looked over at her. "I know it changes me, and that's why I am sorry."

"Me too." She forced a smile. "Perhaps someday it won't."

"Yeah," he looked up at the canopy, "perhaps."

The sun settled below the tree, and dusk gave way to night. The cooks had moved the cauldron above the fire, and the smell of stewing meat drifted through the air, setting their stomachs to growling.

"What now?" Isabella stood, stretching her lithe arms.

"We let them eat, and hopefully drink a little. Then sleep." Marcus stood and pointed to the corral. "You're going to cut all their horses loose. While they're distracted, I'll go in and kill Allard."

"That's your plan?"

"Yes."

"That is a terrible plan. Of course you're going to die. Are you sure it's worth it?"

"Yes." Marcus glared at the distant campfire.

Several hours later, the voices around the flames had faded, and the glow of the embers was hardly visible from the trees. Most of the men were lying on the ground, except for two sentries. One by the main pavilion, which Marcus assumed contained the duke, and a second guard who walked around the camp's perimeter.

"Wait until I am on the far side." Marcus had slipped on a dark cloak, not unlike the one the guard was wearing. "Cut the horses loose. Don't get caught up with them. Leave as soon as you have created the distraction."

"I will."

Marcus hugged her, breathing in the scent of her hair. He pushed the emotions aside and pulled away. "Be careful on the way back. Stay in towns and don't ride at night."

"I will." Isabella smiled at him, her eyes sparkling. "You be careful up north."

"I will."

Marcus stepped away and disappeared into the darkness,

moving along the edge of the tree line. He came back upon the trail and knelt, waiting for Isabella. As if on cue, the neighing of a dozen horses broke the silence. A few moments later, a guard called the alarm and men scrambled to their feet, tossing aside blankets and reaching for weapons.

Marcus stood and headed toward the fire as most of the men ran off toward the corral. As he went through the camp, he leaned over and picked up a helmet next to a bedroll. He slipped it on his head and moved to the smaller pavilion ten feet from the larger one. The guard who had been watching the main tent had slipped away, but returned as Marcus neared the tent opening. He was a teenager.

"What's going on?" Marcus asked.

The kid looked up at him. "I don't know. Something with the horses."

"You better check on the duke's horse. That's his favorite."

"It is?"

"Yes, go!"

The kid scrambled toward the corral.

"The duke does not have a favorite horse."

Marcus turned to find Allard standing at the pavilion opening, wearing a pair of trousers and no shirt. His muscled upper body glistened in the firelight as he lifted his sword and pointed it at Marcus.

"You." He squinted. "You'll never get out of here alive."

"Deal."

Marcus pulled his weapon and rushed Allard. The latter stumbled back, nearly tripping over the pavilion as he raised his sword to block the attack. The swords clanged as Allard regained his balance and counterattacked.

He was a superb swordsman. Marcus was too strong and too fast, and it was clear within a few strokes who would win. But Marcus knew he had to finish it quickly, as the clang of metal would draw the guards back to the camp.

"Over a woman?" Allard grimaced as he covered a large slice in his forearm with one hand and spat on the ground. "You'll die over a woman?"

"You raped her." Marcus flicked his sword, the tip slicing through Allard's cheek.

"It's not rape. She was my ward." He grinned as several guards came running back to camp. "I consider it payment for my protection."

At that moment, the duke stumbled from his tent wearing a long, white nightgown. "What's going on?"

Marcus's gaze never wavered from Allard. "I'm going to kill your son."

"Like hell you—"

Marcus knocked Allard's sword aside and plunged his own blade into his bare chest.

The duke ran forward and grabbed his son as he fell to the ground. Marcus felt a tinge of guilt, but remembered the look on Rebecca's face. The guilt disappeared.

"You bastard!" the duke raged at Marcus. "You'll hang for this!"

Marcus looked down at his bloody blade and the guards standing around him. "There will be no hanging."

The duke looked at Marcus and then to the guards. "Kill him."

Marcus parried a few strokes, but he did not attack. No need to kill innocent guards. Several of them buried their blades in him, and at least one of them was fatal. As Marcus fell to the ground, he drifted into death's dark, icy grip.

He opened his eyes before shutting them when he realized where he was. The earth that surrounded him was moist and moldy. There was no unbearable weight, which meant he was not buried very deep. He lifted his arms, and both broke the surface. Within seconds, his upper body was free.

It was cold and dark. Marcus pulled himself from the soil and brushed the dirt from his body. After a few minutes, his eyes adjusted to the darkness. He was in a small room, a fraction of moonlight filtering in through tiny gaps in a nearby door. He stood and shuffled away from the door, toward the back wall, one hand extended. When his hand reached the thatched wall, he made his way to the right, using his hand to find the corner of the room. He was careful not to walk too close to the wall, having stubbed his toe on the crate stored in the corner the last time he was here.

When he reached the corner, he knelt and found the large wooden box. Opening the lid, he reached inside, his hand searching for one of the woolen sacks. He found one, and a second. That was all. He made a mental note to replenish the stash as he pulled one out and closed the lid.

He opened the bag and pulled out a tunic, which he slipped on. Then trousers, followed by a pair of boots. He removed a sheathed dagger, shoved it into his boot, and left the other items in the bag, including a pouch stuffed full of silver coins and a blanket. He slung it over his shoulder and made his way to the door, almost tripping as he stepped into the hole he had left in the ground.

Marcus ran his hand along the edge of the door and found the latch that secured it shut. It had taken several attempts, but he had developed a mechanism that would lock once the door was pulled shut. It was nearly impossible to gain entry to the room, making it difficult to replenish his stash, but it kept prying eyes from it.

The room was attached to a stable, which Marcus had also built. It was part of a small working farm he had asked a local farmer to run. It was officially part of the local diocese, which protected it from the greedy nobles. Marcus allowed each

HAMMER OF GOD

family to stay on the farm for five years, rent free. Then he would purchase a plot of land for them hundreds of miles away and replace them with another family. The process had worked well for the last hundred years, providing a bit of stability to this resurrection.

Marcus pulled open the door, slipped out into the night, and closed it behind him, ensuring he heard the latch click. Spinning around, he found himself face to face with a small boy, no older than six.

The young lad was holding a wooden bucket, the water sloshing over the edge as he stared up at Marcus, the whites of his eyes visible in the pale light.

The Roman smiled and held one finger to his lips. The boy continued to stare at him without moving. Marcus waved at the boy and continued to the stable. He glanced back over his shoulder to see the child had not moved. He pulled open the stable door, moved inside, and made his way to a pen where a massive work horse stood. Opening his bag, Marcus took out one gold coin and placed it on the railing, knowing it would more than pay for a new horse.

He grabbed a rope bridle from a peg on the wall, slipped it over the horse's snout, and secured it under his ears. He led him from the pen and out of the stable, closing the door behind him. The boy was still there, holding the bucket. Marcus ignored him and grabbed a handful of mane as he hopped up onto the horse's bare back. Not used to riders, the horse neighed and took a few steps back. Marcus leaned forward and rubbed his neck, whispering something in Latin into the steed's ear.

The horse seemed to settle, and Marcus waved at the young boy as he guided the horse to the path leading off the farm.

The moonlight was enough to illuminate the path that led to a wider trail. He rode past several farms before the trail entered a thick forest. He slowed his pace, as he could barely see a few feet ahead. After about an hour, he exited the forest and followed the road down to a small village. The only sign of life was a few wisps of smoke rising from several buildings.

He continued, moving through the narrow streets until he found a stable. Sliding from the horse, he stepped forward and pounded on the door.

A few minutes later, it creaked open.

"Who the hell is pounding on my door at this hour?"

"A traveler."

The man was seventy years old, if he was a day. He came to Marcus's chest and was skinny as a rail. His shoulders leaned to the left, like he was reaching down to the ground to pick something up.

He glared up at Marcus. "I like travelers who arrive during the day."

"I'm sure you also like travelers who pay in gold." Marcus shook his pouch, the coins rattling.

The man's expression changed. "That I do. What do you need?"

"Bed down my steed. A saddle and proper reins."

His face scrunched. "What happened to his saddle?"

"It fell off." Marcus shuffled the bag so he could hear the coins again.

"That's unfortunate." He stepped past Marcus and took the reins. "I have the perfect saddle for this beast, and it will not fall off." The old man led the horse away. "I suppose you will want dinner and a place to sleep." He thumbed back over his shoulder. "Down at the next corner. It's the only inn we have."

"Thank you."

"You're welcome." He disappeared into the stable. "You can pay me in the morning."

CHAPTER TWELVE

In the middle of the journey of our life I came to myself within a dark wood where the straight way was lost.
—Dante Alighieri

Fall, 716 A.D.
Neustria

Marcus reached the town of Bononia eight days after rising from the dead. He knew it as Gesoriacum, a major port used by the Romans to supply the province of Britannia.

At the mouth of the Liane River, the town did not possess a natural port in the classical sense. The river formed an estuary, which provided some protection from the sea, but the reason it was chosen as a port was its proximity to Britannia. It was less than twenty-five leagues across the channel, and when the weather cooperated, the journey could be made in six or seven hours.

As he trotted through the main gate, Marcus looked up at a

giant stone tower looming above the town. Over seven hundred years old, the Romans had built the lighthouse to guide ships through the night. It appeared as if someone had stacked a series of six-sided discs on top of one another, each one smaller than the one below it. Each level had small windows for natural light to enter the tower, and a massive iron cauldron sat upon the top.

The town itself was small, but Marcus knew that traders from all over Northern Europe visited the port. It was the best place to find a trader heading north, and that would avoid traveling by land through hostile territory.

The first thing he needed to do was find a stable where he could sell his horse, then an inn for food, wine, and lodging. He found the stable near the center of town, and Marcus fetched a less than fair price for the steed.

The Roman left the stable with a few extra coins and made his way through the light traffic, finding an inn that looked out over the docks. A dozen ships were moored to the wooden piers, some unloading goods, while others took on new cargo. It was late afternoon when he entered the inn, glad to get out of the summer sun. The inside was cooler, the open wooden shutters allowing the channel breeze to drift through the room.

Marcus took one of the empty tables in the corner and motioned for the barmaid. She was a tall, thick woman, her dress straining to contain her large bosom.

"What can I get you, sir" She had a tray folded in her arm, resting on her hip.

"A pitcher of your finest mead."

"We only have one mead, so that would be our finest." She disappeared before he could reply.

A few minutes later, she returned with a wooden pitcher and a cup. She poured Marcus a cup and set the pitcher down. "Anything else?"

HAMMER OF GOD

He took a long pull, smacked his lips. "What do you have for food?"

"Stew."

"With meat?"

She grinned. One of her front teeth was missing. "No luv, no meat in the stew. Some bits of fish."

"Do you have any meat?"

She studied him for a moment. "What are you paying with?"

He plunked a bag of coins on the table. "Silver sceattas."

She grinned. "Rabbit or mutton?"

"Rabbit."

"Rabbit it is. And a trencher of stew."

As she moved away, Marcus called after her. "And a loaf of bread."

She frowned at him. "Are you expecting others?"

"Nope, I'm thirsty and hungry."

She shook her head and disappeared into the door behind the bar.

The stew came out first, with the bread. Followed a bit later by the roasted rabbit. He finished the pitcher of mead and ordered a second. A few minutes later, she set the second pitcher down.

"You want to square up before you drink yourself under the table, luv?"

"Do you have a room available?"

Her eyebrows raised. "Thinking ahead, are ya?" Without waiting for a response, she said, "Yes, shared or your own room."

"My own please."

"I'll get it arranged."

"And..."

"Sorry, luv, I'm married."

Marcus grinned. "My loss. He is a lucky man." He nodded

around the room. "I'm looking for a ship to take me north. Do you think any of these men could help me?"

Her eyes dropped to the pouch.

He followed her gaze and grinned. "Of course, I will make it worth your while to find out."

"I'll be back."

As the sun disappeared, the room filled up with crew members from the ships that were not ready to disembark. A half hour later, the barmaid pointed to one man sitting alone at a nearby table. "That is Captain Holger." She set down a fresh pitcher of mead. "I believe he leaves tomorrow." Her eyes moved from the pitcher to Marcus. "Not that you'll be in any shape to travel."

"I'll manage." He picked up the pouch and dumped several coins into his hand, then handed them to her. "Thanks, luv."

Mouth open, she accepted the coins.

Marcus pocketed the rest and picked up his full pitcher, the ale sloshing over the top. He moved over to the table where the captain sat. He was older, perhaps in his early fifties. His hair was gray, pulled back in a ponytail. The sun had baked the skin of his scalp and face into a bronze, leathery hide. He looked up at Marcus, lips curled in a sneer.

"I'm sorry to interrupt your dinner, captain," Marcus found the right words in German, "may I offer you a free cup of ale?"

"Who's asking?" The words were Germanic, but spoken with a thick, guttural accent.

"A potential paying passenger."

He glanced at his empty cup, then at the full pitcher, and nodded. Marcus filled his cup and sat down.

"I'm told you are sailing north. Are you going to Ribe?"

"Maybe." He took a sip of ale.

"I pay in silver." He dropped the bag on the table.

The captain set the cup down and picked up his spoon, shoveling another spoonful of stew into his mouth. He chewed for a moment and swallowed. "You sleep on the deck."

"Fair."

"Why Ribe?"

Marcus paused, and Holger noticed.

"It's a fair thing to ask."

"It is." Marcus met his gaze. "I am going north."

"I know. Ribe is north."

"No, further north. Beyond the sea."

He set down his spoon and studied Marcus through narrowed slits. "Why?"

"I'm a merchant, looking to establish a trade."

"Trade goes through Ribe."

"It does now, yes. But I want to talk to the men who make what we seek."

"And that is?"

"Stockfish."

The captain choked on his drink. "Stockfish?"

"Yes. What's so funny?"

"They make stockfish at the end of the world, where the land meets the endless sea." His smile faded. "It is quite the journey. Even I've never been that far north."

"Will you take me to Ribe?"

"Yes, I will. If only to learn about the man who wants to sail into oblivion."

Marcus met the captain on the dock the next morning, as instructed. As they arrived, the older man nodded towards a gigantic pile of fur pelts stacked nearby.

"You should buy one." He pointed toward the man standing next to them. "He will tell you the price."

"Why do I need that?"

"Sleeping. Much more comfortable than the deck planks."
He looked at his large sack. "I assume you have blankets?"

"Yes."

"Probably not warm enough for the trip north, but they will do for the journey to Ribe."

Marcus walked over to the stack of pelts.

"I have beaver, fox, bear and otter." The man's accent was even thicker than the captain's.

Marcus studied the pile. "Fox please."

The man dug through the stack, pulling a pelt free. He handed it to Marcus for inspection.

The Roman looked it over. "How much?"

"Ten sceattas."

Marcus reached for his coin bag.

Holger took a few steps toward them, having watched the conversation. "Frode. We are selling those fox pelts for five sceattas."

"I know, captain, but that's to the merchants."

"Five." Holger did not flinch.

"Yes, sir."

"Thank you," Marcus said.

"Don't thank me." The captain pointed at the pile. "Those are two each in Ribe. Everything is more expensive the farther you get from the source. Remember that when you head north."

Once the transaction was complete, Marcus gathered his pelt and sack, and followed Holger onto the ship. It was over fifty feet long and fifteen feet wide near the middle of the craft. A single mast, sail lowered, occupied the dead center of the ship. Loaded, it had a three-foot draft, allowing it to navigate most rivers. The waterline to gunwale was another three feet, which did not look like much protection from stormy seas.

The fore and aft cargo sections were loaded with sacks of grain. In between, two benches sat on either side. A pair of oars were stored across the benches, and the floor beside each one was covered with pelts.

"Each rower sleeps beside the oar he mans." The captain pointed to a gap between stacks of grain. "You can sleep there."

"How long to reach Ribe?"

"Nine days, maybe less. Maybe more." He looked up at the sky. "Depends on the wind."

Marcus stowed his gear, then watched the crew finish loading and securing the provisions – barrels of water, dried meats, and vegetables. One of the crew dropped a sack, and a biscuit rolled out. It was very similar to the *bucellatum*, or hardtack bread he used to eat when on campaign with his legion.

Next to be loaded were the livestock. A dozen chickens in four cages, plus two goats for milking. The last to come on board were wooden barrels. Marcus smiled as one barrel was secured beside the spot where he was sleeping.

Holger saw his smile and wandered over to him. "That is for the king."

"You have a king?"

"Well, a king of sorts." He shrugged. "He rules most of Jutland. And what he does not rule, he plans to rule."

"So, you don't have your own ale?"

"What?" The captain's brow furrowed. "Do you think we are savages? Of course, we have ale." He pointed to the king's barrel. "That's wine, from Italy."

Now Marcus was really interested, but only smiled in response.

Holger shook his head and walked away.

With the barrels secured, the captain gave the signal, and the ship pushed away from the pier. Marcus moved to the bow of the ship and watched as Holger maneuvered the vessel out of the port and through the narrow gap that formed the mouth of the estuary.

Once into the channel, he barked at his sailors, and soon the large square sail was hoisted and secured, the ship bucking as the wind filled the canvas and jolted them forward. The sea was calm, and the round bow of the ship slid through the swells, periodically smashing into a taller wave. The resulting spray was refreshing; the sting of salt, bitter on his lips.

They sailed most of the day, staying within sight of land as they followed the coastline north. Near dark, they found a shallow indentation in the shoreline with a sandy beach. They put ashore, and the men drew lots to see who would cook dinner. Most of them groaned when they saw the loser, as he was a terrible cook.

Some men grabbed their pelts and blankets, setting them up in a small circle around a fire pit that others were building. The unlucky cook was cutting vegetables.

"I thought we slept on the ship?" Marcus asked the captain as they spread their pelts on the sand.

"If we have to, yes." He motioned toward the sand. "Much softer to sleep on. Sometimes we find a place to moor when we cannot beach the ship."

"You don't sail at night?"

Holger looked up at the dark sky. A million stars looked back at him. "No moon and too many shoals."

The crew members were right. The food was terrible. It was salty, half of the vegetables were raw, the other half overcooked and mushy. The young lad looked around at the others and smiled.

One of the older sailors sitting next to Marcus leaned over to the Roman. "He thinks if he cooks terribly, we won't let him cook."

"Is that true?"

"Of course not." He grinned, one of his front teeth missing. "This is the third night in a row he has drawn the short lot."

"Very unlucky, indeed." Marcus swallowed what he was

chewing. "Why do you do it? It must be horrible eating this every night."

"Oh, it's much better watching him be miserable." He stopped the spoonful of stew heading for his mouth and winked. "You'll find Norsemen are happiest when others are suffering along with us. A character flaw, I'd say."

After dinner, they drank their allotment of ale as the fire faded into the night. One by one, they lay down beneath the stars, the soft ocean breeze lulling them to sleep. Marcus was up before the sun, walking inland to stretch his legs. He did not encounter a soul unless you counted the two squirrels and a deer with her two fawns. He walked back toward camp as the dawn broke, his stomach growling. They ate dried fruit for breakfast, washing it down with a few cups of water.

The tide had receded during the night, leaving the ship halfway up on the shore. But it was returning, and by the time they were loaded back on board, just the bow was buried in the sand. Marcus stowed his gear and walked back to see how the crew would free the ship.

It was not as difficult as Marcus expected. Holger had dropped anchor aft of the boat before beaching. The men lined up along the rope, and with a few coordinated heaves, the flat bottom slipped free from the sand and drifted into the shallow bay. A few more heaves and the anchor was onboard.

The men manned the oars, and following the commands from the captain, spun the boat around and rowed toward the channel. Once in open water, the sail was raised, and they were underway.

The next few days found the same pattern repeated. On the fourth night, they could not find a beach suitable for landing, so they anchored fifty paces from the shoreline and had a cold meal of hardtack biscuits, stockfish, and ale. The captain allotted a double portion of the latter to make up for the cold meal.

They hit a summer squall on the sixth day, which kept them beached the entire day. The crew used a spare sail to set up a shelter, protecting them from the rain. They taught the newcomer a popular dice game; the sides were made of wolves, bears, sheep, and men. Marcus was terrible at the game, never winning a single round. A pang of sadness settled on him as he thought of Ander and his affinity for games of chance.

"Something wrong?" Holger held the dice out to Marcus. It was his turn to throw.

He took the dice, forcing a smile. "I was thinking about a friend. He used to play these types of games."

"Used to?"

"He is dead." He looked down at the wooden dice.

"Did he die in battle?"

Marcus looked. "No. It was in a fight, but not a battle."

"That is too bad."

"Yes, it is." He took a breath and tossed the dice.

Around noon on the tenth day, Marcus was sitting near the bow, chewing on a piece of dried venison.

"Jutland!"

The cry came from the terrible cook. He was pointing straight ahead.

Marcus moved to the railing and squinted at the horizon.

The shore to his right disappeared into a massive river that spilled into the channel. On the far side of the river, the shore took a drastic ninety-degree turn, and if Holger maintained his course, they would run straight into it.

But of course, he did not. He angled the vessel to the right, which unfortunately reduced the wind in the sail. The crew, having made this journey before, jumped to their benches and rowed.

For the next three hours, the men maintained a steady, if not brisk, pace. Though they did not move as fast as they did under sail, the ship still cut through the water with precision

HAMMER OF GOD

and efficiency. They passed a series of islands to their right, where men on small fishing boats tossed and retrieved small nets. By late afternoon, they were rounding the corner of a sand-covered island and turning toward shore. They circled a small island to the left as a small town came into sight.

Three wooden piers extended from the shore out into the water, one of which was straight, the other two splitting into a "T" shaped dock. A long, narrow ship occupied the straight pier. A dozen warriors stood on the dock, watching them make their way toward the town. He had heard about, but never seen, a longship until that moment.

It was sleek and menacing, like a hungry wolf on water. The bow and stern curled up toward the sky, the face of some creature carved into the wood. It was much narrower than the cargo ship they were on, and perhaps twenty paces longer. The warriors standing around it were almost as threatening. They were shirtless, thick muscles glistening in the afternoon sun as they toiled around the ship. Most of them had long blond hair and braided beards.

A second pier was empty, while the last one had two cargo ships. The captain angled the ship toward the empty dock, and one of the crew hopped onto it as they closed the distance. Holger barked orders to the men as Marcus studied the town of Ribe.

It was not much to behold. There were forty, perhaps fifty, permanent structures by the shoreline. Mud or stone buildings with heavy thatched roofs. Those on the left seemed to be homes, with each one having a small pen area for livestock. To the right, black smoke from a small forge drifted into the blue sky. The steady clank of iron on iron competed with the other sounds of the bustling port.

A wooden walkway ran the entire length of the town and had several offshoots that led further inland and to the piers on which they were docked. A large area was reserved for building or repairing ships. One ship was propped up on all sides by giant timbers, as two workmen cleaned the keel. A second ship, a skeleton, consumed the attention of a half-dozen men.

Beyond the initial structures, Marcus could make out a wooden palisade, and buildings within.

"The main town." The captain pointed to the palisade. "That is where you will get permission to go north."

Marcus looked over at Holger. "Permission?"

"Yes. No captain will take you north without the local jarl's permission."

"Will that be difficult?"

Holger smiled. "Everything you do with Norsemen will be difficult, my friend." He clapped Marcus on the back. "Let's get you settled. You'll stay with me, in my home."

"I don't want to impose," Marcus said.

"Where else would you sleep? Outside with the sheep?"

"An inn or tavern?"

The captain laughed. "We have no need for such places. If you are welcome in our town, you are welcome in our homes. And trust me, the ale flows much better in my home."

"Well, then I accept."

Marcus gathered his belongings and followed the captain onto the dock. Holger led him along the wooden path, which was about two feet above the ground. The ground was covered with a short green grass, but not much other vegetation. Thin, muddy paths led from the decking toward each of the homesteads. Some paths led to temporary tents, in which Marcus assumed sailors or soldiers lived.

The path meandered toward the town, past a single tree. It was out of place and had somehow avoided being chopped down for firewood or housing material. Marcus was going to ask about the tree, but he was distracted by a pack of small children running toward them.

"Papa, papa!" the youngsters screamed in unison.

Holger grew a huge smile on his weathered face. He knelt as the first boy arrived and flung his arms around his father's neck. Two other boys and a girl soon joined their brother. They ranged from three to nine years old.

The first to arrive, who was also the largest, leaned back and looked at his dad. "You are late."

"Am I? How did you determine that?"

The boy held up his fingers and counted. "The voyage south should have taken ten days, perhaps eleven if the winds were stronger than usual. Two days to unload and load, nine days home." His lips moved without speaking as he counted his fingers. "That is twenty days, maybe twenty-one. It has been twenty-five days."

"Yes, papa. Why are you late?" another boy asked.

Holger stood, looked at Marcus, and shook his head. "On the ship, I'm the master. Here on land, I am beholden to a six-year-old."

Marcus grinned. "If you get these questions from the children, what will your wife say?"

The captain exhaled and closed his eyes. "The same, but worse." He motioned for Marcus to follow. "We should get it over with."

Holger picked up the girl and plopped her on his shoulders. His oldest boy hefted the captain's bag, using both hands, and stumbled after his father. The two other boys walked by his side.

"Who is this man?" one of the younger boys asked.

"He is my guest."

He shot a glance back at Marcus. "He doesn't look like us."

"Not everyone will. But since he is my guest, you will treat him like one of us. Understood?"

"Yes, papa."

"Now, run ahead and tell your mother I'm home."

He looked up, confused. "She already knows. We watched you dock."

"You did, huh? And why didn't you come to get my bag?" He glanced back at his older son, who was nearly dragging the heavy sack.

"Mother wouldn't let us."

"That's an excellent reason."

The wooden path led up a small hill, ending at the open gates of the palisade. The fence was made of twelve-foot tree trunks, the tops chopped into a sharp point, and the oblong enclosure curved away in both directions. Smart, as the lack of corners made it less susceptible to battering rams.

The gates were open, with a single guard watching people come and go. He nodded as Holger approached, his gaze lingering on the newcomer.

"He is with me," the captain said.

The man's expression did not change.

"He will be a guest in my home, and I will take responsibility for his conduct."

The guard's eyes shifted to Holger. He grunted and motioned with his head for them to continue.

The captain looked back. "No fights unless I start them. And if I do, no weapons. Only fists."

"Understood."

"Good."

They passed a half dozen longhouses, tall rectangular buildings made of wood and thatch. The peaks of the roof boasted wooden carvings, each one different from the others. Bears, wolves, boars, and horses were a few Marcus saw.

He expected more people, but only saw a couple of kids and a few older women.

"Where is everyone?"

Holger looked back. "The men are working on ships, out fishing, or away on trips. The women are cooking or tending to the herds." He smiled. "Our towns do not come alive until after dinner."

They made one last turn, and the captain stopped in front of a door leading into a longhouse. Lifting his daughter off his shoulders, he reached forward and pulled open the door. The children ran inside as Holger motioned for Marcus to enter.

The interior was dark and filled with smoke. Three massive posts, spaced across the room and buried in the straw covered ground, supported the roof. A few lanterns hung from spikes driven into the posts. A long fireplace, the primary source of the smoke, occupied the center of the room, where large, square stones kept the embers in place. A small hole in the roof was meant for venting the smoke, but did a poor job, and a massive cauldron hung above the fire, where two women in long woolen dresses tended the contents. One was stirring, while the other added herbs.

The children ran past the fireplace, alerting the women to the newcomers. One of them smiled at the captain and placed the herbs back into a basket. She wiped her hands on her dress and walked over to Holger.

She was probably ten years younger than him, perhaps more. Tall, with a sturdy frame and bright blonde hair arranged in double braids, she leaned forward and kissed him. "You are late."

"So I'm told." He huffed. "The children have already grilled me. We hit storms going both directions." Her face never changed expressions. "You know how unpredictable the channel can be!"

"A good captain plans for unpredictability."

He paused for a second, his mind unable to process the contradiction.

"Maybe one of those Gaelic women caught your fancy."

His mouth was open, but he did not know what to say. She glared at him and burst out laughing. "You're too easy, my luv."

She shook her head and looked at Marcus. "And who might you be?"

"A witness to the storm." Marcus smiled.

She grinned. "He is getting smart. Bringing a witness."

"This is Marcus, a passenger I took on Bononia." He motioned to the woman. "This is my wife, Edda."

"Are you here for dinner?"

Holger grinned. "He will stay the night and talk to the Jarl tomorrow."

She eyed her husband. "Talk to him about what?"

"He wishes to go north."

"How far north?"

"All the way," Holger said.

She raised her eyebrows and studied the Roman. "Not dressed like that, I hope."

"We shall get him warmer clothes."

"I wouldn't bother." She shrugged. "I doubt my brother will approve. He doesn't like strangers, especially Gauls."

"What makes you think I'm a Gaul?" Marcus asked.

"You're from Bononia? That is in Gaul."

"I only traveled through Gaul."

"Where are you from?"

"I'm Roman."

There was a long silence. The captain looked from Marcus to his wife. It was the latter who asked, "You speak our language?"

"I've spent time in Germania."

"Fighting," she stated.

"Mostly."

"Good." She smiled. "You kept the Goths and Vandals busy, which meant they left us alone."

"Will that help with your brother?"

"Perhaps. He's like the channel."

"Unpredictable?" Marcus asked.

"And deadly." She smiled. "But we worry about that tomorrow. Tonight we eat! I assumed my husband would be home today, so we prepared a meat stew."

"What?" Holger exclaimed. "I thought you said I was late?"

"You were." She winked. "Predictably late."

They ate stew from wide, flat bowls, accompanied by dark bread made from barley and wheat. Half of them sat on slabs attached to the walls, while the other half sat across the table on benches—the kids on one end, the adults on the other. Marcus learned that the other woman was Edda's older sister. Her husband was also a ship captain, and two weeks overdue. She was understandably quiet. Two of the children at the end of the table were hers.

After dinner, Holger retrieved his bag and pulled out gifts he had purchased in Bononia. The first was a doll, which he presented to his daughter. Next were two wooden swords, the hilts of which looked very much like those of a gladius. More Roman influence on the Gauls, Marcus thought. The boys ran to an open part of the chamber and began an epic sword fight.

The last gift was a bright green dress with gold thread inlay. He handed that to his wife.

She blushed, one hand covering her mouth. "You should not have!" She held it up in front of her, studying the intricate pattern. "We cannot afford this!"

"I made a little extra this trip." He looked over at Marcus.

She pressed it against her shoulders and looked down at it. "It's beautiful!"

"I'm glad you like it." He took a long pull of ale, leaned forward, and refilled all their cups.

There was an hour or so of small talk. When the children

had gone off to bed, Marcus refilled his cup again. "How do I convince your brother to let me go north?"

Edda twisted her face in thought. After a few moments, she said, "He's not a greedy man, so you cannot buy your way north." She exhaled. "And he does not seek power. He is comfortable with his position. That may be your best option."

"I don't understand."

"He wants to be the Jarl as long as he can, and not have to worry about losing his position. We need to find a way for you to provide that to him. Then, maybe then, he will support your venture."

Marcus held his cup in two hands, biting his bottom lip. He nodded and said, "Perhaps I have an idea. When can we meet him?"

"I have already arranged dinner tomorrow night," Edda said.

"What shall we do tomorrow?"

Holger smiled. "Do you like to hunt?"

CHAPTER THIRTEEN

*The risk of a wrong decision
is preferable to the terror of indecision.*
—Maimonides

FALL, 716 A.D.
RIBE, JUTLAND

It was a two-hour ride to the nearest forest. They left before dawn, the two of them, plus several of Holger's neighbors. The horses were smaller than Marcus was used to, with thick fur and heavy manes. A half dozen lean hunting dogs paced alongside the group, and a teenage boy trailed behind, leading a string of extra horses, one of them laden with long, stout spears. The prey was wild boar.

Marcus rode beside Holger as they followed a wide dirt rut that served as their path. The Northman held his reins in one hand, and the other rested on his hip. He seemed as comfortable on a horse as he was on his ship.

"You're familiar with a horse. You don't spend all your time at sea?"

Holger grinned. "We are warriors first. All the trades are secondary. From a young age, we are raised to fight and ride, then sail. I am a better sailor than I am a warrior, so I captain a ship."

"Is the ship yours?"

"No, it belongs to our Jarl." He glanced at Marcus. "My wife's brother. I pay him a tithe to use the ship. The rest of the profit I split amongst myself and the crew."

"Seems fair."

"Yes, I have a better arrangement because he is my brother-in-law. Most pay twenty-five percent."

"That is steep."

"Indeed. Nothing in this world comes easy." Holger's grin shifted to a smile. "Especially the farther north you go."

"That is what everyone keeps saying."

"What about you?" He glanced over. "You are not a typical merchant."

"Why do you say that?"

"All my kin are warriors, so I know one when I see one. It's the way you carry yourself." He nodded to the weapon strapped to Marcus's saddle. "Your sword is well made, but not flashy. It's not for show."

"You're right. I'm not a trader or a merchant." He paused. "Let's say I'm doing someone a favor."

"That's a big favor, going to the Northland. You must be in debt to this person."

"You could say that."

"Well, I doubt you will get permission to go, so it might not matter."

"About that. Do you have any advice on convincing the Jarl to let me go?"

"He's a plain man, and he likes straight, honest talk. He's not cunning at all." Holger frowned. "It's surprising he is still the Jarl. But he has strong relations with the other Jarl's, and none of them see him as a threat, so maybe that's why."

"Good to know."

"Your chances will improve if the hunt is successful. He loves boar meat." He nodded to the thin line of greenery on the horizon. "And that is where we shall find them."

Twenty minutes later, they came to a halt a hundred yards from the edge of a thick forest. They all dismounted as the dogs wandered around the open field. Holger and the teenager unstrapped the spears and gave one to each man. They set the spares on the ground.

Holger motioned to the young teen. "Take the pack horses back out across the field. I don't want them gored." Holger glanced back at Marcus. "Have you ever hunted boar?"

"No."

"We will send the dogs into the forest," he pointed to the distant tree line. "They will sniff out a pack of boar, then drive them toward us. We will know they are coming because the dogs will be barking." He pointed across the field. "We will line up at an angle to the trees. When they come out, we charge them. Don't go too fast, as it makes it much harder to spear them. They may be fat, but they are agile. This is the most important part. If you fall from your horse, don't run. These bastards are fast. Keep them in front of you and avoid their tusks."

Marcus grinned. "That is your advice? Avoid their tusks?"

"Yes. Or better yet, don't fall off your horse."

The group remounted, and one man gave the dogs a command. As one, the pack darted toward the trees and disappeared into the heavy brush. The men guided their horses into a line, each man holding their spear straight up in the air.

The spear was about half again thicker than Marcus was

used to. The tip was not metal, but was hewn to a fine point. Not effective against armor, but cheap and easy to make.

Fifteen minutes later, they heard several dogs baying, soon joined by the others in the pack. The clamor grew louder as the pack pushed what they hoped were boar towards them.

"Get ready." Holger lowered his spear, nestling it up against his hip.

The others did the same, and within a minute, they heard a loud thrashing in the underbrush.

Marcus held the reins with his left hand, gripping the spear as the adrenaline flowed. Seconds later, the first boar burst from the tree line, barreling across the open field. He was half as big as a standard cow, with more muscle and a heavy coat of fur running along his back. A pair of tusks, the size of daggers, curled away from his lower jaw.

"Let's go!" Holger spurred his horse forward, the others in close pursuit.

Several other beasts burst from the trees, following the same line as the first boar.

The lead boar looked like he would escape the approaching riders, so they angled in on the others. One of Holger's neighbors was the first to reach one of them, but his spear thrust missed the beast. It bolted to the side and past the rider.

Holger was next. His thrust was true, catching the boar near the shoulder. As the spear pierced the thick hide, it let out a painful squeal. The force of the collision knocked the boar to the ground and unseated Holger from his mount. The horse continued as the Northman tumbled onto the mossy earth, the wind knocked out of him.

Marcus saw him fall from the corner of his eye and saw a second boar angled toward the fallen man. Pulling the reins of this horse, Marcus did his best to judge where to intercept the beast.

Holger had regained his feet in time to see the approaching

beast. He was about to dive to the side when Marcus buried his spear into the side of the animal, letting go of the spear right after contact. The shaft slid between two ribs and flipped the boar onto its side.

Holger grinned as Marcus pulled up beside him. "Good timing."

"I had an excellent trainer."

The first boar, though incapacitated, was still alive. Holger pulled out his dagger and, careful to avoid the thrashing tusks, slit its throat. The one Marcus had speared was instantly killed.

In all, the group had taken three boars.

The men dressed the carcasses, tossing scraps to the dogs, and secured them to poles that the spare horses would drag back to the village.

They arrived after noon, and the boars were taken away to prepare for dinner later that night. They handed their horses' reins to the teenager who had accompanied them, and Holger led them to a water trough where they stripped off their tunics and washed away the grime of the hunt. Holger dipped his head into the trough, then threw it back, his long hair flinging water everywhere. A big grin on his face, he grabbed a nearby cloth and dried off his face.

"Thank you for killing that boar." He continued to dry his neck and shoulders. "It was putting me in a tough spot."

"I was more concerned you were mad at me for taking your kill." Marcus grinned. "I figured you were going to *avoid the tusks* and kill him with your knife."

"Yes." He tossed the cloth onto the pile of dirty tunics. "That was my plan."

As they shrugged on fresh tunics, Holger placed one hand on Marcus's shoulder. "Now, we shall partake of the best part of a successful hunt. Mead."

Marcus grinned. "You know me quite well."

They spent the afternoon putting a dent into a barrel of

mead. As the sun set, the aroma of roasted pig wafted through the town. Edda cut them off before they became too drunk, promising more mead at the feast.

Despite his protests, Edda spent a few minutes combing Holger's hair into something presentable. Marcus took the hint and used a small mirror to do the same. They were ready to head to the main hall when Marcus stopped to retrieve something from his bag. It looked like a sword wrapped in linen.

Holger eyed him suspiciously, to which Marcus replied, "A gift."

"Trond is not a swordsman, but I'm sure he will like it."

"I thought you were all warriors?"

"Well, of course he is. But much like me, he was enamored with the sea. When he was young, he ventured further than any man I know. And survived more storms than I can remember. He had a keen sense of when to put ashore, and when to ride out the storm. Never panicked, hence his name."

"Which is?"

"Trond The Anchor."

"We should all have such names."

"You already do." Holger grinned. "Marcus The Boar Killer."

"I've been called worse."

"I'm sure you have. Let's eat."

The Jarl's lodge was in the center of town, and was several times as large as any other building. Marcus noticed it had open ports in the wall, spaced around the perimeter. The door leading into the lodge was tall enough to allow a man riding a horse to enter, and twice as wide. But it was sturdy and had several large beams that could be used to lock it.

"Here is where we make our last stand, if the walls are breached." Holger pointed a thumb back over his shoulder. "You saw the ports. Archers can fire at all angles. Though if they got this far..." Holger shook his head as his voice trailed off.

HAMMER OF GOD

"Last stands rarely end well." Marcus frowned as he studied the inside of the lodge.

It was dark, despite the two dozen torches. A long row of massive posts held up a network of thick trusses that supported the roof. As in other lodges, a long fire pit occupied the center, currently roasting the three boars they had killed. A dozen tables ran on each side of the pit, with a long table at the far end of the room. Most of the seats were already taken, the occupants laughing and drinking as they waited for the feast to begin. They stopped talking when Holger and Edda led Marcus to a table near the front.

The main table was empty, so Marcus leaned forward and grabbed a cup, which a young teenage girl filled with mead. She had raven hair and a dark complexion, the opposite of those seated around the fire. It occurred to him that she was a slave. He swallowed past the lump in his throat and nodded to her, avoiding eye contact.

Slavery was a common practice in every culture. As a Roman, he had grown up with slaves in his household, and they were a critical part of the Roman economy. But the years he had spent chasing down slavers were some of the darkest days of his life. He did his best to push the thought from his mind and focus on the task at hand.

That was made easier by the arrival of the Jarl. A door in the back of the room sprung open, and everyone stood. A pair of male teenagers emerged, plus a girl who looked in her early twenties. A man, who would be considered below average height for a Northman, quickly followed them. What he lacked in height, he made up for in girth. He was stout, to say the least, with long gray hair and a matching beard. Two women followed him out, one about ten years older than the other.

Holger leaned over and whispered into Marcus's ear. "Trond has two wives. Grid is the older one, and she runs the family, if not the town. But she only gave him one child, his daughter. Hilda is the mother of his two sons."

Marcus nodded and took another sip of wine as the Jarl and his family sat at their table. Marcus sat down. "Do they like each other?"

Holger grinned. "What do you think?"

Marcus chuckled and took a sip of mead. Wiping his mouth, he said, "How is this going to work?"

"Trond will welcome everyone to the feast, then my wife will introduce you."

"Is that when I ask about going north?"

"By the gods, no. He would have to reject you out of tradition." He took a drink from his cup. "We'll do that after. You can give him the gift now though."

As if on cue, Trond raised his cup and, with a voice that did service to his stature, bellowed, "Welcome to our feast! And boar, my favorite!"

The attendees cheered and pounded their fists on the table as they drank.

"And quite a successful boar hunt! Three were taken, including the one that almost made my sister a widow."

The crowd laughed, and even in the darkness, Marcus swore Holger was blushing.

"Where is this Roman that saved me the trouble of finding another brother-in-law?"

Edda stood, replying to her brother, "I found my first husband, and I'll find another if the gods take this one, thank you."

"Ah, older sisters have quite a tongue. But what can I do?" He squinted at the table she was standing at. "And this Roman?"

Holger elbowed him, so Marcus stood.

Edda slanted one hand toward him. "This is Marcus. And yes, he is the Roman, but comes to us from Gaul."

"And for what reason has he come to us?"

"To save Holger from the boar!" someone from another table yelled before Edda could reply.

There was a long round of laughter, and when it died down, Marcus redirected the conversation.

"Trond the Anchor." The Jarl raised his eyebrows, surprised Marcus could speak his tongue. "I bring you a gift from Charles Martel, Mayor of the House, Protector of Austrasia. May I approach?"

"Of course." Trond grinned. "Though gifts are rarely free."

Marcus retrieved the sword and walked around the end of the table, stopping in front of the main table. The Jarl stood as all eyes focused on them.

Marcus held the sword like a baby as he unwrapped the handle. "The finest smith in Gaul forged this." He angled the handle across the table. "I'm pleased to present it to you."

Trond reached for the hilt and pulled the sword from the linen. The blade glistened beneath the torch flames.

"It is well balanced; and we hear about the purity of the Gaul steel. It appears to be a fine weapon." He nodded. "Thank you."

"My pleasure." Marcus bowed and retreated to his seat.

That is when the feast began. Platters of sliced boar, root vegetables and bread appeared at each table, along with fresh pitchers of mead.

It's very difficult to get drunk men to leave a party. The task is nearly impossible when free alcohol is flowing. After several hours of feasting, the Jarl cut off the libations, and gave word to his councilors to send the guests home. That message was not relayed to Holger's table.

As the others filtered from the lodge, the room grew deathly quiet. Marcus took a long pull of mead, the once crackling fire having settled into a long, quiet burn. The Jarl broke the silence. "Come, bring your chairs to my table." He pointed in front of him. "Let's find out why a Roman has come to the Northland."

Edda, Holger, and Marcus stood, grabbing their chairs with one hand, cups in the other. They circled the long tables and positioned their chairs across from the Jarl and his family. Holger pushed Marcus to sit across from Trond.

They stared at each other for a moment, Marcus finally speaking. "I come to ask for your permission."

"My permission for what?"

"To sail north."

"How far north?"

"Hålogaland," Holger said.

Trond sat back, as if someone had pushed him. He sucked air in through his lips, his thick mustache curly. "For god's sake, why?"

"Fish." Holger took a pull from his cup. "Stockfish."

"I have stockfish here."

"Not as much as he needs." Holger set his cup down. "Tell him."

"I need a steady supply of stockfish. For that, I need to go to the source," Marcus said.

Trond frowned and shook his head. "Only Northmen go north."

"I'm told you can grant me an exception."

"And why would I do that?" He leaned forward, elbows pressing into the table.

"I'm sure the boats coming south would prefer to unload here and not deal with the channel." Marcus smiled. "You, of course, can profit from that transition."

"I make plenty of profits now."

"I'm sure you do. And the Saxons and Frisians know that. It would be wise to have a powerful ally."

"We have lived beside the Saxons or Frisians for a long time. Why should I worry about them now?"

"Charles is consolidating his control over Gaul. His neighbors will look to strengthen their position."

"So, he is creating this problem for me?"

"Perhaps it is an opportunity."

Trond studied him for a long moment. "I have no love for the Frisians or Saxons. Your kin kept them from focusing on me, and with that threat gone, we may need a new ally."

"Charles would like to be that ally."

"I'm sure he would." Trond chuckled. "I will sleep on it." He stood, all the others standing as well. "I appreciate you saving my brother-in-law. Listening to my sister whine would have been insufferable."

"Be careful," Edda warned, "you may be Jarl, but you are still my little brother. I'll pluck all your beard hairs with my bare hands."

"I know." He thumbed at his wives. "And they would both help you."

Without another word, he motioned for his family to join him, and they exited the back door toward their living area.

Holger shrugged. "He didn't say no. That's promising."

"If he says no, do I have any other options?"

"How far can you swim?" Holger started toward the door. "No, even if you survive the journey, they will kill you as soon as you land."

"Well, that would be disappointing."

Holger laughed and pushed open the door.

They slept well into the morning. Marcus pushed his fur from his body and swung his feet to the ground. There was less smoke than usual in the lodge, as only the fire was burning. He stood and slipped on his tunic, then his boots.

Edda appeared out of nowhere and handed him a bowl full of porridge and berries. She tilted her head toward the door. "The others are outside."

"You think he will deny my request?" Marcus shoveled in a mouthful of porridge.

"I'm not sure. My brother is fickle, despite his nickname. But either way, you would need to leave soon to take advantage of summer."

"Why is that?"

"No one crosses the sea after summer, and he knows that. He will decide quickly."

"Understood." He smiled and took another bite. "Thanks for breakfast."

"My pleasure."

He took the bowl with him as he exited the lodge and heard the familiar sound of wooden swords clashing. Looking to his left, he saw the boys hacking away at one another.

Marcus stopped next to the pair. "You should spread your feet a little wider."

They stopped and looked up at him, the older one replying, "What?"

Marcus set down his bowl and moved to the younger boy, adjusting his feet and stance. "Quick, but not fast." He angled the boy's sword forward as the other watched. "Try again." Stepping back, he picked up his bowl and took another mouthful.

They sparred for a few minutes, then he stopped them and gave more instruction. The lesson lasted an hour or more, both young boys were covered with sweat when Holger appeared by his side.

"How are they doing?"

Marcus glanced at the smaller of the two. "He's a natural. Quick hands, steady feet."

"And the other?"

He smiled at Holger. "You should teach him to sail."

The Northman chuckled, and said, "I have news."

"Good news?"

"If you want to freeze to death, yes."

"The Jarl has approved my journey?"

"Yes," he paused, his face twisting a bit, "with conditions."

"What conditions?"

"Well, he wants me to sail you north."

"I thought you had never been north."

"I've never captained a ship going north. I've done at least a dozen trips with Trond."

"And why does he want you to go?"

Holger pursed his lips. "He doesn't trust his son to any other captain."

"His son? Bloody hell, no. I don't want to babysit some kid!"

"He is not a kid; he is a teenager. And it's one of the conditions. He feels it will be a good experience for him." Holger added, "The lad is an excellent sailor."

Marcus frowned at him. "And what if something happens to him?"

Holger exhaled. "Then we are both in deep shit."

CHAPTER FOURTEEN

*Ocean is more ancient than the mountains,
and freighted with the memories and the dreams of Time.*
—H.P. LOVECRAFT

FALL, 716 A.D.
RIBE, JUTLAND

Preparations to sail began that day. The Jarl gave Holger his choice of boats to outfit, and a small team of men to ensure the vessel was ready for the rigors of the journey.

While he worked on the ship, Edda focused on the provisions required for the journey. That included the object of their voyage, a healthy supply of stockfish. In addition, they packed a watertight barrel full of grain and another with root vegetables. Smaller containers contained honey, nuts, and butter. Livestock included a half-dozen chickens for eggs and a pair of goats for milking. Lastly, the Jarl allotted them a small cask of mead, much to Marcus's delight, and a full barrel of ale.

HAMMER OF GOD

Another major task was outfitting the Roman for winter in the Northland. Since the journey would take at least a month, if the weather cooperated, there was no way they could return before the spring.

Edda led him out of the small town and toward the assortment of buildings lining the walkway to the docks. They turned down onto the wooden walkways, stopping in front of a worn shack that leaned a bit toward the left. She knocked and waited. When there was no response, she pounded on it again.

A few moments later, a woman pushed open the door and poked her head out. "Who's making all the noise?" She was short and thin, two rare traits in Jutland.

"It's Edda. I have a customer for you." She glared at the woman. "He is a guest of the Jarl. Don't swindle him like you do the others."

"What others?" The wrinkles in her face deepened.

"The furs you sold to the Saxons last month."

"It was a fair price!" she growled, several of her front teeth missing. "Plus, the bastards haggled on everything."

Edda pointed at her. "A fair price."

The corner of the old woman's lip curled upward as she glared at Marcus. "What does he need?"

It was Edda who replied, "A pair of heavy trousers and two fur lined tunics. Do you have any fur-lined boots?"

"What does he have to trade?"

Edda glowered back at her.

"Yes, I have some with squirrel fur."

"No beaver?"

The woman bit her lip and nodded. "Yes. What makes this one so special that he needs beaver fur?"

Marcus grinned. He kind of liked the old hag.

"Hold your tongue, woman." Edda continued, "Woolen socks, two pairs. And mittens. A wool cloak as well."

"Wait here. I'll see what I can find."

As the pair waited, Marcus studied the distant shoreline. The town was situated so that it was protected from the open sea. The beach by the docks was calm, with tiny waves creeping up onto the sand. The dark water beyond was almost black. Several boats were moored to the various docks, but only one of them had men cleaning or making repairs. Marcus spotted Holger walking along the deck, giving instructions to the men.

He turned back when the door opened again, the old woman invisible behind a tall pile of fur and cloth. She dropped them down on the wooden walkway. Rummaging through the pile, she handed several items to Marcus. "Try these on."

He pulled off his thinner tunic and slipped on the heavier garments. Once satisfied they fit, she handed him trousers. Marcus looked at Edda.

"What? Do you think you have something down there I haven't seen before?" The old woman glared at Marcus. "You can't try on the trousers unless you take your other ones off."

Marcus shrugged and dropped his trousers, slipping on the heavier version. They fit well.

They continued at it for a while, and that was when the haggling began.

"How are they paying?"

"I have silver coins. Sceattas."

"I can't eat silver."

Marcus looked at Edda.

She frowned. "You can pay Trond. I'll pay her with goods from Trond's warehouse."

"Will he be alright with that?" Marcus asked.

"Of course, he's my little brother." Her grin disappeared as she looked back at the old woman. "I'll give you five marks of grain, two marks of butter, and a small cask of ale."

"Pfff, that barely pays for the beaver."

Edda's eyes narrowed. "I'll give you eight marks of grain,

three of butter, and the cask of ale. Plus, one boar leg, roasted. He will throw in a few silver coins in case the traders come back. You can buy some spices from them."

The lady stood with both hands on her hips, her tongue running along her narrow lips. She glared at Marcus. "Ten silver coins."

"Three." He dug into his leather pouch.

"Five," she countered.

Marcus pulled his hand from the bag and dropped the coins into her outstretched palm.

He picked up his old clothes and walked with Edda back to the town.

"The lot wasn't worth three coins." She glanced over at Marcus.

He looked back at the old shack, then at Edda. "Where I'm going, that silver won't do me any good. Plus," he winked, "there is plenty more where I got that."

"Next time bring spice, it's worth more than gold or silver."

"Noted."

They passed through the gate and went on to their lodge.

That night, they packed and went for a much smaller dinner in Trond's lodge. Marcus met Bjarne, Trond's oldest son. He was sixteen, and already taller than Marcus, with a wiry frame, thick blonde hair and bright blue eyes.

He was quiet, yet answered questions when asked. Mostly he listened as Marcus updated Trond on developments in Gaul, Rome and beyond. They ate leftover boar stew with toasted flatbread and honey as a dessert. And, of course, mead.

A servant moved to add another chunk of dried peat to the fire, but the Jarl held up his hand. "We finish early tonight. They must leave with the tide in the morning." Trond set down his mug and looked Holger in the eyes. "I entrust my son to you." He shifted to Marcus. "And to you."

Holger placed his fist over his heart. "I will protect him as my own."

"As will I," Marcus stated.

"Good, I know you will." He looked over at the teen, then back to his brother-in-law. "I send him as a warrior, not a son of the Jarl. He will be treated with equal share in the work and spoils." He shifted to Marcus. "I hear you are a fine swordsman. Perhaps you can teach my Bjarne."

"I am adequate." Marcus grinned. "And I will be honored to train this fine young man."

"Excellent!" Trond lifted his cup. "To a safe and fruitful journey!"

They all clanked cups, drained the contents, and stood from the table. Within an hour, they were all asleep.

They woke before dawn, the dogs stirring first, then Edda and her sister. The ladies warmed up breakfast, while the men dressed and rolled up their bedding. They ate in silence, Edda glancing at her husband. This was not a normal trip for her. Everyone around the table understood the dangers ahead.

They finished their meal and sipped down a warm brew of berries and herbs. As they all stood, Marcus grabbed his bedding and stepped outside, leaving Holger in private to say goodbye to his wife.

It was a cool morning, a simple reminder that fall, and soon winter, were just around the corner. Streaks of pale orange filled the cloudless skies, a shallow breeze drifting in from the sea beyond.

Marcus looked down from the sky and saw a pair of figures emerging from the darkness. It was easy to identify the shape of Trond, and Marcus assumed the other was his son.

HAMMER OF GOD

"Is Holger giving my sister a proper farewell?" The Jarl angled his head toward the lodge.

"I can only assume so." Marcus turned to the teen. "Good morning, young Bjarne."

"Good morning, sir." He set his pack.

"No reason to call me sir. We are comrades on this journey."

"Yes, sir."

"Let's head to the ship." Marcus started toward the main gate. "Who knows how long Holger will take to say goodbye."

The other households were stirring as they headed to the docks. The amount of smoke rising from each building increased as fuel was added to the dying fires. Outside the city walls, they spied a dozen men and a few boys walking to the fishing vessels tied to the nearest dock.

They continued to the large, central dock to which their ship was moored. The vessel swayed with the shallow swells, the ramp leading to the deck sliding back and forth on the wooden planking. They were the first to arrive, the goats bleating at them as they topped the ramp and stepped onto the boat.

The craft was a full thirty sections, the space between the ribs of the frame. They stowed their bedding near their other gear and met near the mast. Trond stood with his hand on the massive timber.

"The finest shipbuilders in all of Jutland made this ship." He rubbed the worn surface of the mast. "This came from deep in the Northland, and I was told it is one of the strongest masts the builder had ever seen." His gaze fell on Marcus. "I hope it serves you well on this journey, and more importantly," he shifted his stern expression to his son, "brings me back a man in place of the boy I send."

Bjarne held his stare for a moment, nodded and dropped his eyes to the deck.

"Why so somber?" Holger hopped onto the deck, a smile splitting his brown-gray beard.

"Not all of us enjoyed the same farewell you did." Trond grinned and looked back at Bjarne. "We were discussing the journey and how it can change a man."

"Ah, no worries." Holger placed his arm around Bjarne, patting his shoulder. "Bjarne is a fine sailor and takes to the water like a delfin."

"A what?" Marcus did not recognize the word.

"A delfin." Holger pulled his arm free and held both hands wide. "A big fish." He moved his hand up and down in a circular motion. "They jump in and out of the water."

That did not solve the puzzled look on Marcus's face.

"I'll show you later." Holger extended his hand to Trond. "Your son will be better for the journey, I promise."

The Jarl returned his grip and did the same with Marcus. Lastly, he gave his son a big hug, the young teen's arms barely able to reach around his father. Pushing him away, he held both his shoulders. "Farewell, and may the gods sail with you." He scanned the group. "Tonight, we will make a sacrifice, and ask for a safe and speedy journey."

He climbed up the railing and onto the ramp as other crew members arrived. Holger counted them and gave directions, then whistled. In the nearby patch of grass, a medium-sized gray hound stuck his head up and peered at Holger. The dog sprinted to the dock and up the ramp. He sat next to Holger when the captain raised one hand.

"I see we have a companion?" Marcus said.

"Yes, I take him on my longer journeys. He will help hunt and guard the camp if we sleep ashore."

"I'll take all the help we can get." Marcus rubbed the dog's head, taking a moment to scratch behind his ears. "What's his name?"

"Njördur." Holger pointed to the open water. "God of the sea."

"Good choice."

"I know." He started giving directions to the crew, Njördur right on his heels.

A small crowd had gathered on the dock to watch them leave, including Edda and the kids. Marcus nodded to Edda and placed his fist over his heart as several crew members shoved the front of the boat from the dock. She nodded in return, her hands clasped around her youngest daughter.

When they cleared the dock, Holger ordered the oars to be dropped into the water, and soon the boat was slicing through the surf. He guided them between two islands, angled the ship around the rocky shore, and turned the vessel northward.

"Sails!" Holger ordered as they entered the channel.

The rowers retracted and stowed the oars, as several others scrambled up the mast and across the yard to loosen straps holding the rolled-up canvas. The wind filled the unfurled sail and drove the ship forward, the sleek keel plowing through the larger swells. Holger kept them well within sight of land, adjusting the course to the curvature of the shore.

They had finished a lunch of hardtack bread and dried fish when Holger called from the boat's stern. Marcus gave Njördur the last bit of fish, and wiping both hands, made his way to the captain.

Holger had the end of the steer board tucked under his armpit, his hand wrapped around the rounded top. He adjusted it, then pointed to the open ocean with his free hand.

"Delfins."

Marcus squinted against the noonday sun, eventually seeing a pack of shiny, gray creatures jumping in and out of the waves. He turned back to Holger. "You mean dolphins."

"Yes, that is what I said. Delfins."

The pod had moved closer to the ship, and several were riding the vessel's wake.

Holger leaned over and smiled. "Not as tasty as whales."

"Whales?" Marcus looked back at him.

"What? You don't know about whales?"

"No." Marcus leaned against the railing. "What are they?"

"Big, big delfins. You will see." He winked and made another adjustment to the steer board.

The weather held for the first few days, but a storm caught up with them on the afternoon of the third day. Holger found a shallow bay where they beached the ship and set up camp on the shore. The rain hit at dusk, extinguishing their fire, and leaving them with cold saltfish and ale for dinner.

It continued for most of the second day, the wind blowing back toward Ribe and making it impossible to put back out to sea. During temporary breaks in the downfall, Marcus took Njördur on walks inland and trained Bjarne, trying to break the monotony of the camp.

The storm lifted that evening, and they enjoyed a warm meal of roasted rabbit and boiled vegetables. Holger even allowed the men a cup of mead. They were back on the water and heading north the following morning.

The pattern continued, sometimes anchored in the bay, sometimes on shore. On the eighth night, they put into a small town on the tip of Jutland. Holger and Marcus went into the town to speak with the locals, while the men stayed back on the ship.

Holger had hoped one of the two other ships docked was from the north, and perhaps they could sail together. But that was not the case. As a result, they would be sailing alone.

The others were asleep when they returned, and Marcus grabbed the captain's arm before they climbed back onto the ship. "That man laughed when you said you were sailing north."

"Yes."

"Why?"

Holger turned away from the ship, his voice lowered. "We should have started a week or two ago. That last storm was the beginning. They will only get worse."

"How bad?"

"The next stretch is the most dangerous. Open water for at least five days. If we make that—"

"If?"

"When we make that crossing, we can follow the coast north and put ashore for any storm."

"So, we need five days of good weather?"

"Yes."

"Now I feel better."

Holger raised his eyebrows, smiled, and patted the Roman on the back as they made their way up the gangplank. "I wish I could say the same."

They had one full day of good weather. The day after they left Jutland, a dark cloud bank swept in from the east. Holger gave the order, and the crew ensured everything was secured to the deck.

Marcus joined Holger next to the steer board. "Any advice?"

Holger grinned. "Don't eat."

"Why?"

"It's a waste of food."

The storm hastened the night, blocking the dying rays of sun and plunging them into darkness. First came the wind, snapping at the sails and rigging. Holger gave up holding his course, focusing on keeping the boat's bow aimed toward the waves.

B. K. GREENWOOD

"We have to drop sail!" Holger pointed to the rippling canvas.

Nodding, Marcus motioned to several of the crew. As they climbed the mast, Marcus helped loosen the straps holding the sail in place. The crewman pulled the canvas up, lashing it to the yard, while others clambered down the mast as the vessel rolled with the increasing swells.

The rain followed soon after, a cold, stinging downpour. Marcus stayed with Holger as the waves increased, several crashing over the railing and onto the deck. It was impossible for the captain to steer with no sail, leaving them at the mercy of the storm.

The gale tossed them around like a child's toy. Marcus lost all sense of direction, the waves coming from his right, and then his left. They would smash the vessel, the ship almost capsizing. But each time, the vessel seemed to defy gravity and right itself. Other times, the ship rode straight up the face of a massive swell, then came crashing down the other side, burying the bow into the water.

The storm seemed to last days, but it was still dark when it broke. The sheer tranquility of the after storm was a stark contrast to the fury of the tempest. Despite being soaked to the bone, the entire crew, including Holger, lay down on the deck and slept.

Marcus woke to find a seagull sitting on his chest. The giant bird glared at him with dull, black eyes with yellow rings. He craved roasted bird. That was when he realized how famished he was.

As he shifted on the hard deck, the bird let out a low croaking noise, lifted both wings and tilted its head to the side, staring at him with a single eye. When he lifted one arm, the bird flapped both wings and hopped from his chest, a few feathers floating down where it had once sat.

Marcus sat up and looked out across the boat's railing. The

ocean was smooth, like the surface of the water in a barrel. The sky above was gray, the sun a blotch behind the thick clouds. He rolled over to his knees, and reaching for a nearby bench, pulled himself to his feet. His cold, wet clothes clung to his shivering body.

The boat shifted as he stood and moved to the railing. He was staring out across the horizon when a dolphin shattered the pristine surface of the water, splashing Marcus and startling him so badly he nearly fell back onto the deck.

"They love to do that." Holger was standing next to him, stretching his arms above his head and yawning.

"Why?"

The captain shrugged. "Maybe they think it's funny." He looked up at the dull sky, then at the mast. "I'll wake up the boys. We may have to row for a bit until we get some wind."

"How do you know which direction to row?"

Holger pointed two fingers at the orange blob that was the sun. "I'll watch that for a bit. Perhaps I'll know which way to go."

"That's it?" Marcus raised one hand. "We could row straight out to sea."

"You have a better idea?" Holger's face crinkled. "When the clouds break and the sky is clear, I'll get better bearings."

"What about breakfast?"

"That is one advantage to calm seas. This is the rare occasion we can use the fire. I'll get one of the boys on it."

The men began moving around the deck. They stacked flat stones near the center, in front of the mast. They uncovered a metal brazier and set it on the stones, adding kindling and wood. Soon, a small fire was going, and a frying pan was suspended above the flames.

Marcus watched one of the men prepare breakfast. "What are you making?"

The older sailor looked up at Marcus and smiled. "Ship biscuits." He nodded to the pan. "We fry up smoked pork and onions. Next, we add them to a bowl with flour, wheat meal and salt." He motioned with his hands. "We roll them up, then flatten and fry again. Very good with butter."

"Sounds delicious." Marcus's stomach growled.

The sailor smiled. "Everything sounds delicious when you're hungry."

The meal was supplemented with fried eggs and a bit of honey for the biscuit. Holger opened a cask and allotted each man one cup of ale to wash down breakfast. Once the fire was extinguished and all the animals were fed and watered, the men settled onto their benches and rowed.

Marcus insisted on rowing and sat next to a more experienced sailor. The pace was steady, if not fast. The sharp lines of the ship's hull sliced through the flat surface. They had been rowing for about two hours when the first hint of a breeze caused the sheer surface of the water to ripple.

Holger had them row a bit further, then ordered them to stop. He motioned to several men who scrambled up the mast and unleashed the massive sail. Once secured, it billowed enough to drive the boat forward. Within an hour, the wind had picked up enough to engage the sail, and they were moving near top speed.

The wind also cleared away the clouds, revealing the warm sun's rays, so men pulled off their shirts and trousers, securing them to the railing or mast so they could dry.

The next two meals consisted of salt fish and leftover biscuits. By the time the sun set, most of the men had laid out their bedding and gathered to play dice games. Marcus wandered over to Holger as he adjusted the steer board with one arm and picked up a pouch on the deck with the other. He tossed the pouch to Marcus.

"What's this?"

"Pipes. Do you smoke?"

"I have, yes."

HAMMER OF GOD

"Good. Fill two up with the herb in the smaller pouch."

Marcus opened the small leather bag and took out a pinch of the herb. It was earthy, with a rich musky scent. He stuffed some into each pipe and looked at Holger.

"There is a flint in the bag."

Marcus pulled it free and put a pipe into his mouth, sucking in as he struck the flint near the bowl. After a few sparks, the herb glowed orange. He took in a few puffs, the smoke tickling the inside of his mouth and throat, gave the pipe to Holger and repeated the process for himself.

They smoked in silence, Holger leaning against the railing, Marcus one foot up on the nearby bench. A sense of peace settled over him as Marcus watched the wind ripple through the sail and the ship rise and fall with the waves.

"I've been sailing all my life," Holder said, the pipe dangling from his lips. "But these Northmen, they are real sailors. You will see. The mountains make it impossible for them to travel by land. So, they sail as wee lads." He put his hand down to his knees. "They handle boats like you do a sword."

Marcus frowned.

"Aye, I know. You are better than most men. The quiet ones always are."

Marcus nodded; the pipe clenched in his teeth. He pulled it free. "What else should I know about them?"

"They are honest, but impatient. They respect strength, despise weakness." He let out another cloud of smoke. "And they grow restless. Life is very hard, this far north. Many of the men talk of moving to easier places to live."

"And why don't they? Doesn't sound like they are afraid of anything."

"They are not." Holger shook his head. "I don't know why they have not left. Perhaps tradition? They are a very superstitious lot."

"Yes, they still believe in the old gods."

"Old gods?" Holger asked.

"Most people have embraced the concept of a single god."

"Including the Romans?"

"Yes, especially the Romans."

"One god." Holger chewed on his pipe. "What is he the God of?"

"Everything." Marcus grinned. "It's much less confusing."

"Sounds boring." He tilted his head to the side. "And you believe in this one God?"

Marcus paused, looking down into the tiny orange glow of the pipe, then back up at Holger. "I suppose I do."

"Suppose?" Holger smiled, the whites of his teeth visible. "Doesn't sound very convincing."

Marcus smiled back. "No, it doesn't."

"Land!"

Five days after the storm, the exclamation shattered the morning stillness. Marcus looked back at Holger, who was seated near the stern. The captain smiled, and instructed Bjarne, who was now manning the steer board, to angle the ship toward the shore. The night before, Marcus had asked Holger if they would ever step foot on dry ground again, to which the other man had only laughed in response.

It was not the first time Marcus had failed to trust a sailor, and probably not the last.

Marcus stood next to Holger, one hand on the railing. "I'm sick of the ocean."

Holger took a deep breath and gazed out over the narrow swells. "It's where I'm most at peace."

"I can see that."

"But don't worry, we will put to shore this afternoon."

HAMMER OF GOD

"And then how far north?" Marcus looked toward the distant shoreline.

"Two weeks or more." Holger frowned. "It depends on weather and wind." He glanced at the Roman. "What's your plan when we get there?"

Marcus shrugged. "I hadn't thought that far ahead."

Holger studied him for a moment. "You should start thinking about that."

He moved back to chat with Bjarne, and Marcus watched a pair of gulls drift on the wind next to their ship.

A few hours later, what was once a dark line against the choppy sea took shape. The coastline was barren rock, gray granite with veins of green turf scattered along its surface. The shore was rounded, worn smooth by thousands of years of water and wind. There was no sign of life or settlements.

"We'll keep sailing north," Holger pointed to the left, "and find a nice bay. Tonight, we sleep by the fire, with grass beneath our heads and a hot meal in our bellies."

Marcus glanced at the small wooden barrel. Holger followed his gaze and added, "And mead to celebrate the crossing."

The Roman smiled.

By late afternoon, they had found a bay with a long, sandy beach. As before, Holger angled the ship ashore, and soon the keel was grinding to a halt in the soft, brown sand.

Njördur was the first off the ship as he leapt from the bow to the sandy beach and disappeared inland. Marcus glanced over at Holger, and the latter smiled.

"He misses running. We will see him later tonight."

The men unloaded supplies and set up camp.

"Should I go look for water?" Marcus asked.

Holger shook his head. "No, we have enough for another week. In a few days, we will reach the upper fjords and there will be plenty of water."

B. K. GREENWOOD

Dinner was a stew of salted boar and root vegetables, along with freshly baked bread. Holger allotted two cups of mead per person. Njördur arrived before dinner was done and licked the wooden bowls clean. Holger went over to the pot and fished out a leg bone, tossing it to the hound, who caught it in his massive jaws and bolted away.

The last remnants of daylight were still fading as the fire died and the crew drifted off to sleep. Morning would come soon this far north, and it was best to get as much sleep as possible.

"We can all rest, no need for guards." Holger nodded toward the dog, sitting on a boulder overlooking the camp, as he gnawed on his bone. "He will warn us if anyone approaches."

"Where are all the people?"

Holger smiled. "In the fjords. They farm any flatland they can find. This far south, the land is barren. Much different inland. You shall see. Get a good night's sleep, my friend."

The next morning brought a cool, crisp breeze and the first sign of summer's demise. They packed the ship and rode that breeze north, skirting along the rocky coastline. By midday, the smooth, flat shoreline gave way to steepening cliffs covered with a mixture of spruce, birch, and pine.

It was late afternoon when Holger guided their longship into a wide channel, splitting two massive cliffs. On both sides, thin plumes of water cascaded down the sharp crags. They dropped the sails and rowed, the keel slicing through the placid surface of the fjord. Another hour brought them to a small cove, and soon the ship was nestled onto the rocky shore.

Several men disappeared into the nearby forest to gather water, while Bjarne and several others took their bows and went with Njördur. Marcus sat on a boulder, awestruck by the fjord's raw majesty.

"We have mountains where I am from." Marcus glanced

over at Holger. "But nothing like this. It's as if God filled the valleys with water."

"Yes, it is." Holger looked up at the nearest peak. "The beauty of this world never ceases to amaze me."

Marcus studied the steep slopes of the mountains. "Where do they live?"

"Anywhere they can." Holger smiled. "They find flat areas on the mountains, or in the valleys beyond. Some make stairs down the mountains, or rope ladders. They travel by boat. It is a very solitary life."

"And villages?"

"Some, few and far between." Holger smiled. "We shall reach one soon."

They ate a dinner of roasted rabbit with a collection of local berries. As the men settled down to sleep, Holger sat next to Marcus and refilled both of their cups with ale.

"In the next day or so, we will start running into locals."

"Is that a bad thing?"

"No." He took a sip of his drink. "I can replenish our stores. They may ask where we are going."

"What will you tell them?"

"I'm still figuring that out."

"And you said I need a plan."

"True, true. These people," Holger waved his cup toward the fjord, "they are very guarded. And competitive. Resources are scarce, and they are all competing for them. That creates rivalries. If I reveal too much, it may put the journey at risk."

"I trust you'll find a way."

"At least one of us does." He smiled, drained his cup and set it down on a nearby rock, and stood. "I'm going to take a piss and go to sleep."

Marcus raised his cup. "I'll see you in the morning."

They were on the water right after dawn. The sun was still behind the towering mountains, casting dark shadows across the fjord. Within an hour, they were sailing north again across open sea. Holger was correct, and by early afternoon they had encountered several fishing boats. They waved as they sailed past, the fishermen eyeing them suspiciously. Soon after, they reached the first settlement, nestled into a cove, surrounded by sheer granite walls.

It was less than a dozen buildings, and a bit of pasture for a small herd of sheep. Several fishing boats were moored to a single dock, and Holger guided the ship toward it. When they had closed to a few feet, several men hopped off the ship and secured it to the dock pylons.

Holger was the only one to go into the village, where several local men met him. After a long discussion, which included several gestures toward the ship, the conversation ended, and Holger returned to the ship. Climbing onboard, Marcus met him as the captain moved to a small wooden chest.

"What's going on?"

"They agreed to sell me some provisions in exchange for spices."

"That's it?"

"One of them asked where we were going, but I was noncommittal. The others were glad to get some pepper, so they respected my privacy."

They stayed the night on the dock, eating leftover rabbit and bread. The next morning, they headed out to sea alongside the various fishing boats. Holger dropped the sail and headed north. They passed several more settlements, all about the same size as the one they had just left. They camped on shore when possible, and when not, they moored inside a small bay or fjord.

Five days after trading for supplies, they reached a much larger town perched on a peninsula near the entrance to a massive fjord. A half dozen docks led to a wooden landing where a long row of low structures sat. Beyond, a palisade protected the rest of the town.

"This is Orland," Holger said to Marcus as he guided the ship toward the dock. "This is the primary trading post for all goods that come from the North."

"But they don't make stockfish here." Marcus studied the walls.

"No, that is much farther north."

"I want to see that."

"We can." Holger adjusted the steer board. "But this is where your deal will be made. No stockfish goes south that doesn't come through this port."

"Is there a Jarl here?"

"No, nothing that formal. I'll find out who is in charge and see if we can speak with him. Preferably over a nice hot meal."

"Good luck. What should we do?"

"Stay on the ship until I come for you," Holger replied with a grin. He made one last change to their course, and the men hopped to the dock and secured the longship. The others on the dock glared at Holger when he sprang to the deck. The captain walked up to one of the men and struck up a conversation. The man looked past Holger's shoulder, staring at Marcus, then paused before pointing to the town.

Holger nodded, clapped the man on the shoulder, and started along the dock.

He was gone for about an hour, and when he returned, he had a slight grin on his face. As he climbed into the ship, Marcus met him by the railing. "So?"

"The man in charge is Herlaug. Or I should say boy, he's barely old enough to grow a beard."

"Will he meet with us?"

"Of course, that is what I went to arrange."

Marcus glared at him.

"He is very excited to meet a Roman. He has only heard of them in stories." Holger frowned. "Did you bring your Roman armor?"

"No." Marcus grimaced. "I wear the same armor as the Franks."

"That's too bad, I think it would have impressed him."

"I suppose I'll have to impress him with my charm."

"No." He grinned. "I doubt that will work."

Marcus placed one hand over his heart, feigning offense. "Then what?"

"Sword play." Holger nodded. "You shall best his champion in a duel."

"What?"

"I might have mentioned you have fine quality iron weapons."

"Oh, *you might have mentioned.*"

"Yes, and he might have suggested a duel." Before Marcus could respond, Holger patted him on his chest. "I'm sure you'll do fine. The fellow is very large, but probably slow."

Marcus rolled his eyes as the captain disappeared down the deck.

Soon after dark, a man came to the ship and asked for Holger. They spoke for a few minutes, then the captain nodded and turned to his crew.

"They have invited us for dinner." The men cheered, but Holger held up his hands. "But it comes with one condition." He glanced over at Marcus. The Roman had a blank stare on his face. "The local chieftain has asked our Roman to fight his champion."

"To the death?" Bjarne smiled.

Marcus glared at Bjarne.

"No, not to the death." Holger grinned.

Marcus bowed. "If it gets us all a hot meal and some fresh ale, I will fight their champion."

The crew cheered again. When they had quieted down, Marcus asked. "What are the rules?"

"First blood, no fatal blows," Holger said.

"Fair enough. Let me get my sword."

The gate guard nodded as they passed through. None of the men could bring weapons, except Marcus. Once inside, they passed a half dozen stout longhouses before reaching the largest of the group on a small rise in the center of town. A pillar of smoke drifted from two holes in the roof, and the aroma of roasting meat hung heavy in the air. There was one peculiar difference between these buildings and the ones in Jutland. These had soil and grass growing on the roof.

Marcus nudged Holger and nodded toward the oddity. "Why is there grass growing on the roof?"

Holger looked up. "Helps keep the warmth in during the winter. Gets really cold here."

Nodding, Marcus followed him through the door. The inside of the longhouse was packed with locals, most of them standing along the edges of the room. As expected, two large fire pits burned at each end, with a large open area between them. A small group sat at a single table on one side of the farthest fire pit.

A young man stood as they entered and motioned them to his table. "Come forward!"

Holger led the way, Marcus by his side. The rest of the crew trailed behind.

"Where is the Roman?" the man asked.

"I am the Roman." Marcus stepped forward.

The young man frowned. He was tall and thin, with long blonde hair and the wisp of a beard. His eyes were crystal blue and reflected the flames of the nearby pit. "You do not look like a Roman."

"Have you ever seen a Roman?"

"No."

"Then how do you know what they look like?"

He grinned, followed by laughter. "You are correct! I suppose your dress confused me."

"I was told I would freeze to death if I dressed like a Roman."

"Very true. My name is Herlaug Ladesson." He looked at the others. "You have agreed to fight my champion?"

"I am Marcus Gracchus, and yes, I have."

"Do you want to see him first?"

"Why would I want to see him?"

"He's very large."

"That means there is more of him to strike."

"Good, I love a confident man!" Herlaug smiled and called back over his shoulder, "Rognvald!"

The residents standing behind Herlaug stepped aside to allow a giant of a man to approach the table. He was shirtless, and at least a head taller than Marcus, with thick, muscled shoulders and arms like tree trunks. His head was shaved on the side, the rest of his blonde hair pulled back into a ponytail. His long beard was braided into three strands with pieces of metal and bone. A shield was strapped to his left arm, and he held a massive sword in his right hand.

He walked around the table and into the center of the room.

"Have you changed your mind?" Herlaug said.

Marcus smiled. "I thought he'd be bigger."

Herlaug laughed. "Rognvald has never lost a match."

"That's impressive." Marcus drew his sword and looked over at his opponent's shield. "Do I get one of those?"

"Of course!" Herlaug motioned for a shield to be brought to the Roman. "These two brave men shall fight until one of them draws blood. No fatal blows!"

HAMMER OF GOD

Holger held the shield as Marcus strapped it on.

"He's big, probably slow," the captain whispered.

"Why do people keep saying that? Are all big men slow?" Marcus tightened the last strap.

"No."

"Then why should he be?"

With a furrowed brow, Holger paused. "Alright, forget about that. Tire him out. That is your best chance."

"Are you drunk?"

"Not yet."

"Go find some ale, and watch."

"Don't get yourself killed." Holger walked away, stopped and said, "And don't kill him."

"Expert advice." Marcus turned back toward the giant.

The two men stood ten paces apart when the Northman raised his sword, and Marcus did the same.

Rognvald was confident, but not a fool. He didn't rush at Marcus and attempt to use his size to overwhelm the Roman. Instead, he crouched and circled to his right, shield raised. Marcus did the same, squeezing the hilt of his Frankish sword. The most skilled smith in Gaul forged the blade, and it was perhaps the strongest sword he had ever wielded. That was what he was counting on.

Rognvald struck first, and he was not slow. He angled his blade toward Marcus's left shoulder, forcing the Roman to counter with his shield. The iron clanked against wood, a chunk splintering away. Marcus focused on the blade, and to his delight, it did not bend, confirming his suspicion.

Marcus feigned a counterstrike, slipped to his left and parried a second stroke from Rognvald. Next, the Roman lowered his sword and swung it in a tight arc, aiming above the hilt of the Northman's weapon. The two blades met with a sharp crack, and it was clear Rognvald was surprised by the strength of the blow.

B. K. GREENWOOD

But Marcus did not want to give away his speed and strength advantage, so he shuffled to his right and let the Northman attack. Rognvald was a fine swordsman, if a little raw. He was faster than his size would suggest, but predictable and limited in technique.

Marcus had spent seven hundred years fighting men with various styles. Romans, who were very precise and fixated on stabbing. Gauls and their propensity to overwhelm their opponents with strength and tenacity. Saracens who relied on speed and their razor-sharp, curved blades. And hundreds of variations in between. Marcus had learned from them all.

Rognvald's style was most like the Gauls, which made sense because they were both descendants of the Germanic tribes. Marcus focused on parrying the Northman, and whenever possible, he struck at the same place on Rognvald's sword.

Both men were dripping sweat when the Roman decided the time had come to end the match. He needed Rognvald to present his blade diagonally, so Marcus stepped forward and used his shield to knock his opponent's shield away from his body. He followed that up with an overhead strike, knowing Rognvald would have plenty of time to bring his sword up in defense. And that is exactly what Marcus wanted.

He put all his strength into the blow, and his sword shattered the Northman's inferior blade, leaving Rognvald with a handle and a blade less than half the length of a dagger. The broken piece twirled through the air and clattered off a nearby table, startling Herlaug.

Rognvald stared at Marcus, and the Roman flicked his wrist, the tip of his blade slicing the flesh on the Northman's exposed forearm. Stepping back, Marcus looked over at Herlaug. "First blood."

The young man, still flustered by the shattered blade, recovered quickly. "Yes, yes of course. Excellent match! I've

HAMMER OF GOD

never seen two finer swordsmen!" He nodded to his champion. "It appears your weapon let you down, Rognvald."

The big man bowed, distraught at losing his first match.

Marcus slipped his sword into his scabbard and stepped forward, extending one hand. "It is much better to lose your first match here, rather than a battlefield."

"Indeed." The giant held Marcus's hand in his tight grip. "You are much stronger than you look."

Marcus grinned. "I get that from my mother."

The Northman looked confused, but soon chuckled.

"Shall we share a pitcher of ale?" Marcus slapped his shoulder.

"Only a pitcher?"

The pair spun back toward where Holger joined them across from Herlaug. The young chief looked from Marcus to his champion. "Let me see." He held out his hand.

Rognvald handed him the broken sword. Herlaug examined the broken blade and looked up at Marcus. "You were trying to break this?"

"Yes."

"Why?"

"Because I could." He pulled his sword free. Several members of the chief's entourage took a step forward, but Marcus put them at ease when he flipped the weapon around and handed it to Herlaug, handle first. "Look for yourself."

Herlaug took the weapon and inspected the blade. It was balanced and razor sharp, the edge free of nicks or blemishes.

"May I?" Marcus reached for the sword.

"Yes." Herlaug handed it back to the Roman.

Marcus held the sword in his right hand and grabbed the end of the blade with his other. As he put pressure on the ends, the blade bent. When he released the tip, it bounced back into place.

"When I first crossed swords with this worthy champion,"

Marcus motioned to Rognvald, "I noticed his blade did not flex. That told me the metal was brittle, and if enough force was applied, the blade would break."

"Our best ironsmith made that blade."

"And his skill is not the issue." Marcus sheathed his sword. "I believe it's the iron ore you use."

Herlaug studied Marcus, eyes prying. "Why do you tell me this?"

"I have a proposition."

"I'm sure you do." He smiled. "But my father told me never to do business on an empty stomach. We shall eat and drink, and if we are still awake, we can talk business."

Plates of bread and cheese appeared, along with cups and several pitchers of ale. As they filled their cups, Holger did the introductions. "This," he motioned to the young man sitting next to him, "is Bjarne, son of Tronden. Someday he will be Jarl." He smiled. "If he lives long enough."

Herlaug nodded and tilted his cup toward Bjarne. "Is this your first journey north?"

"Yes," Bjarne said. "But I have been on many trips to Gaul and Britannia."

"Good." He took a long pull. "I was not much older than you when my father died, and I became chief. You need always be ready when you are called upon."

"I plan to, sir."

Just then, several platters of steaming venison appeared on the table, along with a variety of vegetables. The conversation shifted to their journey north as they dug into the main course. With plates empty, stomachs full, and mugs refilled, they returned to the original topic; why Marcus had come north.

"Your proposition?" Herlaug ran a finger along the top of his cup.

"Yes. You need better weapons. And for that, you need iron ore. I can provide that."

Herlaug stared back at him and took a sip. "In exchange for what?"

"Stockfish."

A silence settled on the table, and Herlaug sniggered. The men sitting next to Herlaug followed suit until all of them were laughing.

Marcus scanned the Northmen. "Did I say something funny?"

"I'm sorry, my friend, but yes." Herlaug set down his cup and scratched above his eyebrow with one finger. "Stockfish for iron. Seems like a very odd trade."

"I have lots of iron ore. I don't have any stockfish."

"But why stockfish? I'm sure you have plenty of other fish or animals you can kill and eat."

"Why do you make stockfish?" Marcus tilted his head to the side.

Herlaug's brown furrowed. "It lasts forever. So, we can take it on long sea voyages. Do you plan to sail far away?"

"No. But Charles, my patron, has a kingdom to conquer. And he needs food stocks that he can store for his army."

"Why not salt? I've had salted pork; it is very good. Much better than stockfish."

"Why don't you have salt pork?"

"Salt is expensive and very difficult to secure."

"Exactly. That is why I need stockfish."

Herlaug crossed one arm over his chest, and rested his other elbow on it, hand rubbing his chin. "And what do you propose?"

"I need someone here in the North who can secure large quantities of stockfish. They will ship them to Ribe," Marcus angled a thumb at Bjarne, "where his father will transport them to Gaul."

"And you will pay with iron ore?"

"Yes, by weight. Ten parts stockfish to one iron ore."

Herlaug frowned. "Ten? We do all the work and take all the risk of transport. Five. And you will send me three parts grain. If I send you stockfish, my people will have nothing to eat. I need grain to feed them."

"Agreed on the grain. But eight parts stockfish for each one of iron." Marcus met his gaze.

"Seven."

Marcus paused. "Eight. And I want to sail north and see how the stockfish is made."

Herlaug frowned. "Why?"

"I'm curious. Deal?"

"Deal," he leaned forward, "on one condition."

"What is that?"

"You must attend my wedding as a guest of honor."

"Your wedding? Why?"

"It's not often a man has foreign dignitaries at his wedding."

"Alright. When is this wedding?"

"One month. Plenty of time for you to sail north and see your precious stockfish."

"And who is the lucky bride?"

Holger shoved a piece of sausage into his mouth and smiled. "She is the daughter of a Jarl farther south. Not only will it bind our two towns, but she is also very beautiful."

"So, you have met?" Marcus asked.

"Yes, I spent a good part of the spring courting her." He glanced at his brethren. "My councilors say too much time." The others nodded as Herlaug continued, "But they have not seen her. Then they will understand."

The server arrived and refilled their cups.

"Well," Marcus said, taking a long pull from his cup, "we better head north so we can be back for this wedding."

CHAPTER FIFTEEN

We sail within a vast sphere, ever drifting in uncertainty, driven from end to end.
—Blaise Pascal

Fall, 716 A.D.
North Sea

The rolling whitecaps were a stark contrast to the dark, almost black, sea. Holger kept them within sight of the coast, but far enough away to avoid hitting any shoals or rocks. At least they hoped so. He had never been this far north, and everything was new.

One of Herlaug's men had drawn Holger a rough map of the coast, but that did them little good while at sea. It had three key markers identified, two of which had already passed. The last was supposed to be the easiest to find. If they followed the coast, they would sail into a massive bay, with land visible on both sides. On the seaward side of the bay, they would find a peninsular, and on that peninsular, they would find one of the primary fishing villages that produced stockfish.

Eight days had passed since they set sail from Orland. Though they had seen several fishing villages, they decided not to stop. They had put ashore most nights, replenishing water stocks, and hunted when possible.

As they traveled north, the green forests gave way to the colors of fall, a riot of orange and yellow hues covering the steep mountains. The nights grew longer, the air colder, and each morning, they woke to find ice on the ropes and railings.

"I thought it was still summer?" A plume of steam followed the question as Marcus stood next to Holger and rubbed both hands together.

"It is, down south." Holger nodded toward the Roman's hands. "Where are your mittens?"

Marcus looked down at his white knuckles and shrugged. "I don't know. I should find them."

"Yes, you should. Being on the ocean is a different cold." Holger turned his weathered face to the wind. "The air is salty and wet... and the wind is always blowing."

Marcus squinted at the horizon. "How much farther do you think it is?"

"He told me eight days with a strong wind." Holger looked up at the sail. "It was not very strong when we started, but has been for the last few days. The actual issue is daylight. I don't know these waters, so I cannot sail after dark. And dark comes sooner with every day."

Marcus studied the pale sky. "We have to put in to shore soon."

"Yes. I think we have at least three or four more days of sailing."

"That means it will get colder."

"Yes." Holger smiled. "Much colder."

Five days later, they were still sailing north, and Marcus was worried. Even Holger wondered if they had somehow missed the bay. Bjarne manned the helm as Holger and Marcus studied the crude map.

"Perhaps we drifted away from shore and missed the opening of the bay." Marcus pointed to the top of the map. "We could be anywhere up along here."

"I don't know how we would have done that." Holger picked his teeth with his thumbnail.

"Should we try to find a local village? They can direct us."

Holger looked up from the map, the wind whipping at the loose strands of his blonde hair. His blue eyes focused on the nearby shoreline. "Yes, if we can find a village. I have not seen one since yesterday morning."

"What's north of this?" Marcus pointed to the top of the map.

Holger grinned and shook his head. "Only the Gods—" he glanced at Marcus, "or one God, knows."

"Well, let's not be the ones to find out."

"I'll have Bjarne bring us closer to the shore so we can watch for villages." Holger stood and folded the map, shoving it into his coat. He was turning toward the helm when one of the men called out.

"A ship!"

Marcus and Holger stumbled across the deck to the railing, where the man pointed ahead of them. Sure enough, a small fishing vessel splashed through the rough seas.

Holger scrambled to the helm and instructed Bjarne to adjust their course. Soon they were closing the gap between them and the small craft. As they drew closer, Marcus could make out three men in the boat, which appeared to be dragging a net behind them.

When they were less than a hundred paces away, Holger

moved back to the bow of the boat and hailed the craft. "Hello!" He waved at the men.

His answer was a trio of scowls. Holger looked back at Bjarne and motioned for him to bring them closer to the fishing boat. As their ship angled forward, the three men on the boat stopped working their sail and glared back at them.

"Hello! We are looking for Lofoten," Holger yelled across the expanse.

The three men looked at one another and back at Holger. They huddled together, and what appeared to be a fierce debate followed. The taller of the three looked like the leader and held up his weathered hands to the others. He leaned over the railing.

"Follow!" he said, pointing to himself.

The other two men had moved back to the net and were pulling it up onto the boat.

Holger looked back at Marcus and shrugged. "I guess we follow them."

Holger had his men reduce sail so they could keep pace with the slower vessel.

Marcus watched them pull their catch, each man leaning over and grabbing the soaked net and hauling it onto the deck. He could not imagine how cold the water must be, and how numb their hands must get. After a dozen pulls, Marcus saw the first signs of their efforts. Thin, silver fish shimmered as they flopped against the netting. With each pull, the number of fish increased, until it took all three men to pull in the bulging end of the net. No longer held back by the net, the fishing boat picked up speed, and Holger added sail to keep pace.

They followed the vessel for an hour, before sighting the speck of a shoreline on the horizon. Holger glanced over at Marcus and winked. "You are almost there, my friend."

The speck gave way to a sharp sliver of a peak. Patches of

snow, glimmering in the fading light, covered the steep granite mountain. Near the base, a flat stretch of land extended to the sea. The fishing boat guided them around a series of islands, most of them single rocks poking from the water, and into a small cove.

Hundreds of seagulls met them near the cove's entrance, shrieking as they hovered above the fishing vessel. A few braver birds dived toward the pile of fish on the deck, but the fishermen were waiting, sticks in hand. Thwarted, the gulls returned to their squawking ways.

A dozen structures huddled near the center of the cove, some half on land, half on large poles that disappeared into the water. A single dock was stuck out from the middle of the small village, two other boats moored alongside. The fishing vessel lowered its sails and glided toward the dock.

Holger did the same, several men ready to man the oars if needed.

One of the fishermen on the boat pointed to the end of the pier, and Holger waved in return. He adjusted the rudder to swing the boat around and docked it perpendicular to the wharf. By the time Holger had maneuvered the ship into place, the tall man from the fishing boat had hopped onto the dock and walked to meet them.

As he approached, he motioned for the docking rope, which Marcus tossed to him. He secured the front, while one of Holger's men did the same near the aft. The man waited for Holger near the center of the boat, hands on his hips.

The fisherman was taller than Ander, though not as tall as the champion Marcus had fought. He was thin, but not skinny. Blonde hair, streaked with gray, was pulled back into a ponytail. His face was tanned and weathered, thick wrinkles cut across his forehead, with similar lines around the corners of his eyes and mouth. He waited for Holger to secure the rudder and make his way across the boat.

B. K. GREENWOOD

"What do you want?" His accent was thick, barely recognizable to Marcus.

"Fish." Holger nodded toward his boat. "We want to learn about fish."

"They swim," the other man said, with a shrug. "We throw in the net to catch them, then we eat them."

Holger looked past him to the structures beyond, focusing on the racks and posts. "I think it's a bit more complicated than that."

The man followed his gaze and turned back toward them. His eyes shifted from Holger to Marcus. After a long pause, he nodded and motioned for them to come onto the dock.

"Come. We eat." He started down the dock.

Marcus looked over at Holger and shrugged. The latter grinned. "Did you expect a warm welcome?"

"I'm glad he didn't tell us to go to hell."

Holger frowned as he stepped over the railing to the dock. Looking back at Marcus. "So, you believe in the Goddess Hel?"

Marcus followed him and chuckled. "It's complicated."

"Religion always is." Holger set off down the wharf.

The fisherman led them to the largest of the structures near the center of the village. It sat on the edge of the water, with four thick pylons holding up the front. The roof was covered with soil and moss, like all the other buildings they had seen. A thin wisp of smoke drifted from the top, promising warmth and perhaps a warm meal.

The fisherman held open the door and waved them in. Marcus had been at sea for so long that he had almost forgotten what it felt like to be in a warm room. The aroma of fresh baked bread and some sort of stew competed with the smoke that filled the room. Two women toiled near a fire, stirring an enormous cauldron, and flipping flatbread cooking on a skillet. They stopped and stared at them, but the fisherman motioned

HAMMER OF GOD

for them to continue working, then guided his guests to a long table on the far side of the fire.

He sat first, Marcus and Holger sitting across from him. The others settled around the table.

"My name is Birger." He moved aside as the woman set a cup down in front of him, along with a pitcher.

"I am Holger." He waved one hand at the Roman as more cups appeared. "This is Marcus."

"Marcus?" Birger poured the three of them a cup of pale liquid. "You are not a Northman."

"No, I'm not."

"But you speak our language?" He took a long pull from his cup.

"I learned it a long time ago." Marcus took a sip.

It was a sort of mead, but much stronger than the mead they had brought from Jutland, and not nearly as sweet. He assumed they had trouble getting honey this far north. A warmth spread down his throat and chest as he took another long pull. Now he saw the benefit.

Before they could continue, several platters of flatbread and cheese arrived. Steam was still rising from the bread as Birger tore a piece off, and, adding cheese, shoved it into his mouth. The others followed suit.

The cheese, like the mead, differed from anything he had tasted. It was sticky and pungent, almost tangy.

"Goat?" Marcus held up a piece of cheese.

"No, sheep." Birger licked his fingers.

After refilling their cups, Birger raised the pitcher toward the woman and looked back at Holger. "So, you want to learn about fish?"

Holger nodded. "Yes. Stockfish."

"Why?"

"We want to trade," Marcus said.

"Trade what?"

"Iron." Marcus took another bite of bread.

"I can't eat iron."

"I will give you grain, honey," he lifted the cup, "and mead."

"Your mead is too sweet." Birger smiled. "I tasted wine once. I would like more wine."

Marcus smiled. "Wine it is."

"How much?"

"More than you can drink."

"You must never have seen a Northman drink." He shrugged. "I will talk to the others."

"Others?" Holger said.

"The elders make all decisions. I am only one of them."

"Fair enough." Holger refilled his cup. "When?"

"I will speak to them tonight, and we can discuss it in the morning." He looked around the table, ending at Holger. "You and Marcus can sleep in my house. But I do not have room for all of you, and I cannot speak for the others. I can offer you a barn."

"I appreciate your offer," Holger said, "but we will all sleep in the barn."

"As you wish. I will show you after we eat."

As if on cue, bowls of fish stew appeared in front of each of them. It was a clear stock, with chunks of whitefish, carrots, and some sort of green leaf. Marcus took a bite, somewhat surprised at how salty it was. He took a piece of flatbread and dipped it into the stew, then shoved it into his mouth. It did not matter how salty, it was warm and filled his belly.

When they finished, Birger led them to a long, low building near the edge of the village. They had to duck to step inside, and even then, could not stand up completely.

Birger, half-stooped, looked around at them. "It is dry and warmer than your boat."

"It is all we need," Holger said. "We appreciate your hospitality."

"We shall talk in the morning." With that, he disappeared.

Marcus looked at Holger. "All we need?"

Holger chuckled. "I've slept in worse."

"In or with?" Marcus grinned.

Holger winked. "Don't tell my wife."

Shaking his head, Marcus moved to the doorway. "Let's get our bedding. And more mead."

Birger was correct, it was warm and dry. It took Marcus about an hour to get used to the smell of straw and sheep shit, but with the aid of several cups of mead, he fell asleep. It was still dark when Holger shook him awake.

"Time to get up, my friend."

Marcus sat up and accepted the cup offered to him, taking a sip. It was a mixture of warm mead and herbs. He looked around at the others, who were still asleep. "Is the sun up?"

"No," Holger said, tilting his head toward the door, "but Birger asked to see us."

Marcus gulped down his mead and dressed, joining Holger outside the barn. Birger was waiting for him, his usual expressionless face hardly visible in the pale dawn light.

"Let's go." Birger started walking toward the docks.

"Where are we going?" Marcus asked.

"To the bay."

"Why?"

Birger stopped and looked at Marcus. "Do you always ask so many questions?"

"Yes." The Roman met his gaze. "I'm a curious fellow."

Birger exhaled, his face scrunching. "We are not so curious. We do what needs to be done."

"And what needs to be done?" Marcus pressed.

Birger pointed to the bay. "One of the fishermen spotted a

wounded whale. We will kill it and bring it ashore. You will help us."

Marcus glanced over at Holger and smiled. "Why didn't you say that?"

They followed Birger to the dock, where a dozen other men were waiting, several of them holding spears.

Birger motioned to Marcus and Holger. "You go with me in my boat." He took a spear from a nearby fisherman and shoved it toward Marcus. "You look like you've used one of these before."

Marcus accepted the spear and studied it in the growing light. The handle was worn from years of use. The tip, about a foot long, was made from some sort of bone and filed to a razor-sharp point. It was secured to the spear with twine or cord of some sort, covered with a dark, almost rubbery, pitch. The wood near the blade was stained, almost black.

He followed Holger onto the boat, and a fourth man from the village joined them. Within minutes, the four small boats were untied and made their way into the bay. One of the craft took the lead, captained by the man who had spotted the wounded whale. Marcus made his way to Birger, who was manning the rudder. "Do you find wounded whales often?"

The Northman shook his head. "No, very rare." He studied Marcus. "We consider it very lucky. Some others think you brought the luck."

"And you?" Marcus grabbed the nearby railing to keep his balance as they exited the safety of the cove.

"We do not have the whale yet."

Marcus grinned and shifted his attention back to the sea. It was cold, steam rising from the dark surface. A tiny sliver of the sun crept over the horizon, driving away the shadows, and offering potential respite from the biting wind.

Marcus alternated the spear between his hands, bringing the empty one to his mouth and blowing into it to keep it

HAMMER OF GOD

warm. They had sailed for about half an hour when they heard someone in the lead boat yell. Marcus could see a man pointing to their left, and moved to the front of the boat, joining Holger.

The Northman pointed to the water. "There!"

A dark red trail dispersed across the surface, so they adjusted their course, and within a few minutes, Marcus saw the source of the blood.

The beast was barely moving, the current carrying it further out to sea. The choppy waves crashed over the whale as it struggled to stay upright. As they approached, it rolled over, a massive plume of water erupting from its spout. Blood seeped from a massive bite mark near its flipper. Next to the laceration, a large, dark eye stared back at the Roman. A tinge of sadness settled upon Marcus, but he realized that tragedy for one often meant a bounty for others. The sooner they put this majestic beast out of its misery, the better.

Birger brought them alongside, as the other fisherman on the boat brought a thin cord to Marcus and pointed to the end of the spear. Marcus lifted the end, and the man pushed the cord through a hole in the shaft, then secured the end. Nodding, he motioned toward the whale.

"I am Knud." He motioned to the whale. "Stick it behind the flipper. That is where the heart is. But do not let go."

Nodding, Marcus lifted the spear above his head and aimed for the recommended spot. Driving the weapon home, he watched the sharp tip slice through the skin and deep into the fat below. He used two hands to push the spear deeper. On the other side of the whale, a second boat had pulled alongside, and a fisherman was doing the same. As the animal spun, it nearly pulled Marcus from the boat. Releasing the shaft, he somehow stayed in the craft.

Knud glowered at Marcus and nodded to Birger. They veered away from the whale, letting the cord unwind as they went. Another boat took their place.

B. K. GREENWOOD

Within ten minutes, the whale was dead. Birger guided them around the end of the animal, and Knud produced a thick rope, tossing one end to another boat about ten paces from them. They let the rope settle into the water as they approached the carcass. The other fisherman tossed the end back when they were just past the flipper. Knud tied a slipknot, securing it tightly. Pulling the loop closed, the rope tightened around the tail, and he secured the other end to the mast.

The boat slowed to a crawl as they dragged the massive carcass through the water. Even with two additional boats tying lines to their boat to help tow them back, the sun was near its apex when they reached the cove. The craft released their lines and headed to the dock as Birger shifted them toward a standing beach near the entrance of the cove and grounded the boat.

Knud untied the line and hopped onto the sand.

Marcus glanced over at Birger. "We leave it here?"

"No." Was his only response.

Within fifteen minutes, dozens of villagers joined them on the beach, plus all of Holger's crew. Men, women, and children grabbed the rope and waited for Birger to give the signal.

The old fisherman looked back at the group, a rare smile on his weathered face. Nodding at Marcus, he yelled, "Heave!"

The group responded, pulling the whale to shore. That was the simple part.

"Heave!"

The tale slid up onto the sand, with several of the young children falling down. Birger waited for them to get back up and grab the rope. It was important that everyone in the village took part in the ritual.

"Heave!"

The carcass moved another foot or so out of the water, this time a large man fell to the ground. The children burst out

HAMMER OF GOD

laughing, and the man grabbed one of the little girls and pulled her to the sand with him.

Usually not the patient type, Birger watched them play and waited for them both to get up and wipe the sand from their clothes.

"Heave!"

Less than a foot.

"Heave!"

Inches.

"Heave!"

By now, the laughter and smiles were gone, replaced by heavy breathing and sweat. Marcus shifted his stance, burying his feet in the sand.

"Heave! Heave!"

Marcus strained against the rope, feeling the rough fibers dig into the palms of this hand. But the whale moved a foot further on shore.

"Heave! Heave!"

Another titanic effort, and a third of the whale was beached. Satisfied, Birger raised his hand into the air, and everyone dropped the rope, some bending over to recover.

"What do we do now?" Marcus managed between breaths.

"We tie it to the rocks." Birger pointed to rocks above the beach. "And the Harvest Festival begins."

"Festival?"

He smiled. "You will see."

By the end of the day, the beach was transformed. Several giant cauldrons were carried from the main longhouse and set above two fires. Tables were brought out, with chairs and a barrel of mead. Linen was laid out on the sand as Birger, a large carving knife in hand, called for Marcus and Holger to join him near the whale. The other villagers gathered around.

"We live and die by Njqror, God of the Sea. Sometimes he takes, and sometimes he gives." He met the gaze of several female villagers. "Most recently, he has taken. And given very little in return."

There was a long silence, punctuated by quiet sobs.

"But today, he has given us this wonderful treasure." He shifted his eyes to Marcus. "And it coincides with the arrival of this strange man from a faraway land. Who am I to question or doubt the ways of the Gods?" He looked around to see if anyone disagreed. Assured they did not, he handed Marcus the knife. "You shall make the first cut."

Marcus took the knife and looked down at the carcass. Leaning forward, he plunged the blade into the thick skin. There was more resistance than he expected, and it was quite a task to make a foot long slice in the blubber. The blood that seeped from the cut was deep red, almost black. A stench, like rotting fish, drifted from the wound.

"Cut here." Birger pointed alongside the gash. "Here and here." He pointed to the top and bottom.

Marcus did as instructed, cutting a long, thin piece from the carcass. Angling the blade, he cut the bottom of the piece and lifted it free. The surface was black, but the next two inches were white, and the next layer below that was blood red. It weighed much more than it looked like it should.

"Well done." Birger took it from Marcus and held it up. "Njǫror, we offer this back to you in thanks for the bounty you have given us. Please receive with our heartfelt thanks."

He took a step forward and threw the piece of meat as far as he could into the sea. The entire village watched it splash into the surf and cheered.

Birger smiled, which seemed to have become a regular occurrence. Marcus smiled back.

"Now that Njǫror has his offering, we harvest. And drink."

"What are we harvesting?" Marcus stepped back and handed the knife to Knud, who had appeared by his side.

Knud took the knife before moving to the carcass. "Everything."

Birger continued, "The blubber we will melt into oil for our lamps. We will trade some to other villages. The meat we will hang to dry, like the fish. This," he motioned to the whale, "will make winter comfortable for us. The insides will smoke and be eaten over the next few weeks. It does not do as well when dried." He pointed to where Knud was skinning the carcass. "The skin is very thin, but strong. We cut that into strips and twist it together for rope. And then we have the bones. We carve knives, shovels, and other tools. But most importantly, Hnefatafl."

"What is that?" Marcus looked from Birger to Holger.

The latter replied, "A game, played on a square board with carved pieces. The defending pieces are carved from bone, the attackers from wood. We play it all winter."

"I would like to learn this game," Marcus said.

"I'm afraid I will be too drunk to teach you tonight." Birger had accepted a drinking horn that was handed to him.

An old lady thrust a similar horn at Marcus. He grinned at her and thought she smiled as he turned away.

Holger had one as well, so they clinked horns and emptied the contents in one long pull. They spent the rest of the day, and a good part of the night, harvesting, eating, and drinking. Though the more of the latter they did, the less of the former got done.

Despite the late night, Birger was up at the crack of dawn. As he pushed open the door of the barn, the morning light spilled into the darkness.

"Roman?" Birger called into the void.

Marcus squinted at the bright opening and turned to where Holger was sleeping. The Northman groaned and turned away.

"He wants you."

"Just a moment." Marcus tossed his blanket aside, the chilled air sharp against his naked skin. The barn was warmer than sleeping outdoors, but barely. He fumbled on a pair of trousers and slipped on his tunic. After pulling on his boots, he grabbed his coat and headed for the door.

Birger, waiting outside the barn, shoved a horn toward Marcus.

The Roman shook his head. "I had enough mead last night."

"Not mead, tea." He pointed a crooked finger at his head. "Helps the pain."

"Thanks." Marcus accepted the cup and took a sip. It was thicker than he expected, and bitter. But it warmed his throat as he swallowed, and he was thankful for that.

"You wanted to see how we make stockfish." Birger had already started walking down the dirt path.

"Yes." Marcus set in behind him.

"I will show you, then we will eat breakfast." He glanced back and smiled. "Whale heart."

Marcus forced a smile and took another long pull of the tea.

Birger led them through the village, away from the cove. As they topped a small rise, the smell hit him like a punch to the nose.

"Whew," Marcus twisted his face and glanced over at Birger, "that is terrible."

The fisherman smiled. "That is why we do it over the hill."

From the top of the rise, Marcus could see a dozen wooden structures spaced across the hillock. Beyond was a massive lake, its deep blue surface sparkling in the emerging dawn. A pair of mountains towered over each side of the lake, craggy peaks spiking into the pale blue sky.

Calling them structures was a stretch. They were nothing

HAMMER OF GOD

more than a series of poles secured by rope, with a dozen additional poles strapped across the top. They stopped in front of the closest set up, and Birger pointed at the fish hanging from the poles. "We caught them the day you arrived. Cod."

Hundreds of gray fish hung in pairs, their tails tied together and slung over the pole. Now and then, a drop of blood dripped from where the heads had been chopped from the body. Birger motioned Marcus to follow to the next set of poles. These fish were more brownish.

"We caught these a month ago." They continued to the last structure. "And these in spring."

"Why hang them here?"

"The wind from the ocean dries them." He reached up and grabbed the nearest fish, peeling a piece of the flesh from the body. Splitting it in half, he took a bite and handed the other to Marcus.

Stomach rumbling, the Roman tossed it into his mouth. Slightly salty, with very little fish taste, it melted on his tongue. It was not as dry and rubbery as the one he had tasted in Gaul.

"Is this finished?"

"No, two more weeks." He nodded toward another structure closer to town. "We already packed up the ones that are ready."

Marcus looked back at the others and nodded to the closest fish. "These are much bigger."

"Yes. In spring we have king cod. Very big, easy to catch." He motioned with his hand. "Just throw the net and pull them in."

"Can you catch more than this?"

"Yes. But why?"

"I want to trade for them."

"How much?" Birger eyed him, his wrinkled forehead creased even more than usual.

"This much." Marcus motioned to all the structures.

Birger grimaced, then a blank look settled on his face as he ran mental calculations. He exhaled. "I would need three more boats. And eight men."

"We can get that."

"Hard men. Fishermen, not boys."

"How long do you need them?"

"Four months." He raised his hand with all his gnarled fingers pointing to the sky. "Starting very early spring."

"What do you want?"

"Wheat. And wine." He shook his head. "But we need to decide how much of each. We can discuss it over breakfast. The entire village must approve."

"Of course." Marcus looked down at his empty cup, his stomach growling. "About that breakfast."

"Yes." Birger turned away. "Let's go."

Whale heart was better than Marcus expected. Then again, he expected it to be awful, so anything above awful was a win. They served it with warm flatbread, nuts, fruit, and more sheep's cheese.

Holger and the rest of the crew joined about halfway through the meal. They all looked like death warmed over, heavy bags beneath their eyes, and their skin pale and shallow.

"Good morning boys." Marcus held up a cup. "Mead?"

Holger glared back at Marcus. "No." He settled down in his chair and rubbed his temples.

Marcus looked over at Birger. "I think they all need the tea."

"Yes, of course." The fisherman motioned to a lady, who nodded and disappeared toward the far end of the lodge.

A few minutes later, she was filling all their empty cups. Holger looked down into the concoction, suspicious.

"Drink. You will feel better." Marcus popped a piece of whale heart into his mouth. "Trust me."

HAMMER OF GOD

"Trusting you is how I got this headache." Holger took a long pull, draining the cup. He nodded and set the cup down. "We have something similar, but not as thick." He glanced over at Birger. "What makes it so thick?"

"Fish bone." He rubbed his fist into his palm. "We grind it into dust and add it to the tea, with some fish blood."

Marcus looked down at his cup, shrugged and took another sip.

As they finished breakfast, Marcus said to Holger, "I think we have everything we need."

"You saw how they make the stockfish?"

"Yes, very interesting. We will need to work with Herlaug to provide ships and men, but that should not be a problem." He looked over at Birger. "You can speak with the elders today?"

"Yes, we should have an answer by dinner."

"Good, we can leave tomorrow." He glanced at Holger. "Will that work?"

"No," Birger cut in.

"What? Why not?" Holger asked.

Birger nodded toward the ceiling.

They looked up to where a giant dried fish hung from the wooden raft by a thin piece of string.

"A storm is coming," the elder said.

Marcus raised his eyebrows and looked over at Holger. The Northman met him with wide eyes.

"The fish told you that?" Marcus raised one eyebrow.

"Of course not. That damn thing doesn't talk." Birger pointed to the head. "The head normally faces the fireplace. But it has spun. When it spins, it means the weather is changing. Probably tomorrow, but maybe tonight."

"For how long?" Marcus set down his cup.

"I don't know, the fish did not say." He grinned and took another sip of his tea.

221

The storm lasted for three days and four nights. At first it was rain; cold, steel rain that pounded on the wooden roof like tiny hammers. Then wind, blowing the rain sideways and through the tiny cracks in the doors. Twice a day, they ventured into the storm and made their way to the main lodge. There, the men had gathered to play Hnefatafl.

Marcus watched at first until Birger agreed to teach him the rules. The Roman was terrible and lost every game he played the first two days. And Marcus was convinced the one game he won on the third day resulted from his opponent letting him win. But, despite the suspect play of his adversary, Marcus enjoyed the hoots and hollers of the other men celebrating his victory.

But you can only play games for so long before going stir crazy, and the Roman was relieved when the storm broke near midnight of the fourth day. They stayed two more days, helping clean up some debris around the cove and securing supplies for the journey south.

The entire town, minus the men out fishing, showed up for their departure. Birger met Marcus at the end of the dock and handed him a weathered wooden box.

Marcus accepted the gift and lifted the lid. It was all the pieces he needed to play Hnefatafl, including a cloth tile used as the playing surface. He tilted his head and smiled at Birger. "Is this your personal set?"

"Yes." Birger smiled.

"I can't accept this." Marcus tried to hand it back to the fisherman.

"It's my gift to you, and you cannot refuse." His face softened. "It was my father's, but I have no children. I would like you to have it." A grin split his wrinkled face. "I will make a new set from the whale you helped us catch."

HAMMER OF GOD

"I would like to see that."

"Then come back next summer," Birger said, and patted him on the shoulder. "When you pick up your stockfish."

"I hope I can." Marcus climbed onto the boat.

Holger bid farewell to their hosts and joined Marcus on the deck, smiling as he made his way to the steer board. The crew untied the boat and pushed away from the dock. The villagers waved as they dropped several oars into the water and made for the mouth of the cove. As they moved out to the open sea, Holger motioned for his men to release the sail. When the wind filled the canvas, he looked over at Marcus. "That went far better than I expected."

Marcus glanced back at him. "What did you expect?"

"I expected some of us to die." He peered out across the horizon. "If not all of us."

"Why didn't you tell me that?"

"What fun would that be?" He winked. "Plus, we still have a long way to go before we get home."

CHAPTER SIXTEEN

There are souls which fall from heaven like flowers, but ere they bloom are crushed under the foul tread of some brutal hoof.
—Jean Paul

Late Fall, 716 A.D.
North Sea

It took them three weeks to get back to Orland. They fought against the wind and current as they sailed south, often resorting to rowing to maintain their progress. Twice they took refuge in a fjord to escape the wrath of an approaching storm, the second time barely outpacing the tempest.

The men were tired and hungry when they spotted their destination. Marcus was concerned they may have missed the wedding celebration, putting his negotiated deal at risk. His concern shifted to dread as Holger guided their vessel toward the dock. There was not a soul in sight, and the town gate was closed. A few torches burned along the palisade, and smoke drifted up into the fading sunlight.

Holger looked as concerned as Marcus felt.

"You stay here, ready to sail," Marcus said to Holger, but his gaze was on the town. "I'll see what's wrong."

The Roman took a few steps and rifled through his belongings, pulling his sword free. Strapping the scabbard belt around his waist, he hopped over the ship's railing and onto the deck. The last fading light had disappeared when he arrived at the gate. He pounded the wooden posts with the bottom of his fist.

There was no reply, so he pounded again.

A few moments later, a torch and the upper body of a man leaned over the top of the palisade and glared down at Marcus.

"What do you want?"

"I'm here to see Herlaug." He took a step back so he could look directly at the man. "I'm the Roman who visited a month ago."

The man squinted at him, then he and the torch disappeared. Marcus stood in the darkening shadow of the wall and debated pounding on the gate again. After a long silence, he raised his hand just as he heard the crossbar being lifted from within. The door swung out, the opening filled by the massive form of Rognvald.

He was dressed for war in bracers, leather tunic, and his round shield. Instead of a sword, he held a long-handled battle-ax. His expression was less than welcoming.

"What do you want?"

Puzzled, Marcus tried to peer beyond the Northman. "I came back to join the wedding."

"No wedding," Rognvald said, lifting his ax, and pointed toward the docks. "You should leave."

"What happened?" Marcus took a step forward.

B. K. GREENWOOD

Rognvald took a defensive posture. A few of the men behind him closed in formation around the warrior.

"Hold on!" A familiar voice called from within the gate, and a figure emerged from the dusk. Herlaug stood in front of his men. "The wedding is off."

"Why?"

Despite the heavy shadows, Marcus saw the myriad of emotions competing on his young face.

"She was kidnapped." His voice lowered. "By a rival."

"Kidnapped? How?"

"They ambushed my men when they were escorting her here."

"And where is she now?"

A puzzled look replaced the other expressions. "Why?"

"Aren't you going to get her?"

Herlaug glanced at his warriors, but it was Rognvald who replied. "They have more warriors than us. We could never capture their town."

"Why do we have to capture it?" Marcus looked from Rognvald to Herlaug. "We sneak in and take her back."

"We?" Herlaug said.

"Yes, we." Marcus set his jaw. "I'm part of this wedding party, so it's my responsibility as well. Where is this town?"

"Up the fjord." Herlaug jutted a finger over his shoulder.

"Are any of your men familiar with this town?"

"Yes."

"Alright." Marcus exhaled. "I'm going to get Holger and his men. Then we will come up with a plan."

"I'll wait here for you."

Marcus nodded and started back toward the dock, using the starlight to guide him. Holger must have heard him approaching and met him on the dock.

"What's going on?"

226

"We have a rescue mission." Marcus's grin was barely visible.

"What? Rescue who?" Holger frowned. "And why *we*?"

"The bride." Marcus placed his arm around Holger's shoulder. "We are part of the wedding party!"

"We?" Holger shook his head. "I knew this was going too well."

"Get the men. We will eat, drink, and plan."

Holger cast him a sideways glance. "Let's plan before we drink."

"Have it your way, but I plan better after drinking."

"That's what I'm worried about."

They sailed two nights later, when the moon was a sliver in the cloudy sky. A tiny fleet of three ships, two filled with three dozen warriors. The third was a smaller craft, powered by six of Holger's best rowers. It raced ahead, so it could drop off its passengers before the other two ships reached the town. Holger steered the vessel, with one of the local men guiding him down the fjord. Marcus and Herlaug sat in the boat's bow, both men dressed in black.

Marcus glanced over at the soot-covered face of his companion. He could sense, more than see, his nervousness.

"This will work," Marcus whispered.

The young man nodded and forced a smile, his teeth visible in the darkness.

Marcus settled deeper onto the deck, adjusting his sword. "Who is this man? The one who stole your bride."

"My older brother."

"Oh, a family feud. They are always complicated."

Herlaug was staring down at the wooden deck. "He killed my father so that he could be chief." He looked up and met

Marcus's gaze. "I challenged him and won, but I could not force myself to kill him. So, I banished him. He has been taking on thieves and misfits from other villages. They raid farms for food and sometimes fishing boats. They are a menace."

"Some men cannot carry the burden of mercy. It eats at their soul and consumes the very person you spared."

"I will not make the same mistake. I will kill him if I can."

"Your bride is the priority." Marcus shifted on the hard deck. "Will he come after you?"

"For sure."

"But it will be on our terms."

"That is what you say. I don't know what you mean." He peered at Marcus in the darkness. "You have fought many battles?"

"That is an accurate number."

"Do you get scared?"

"Yes," Marcus lied. He tried to think back to what it felt like to be scared before a battle. "I focus on those around me. They depend on me, so that helps. The first minute is the worst. After that, it just happens."

"If you live for a minute."

Marcus flicked a finger at him. "A very important point."

"Psssst."

They looked back at Holger, who held up one finger to his mouth and pointed down the fjord, where they saw the first signs of a settlement. A fire glowed near the center of a dozen or more structures in front of a single dock.

Herlaug shifted closer to Marcus, his voice barely perceptible above the soft splashing of the oars. "The palisade goes around the village."

"And you are sure there is a gate in the back?"

"Yes," he looked over at Marcus, "I am sure."

Marcus nodded as he studied the shoreline. It was heavily wooded, with large boulders rising above the water. About

HAMMER OF GOD

thirty paces ahead, there was a break in the boulders. He turned back to Holger and pointed to the gap. The latter nodded, and with a click of his tongue, the men stopped rowing and pulled their oars from the water. Holger guided the bow toward the shore, slipping it along a large, smooth rock.

Marcus reached out to keep the boat from scraping against the stone. It slid to a stop when it hit the thick grass of the shore. Holger joined him near the bow, kneeling on the slick deck.

"I'll turn the boat around and wait for you on shore. The men will be ready to go."

Marcus met his gaze. "Are you sure you can row faster than them?"

"Yes," Holger said, and extended Marcus a hand. "That I promise."

Marcus returned his grip. "Good, otherwise we get to see what kind of warrior you are."

Holger smiled. "I think that will come, no matter what we do."

"True." Marcus looked over at Herlaug. "Let's go."

They moved onto shore, their boots sinking into the spongy grass. There was no trail, so Marcus did his best to keep the shore in sight as he moved through the thick undergrowth. A short while later, they reached the forest edge, two hundred paces from the village. The open ground in front of them lay strewn with rocks, covered with a thick layer of moss. Marcus nodded to his right, and they stayed within the confines of the forest as they moved inland, reaching the steep incline of the mountain.

Exiting the tree line, they hugged the mountain as they crept toward the back of the village. And they were soon within thirty paces of their objective. They found a clump of rocks and settled down on the wet, dewy moss.

"Now what?" Herlaug said.

"We wait for the distraction." Marcus nodded to the fjord.

The clouds faded into the night, revealing a million stars above the jagged peaks of the nearby mountains. The water in the fjord was a black void beyond the flickering fires of the village.

A horn shattered the peaceful night.

"Here we go." Marcus sprang to his feet and started toward the palisade, Herlaug right beside him.

They were at the wall when a series of horns meant Herlaug's warriors were approaching the dock. A few steps brought them to the gate. As practiced, Marcus knelt down and cupped his hands, which Herlaug stepped into. Marcus lifted him up high enough to grab the top of a pole. Pushing both of his feet, Marcus watched the Northman disappear over the palisade.

A few moments later, he heard wood scratching against wood as the beam securing the door was lifted away. Marcus pushed the door open as he pulled a dagger from his scabbard. The Northman leaned the beam against the palisade and turned back to Marcus.

The Roman could hear men yelling and calling the alarm as they scrambled from longhouses. Marcus moved to the closest structure, Herlaug right behind him. The former peered around the corner and spotted several figures outlined by the firepit in the center of the village. The size of the group increased until they had all assembled. Within minutes, they were headed toward the dock.

Marcus nodded to Herlaug, and they snuck along the shadows, moving toward the largest of the longhouses. Kneeling, Marcus pointed to a man standing near the door of the next building over. "I'd guess that is the place."

"Yes." Herlaug looked over at Marcus. "How do we get in there?"

HAMMER OF GOD

"I'm going to move around to that building. When you see me, walk toward him. I'll take care of the rest."

Without waiting for a response, Marcus disappeared back the way they had come. A minute later, he was standing near the corner of the longhouse and waved at Herlaug. The Northman nodded and stepped into the firelight, striding toward the guard.

Marcus heard the guard curse and then saw the large man by him. Tightening the grip on his dagger, he lunged forward, grabbing the man by his hair and shoving the blade into the base of his skull. He was dead before he hit the ground. Marcus pulled the blade free and moved toward the longhouse's entrance.

A single fire burned in the center of the dark interior. Marcus motioned for Herlaug to walk down the middle of the room as he slipped into the shadows. The room was eerily quiet. He paced the Northman as the latter advanced across the room. He was worried they would need to move to another longhouse when Herlaug darted forward. "Astrid!"

Marcus rushed to join him.

Someone had secured her hands with a rope to a ring in the wall. Her dress, or what was left of it, hung from her scratched and bruised body. But she was not alone. There were two other young girls secured to other rings.

"Fuck," Marcus muttered. He looked up at Herlaug, then nodded toward the rope.

The Northman cut Astrid free as Marcus moved to the others.

"What are you doing?"

"I am going to free them as well."

"That will make Gorm mad. He will attack us for sure." He looked at Astrid. "If we only take her, he may not attack."

Marcus took a step forward, the firelight dancing in his

eyes. "Let him come. I will not leave them to his wrath." He spun back toward the others without waiting for a response.

As Marcus cut the others free, they eyed him warily. His response was blunt. "You can stay. Or you can come with us and be free. Your choice, but you must choose now."

They looked at each other and back at Marcus. "We go."

"Good. Do as I say." He nodded to Herlaug. "Let's move."

Once outside, they heard yelling and cursing coming from the dock. As they headed back toward the gate, three figures stepped from the shadows.

"Where do you think you are going?" The tallest freed his sword.

Marcus turned to the others. "Go."

Herlaug ushered the girls away as Marcus pulled his sword and dagger out, then lunged toward the nearest man. The Northman stabbed his blade at Marcus, but the Roman parried the attack with his dagger, twisting the sword to expose his enemy's wrist. A quick strike severed his hand. As he stumbled away, gripping his bleeding stump, Marcus ducked the next attack, and, taking a step forward, planted his foot into the man's chest, knocking him back into the dying fire.

As the man screamed and rolled away from the embers, Marcus dodged a hasty thrust from the remaining Northman. The Roman countered with several blows, before burying his dagger in his man's throat.

Marcus spun around to see the man on fire gain his feet and take off, running toward the water. Seeing more figures in the darkness, he pivoted and ran toward the rear gate. Herlaug and the girls were nowhere to be seen when Marcus bolted through the opening. Instead of taking the path they had used to approach the settlement, he hurried across the field. But the moss was slick, and his boot slipped from a stone into a hole, causing him to stumble.

He stood up, a sharp pain shooting up his right leg. It did

not seem broken, but it was surely sprained. Hobbling forward, he crashed through the brush and along the shoreline. Tripping once over a fallen log, and a second time when he ran into a low branch.

Within minutes, he was covered with sweat, leaves, and mud. The sound of pursuit only added to his predicament. He had resigned himself to making a last-ditch stand when he heard a voice through the trees.

"We have to go!" It was Herlaug. "There were three of them. He could not have survived."

Scowling from the pain and insult, Marcus staggered through the undergrowth. Holger's response heartened him. "I'll die on this shore before I leave him."

Marcus pushed the last of the branches aside. "Luckily, it won't come to that," he said, and gingerly slid down the grass bank.

"See, not a scratch," Holger motioned to a rower. "Help him in."

"No, no." Marcus flicked a thumb over his shoulder and shuffled through the shallow water. "They are right behind me."

Ignoring the sharp pain, he leapt into the boat.

The men buried their oars, and an instant later they were speeding from the shore. And not a moment too soon, as a dozen men emerged from the forest.

"Herlaug! I know it is you!" The man jumped into the water. "I will burn down your village and enslave all your women and children!"

Marcus grinned in the pale moonlight. "I guess that settles that."

Herlaug tried to smile, but it never materialized.

CHAPTER SEVENTEEN

*In the end, we will remember not the words
of our enemies, but the silence of our friends.*
—Martin Luther King Jr.

Late Fall, 716 A.D.
North Sea

"What happened?" Marcus unbuckled his sword and hung it on a post in the wall. Moving to the table, he settled onto the bench.

Rognvald handed him a full cup of ale. "We blew the horn as we approached the village, like we agreed." He took a sip, the ale gathering in beads on his long mustache. "We unloaded half the men on the dock and formed a shield wall. The bastards gathered on the shore and attacked."

"How many?" Marcus asked.

Rognvald looked around the table for Herlaug, but the latter was busy getting Astrid settled. "Eighty, perhaps more."

HAMMER OF GOD

"After they attacked?"

"We held on for as long as we could, but they could rotate in fresh warriors." He met Marcus's gaze.

"I'm sure you did. Were you able to disable their ships?"

"Yes, my men chopped holes in the decks while we fought. But they will repair them."

"But that buys a few days to prepare. Casualties?"

"Two men dead, another six wounded. Mostly when we retreated to the boat." He took another drink of ale. "Three of six can still fight."

"Are you one of the six?" Marcus nodded to the bandage wrapped around his left biceps.

"No, that is only a scratch." He smiled at Marcus. "I hear you twisted your ankle."

"I did." Marcus grinned. "Running from a dozen crazy Northmen."

"Smart choice."

"Evening." Holger plopped down next to Marcus and helped himself to a cup.

"Rognvald was filling me in on the diversion. It seems we can expect eighty—"

"Or more," Rognvald said.

"Or more, warriors," Marcus corrected.

"And how many can you field?" Holger asked.

"Forty men. About half of them warriors. The others are fishermen."

"I have twelve." He tilted his head at Marcus. "And him."

"Thirty-five against eighty, or more," the Roman added before Rognvald could correct him. He picked up his cup, holding it close to his lips as he thought. "I've faced worse odds." He took a long pull.

"And you lived through it." Holger shrugged.

Marcus grinned. "Of course."

The others chuckled, but it faded as Herlaug joined them.

He grabbed the nearby pitcher and an empty cup, filling and draining it in one long gulp. Refilling the cup, he looked around at the others, all but the Roman avoided his gaze.

"How is she?" Marcus asked.

"Tired." He looked into the amber surface of his cup.

"She'll be fine after some rest," Marcus said.

"Will she?" He looked up at him. "She flinches when I touch her."

Marcus set down his cup. "That is normal. She is young, and she experienced things no woman should endure. You need to give her time." He leaned forward and looked into his eyes. "Do you understand me?"

"How do you know?"

He did not know. Though many close to him had suffered similar tragedies, he could not say they would ever be the same. His wife never lived long enough to recover. He never found his daughter, and he left before Rebecca dealt with the trauma. But he would not tell Herlaug that. The best chance this girl had at a normal life was a patient man by her side.

"Because I've experienced this, and the best thing you can do is give her the time she needs."

"I'm sure she blames me for this happening." He looked back down to his cup.

"Perhaps, but you have to make sure it doesn't happen again."

"And how do we do that?" Herlaug glanced around the table.

"Marcus was going to tell us about his plan," Rognvald said.

"I was?" The Roman refilled his cup. "I was hoping you guys had an idea."

"I do." Holger set down his cup. "They don't have enough men to siege the town, so they will have to attack it. We don't have enough men to protect all the walls, and they know that. They will split up and attack from different directions."

"Yes, that is how I would do it," Rognvald said.

"So, we keep them from splitting up."

"And how do we do that?" Herlaug was skeptical.

"I saw something once that I think will work." He looked up back at Herlaug. "But it will require everyone helping."

"Every man, woman and child in the village will help."

"Good." Holger nodded toward Marcus. "I have a special plan for you, my friend."

"Is it dangerous?" the Roman asked.

"Extremely."

"I want to be part of it," Rognvald said.

"No, I have a special plan for you." He looked around the group. "We will pick eight more men, the best we have." He met Marcus's gaze.

"I will take Bjarne."

"Are you sure?"

"He needs to experience battle, not fight behind a wall."

"If you say so."

"Don't worry, I'll keep him by my side." Marcus finished his cup. "As soon as I'm told what it is that I'm doing."

"I'll show you in the morning." Holger looked around. "Right now, I need food or I'll be too drunk to tell you anything."

Herlaug had food brought to them, and they spent the rest of the night eating, with less drink. It was clear they had a lot of work in front of them, and staying up late drinking was not part of the plan.

They spent two days making the preparations. Most of the men dug trenches, while the women and children gathered all the firewood they could. The boats were moved away from the dock and stored in a nearby cove to prevent them from being damaged by Gorm and his men.

Marcus spent several hours each morning and afternoon sparring with Bjarne, focusing on his defensive skills. The young man was a natural swordsman and picked up new skills quickly.

On the afternoon of the second day, they practiced side by side against a half-dozen men. Marcus paused the action several times to give Bjarne instruction. Near the end, Bjarne was tiring and lunged at an opponent, who capitalized on the mistake.

"Stop!" Marcus spun his wooden sword around and buried it in the dirt. He took a step toward the teenager, who was panting and covered with sweat. "You are going to get tired. It's natural." He tapped him on the forehead. "That's why you have to use your head. Conserve your energy, maintain a strong defensive posture, and use quick strokes." He motioned forward with his hand. "Stabbing is easier than slashing. Stay focused and you'll stay alive. Got it?"

"Yes, sir."

"Good, one more time." Marcus retrieved his sword, and they sparred again.

Soon after, he looked up at the setting sun and nodded to the men. "That's enough for today. Let's get something to eat."

Marcus followed Bjarne to a nearby water barrel and waited for his chance to quench his thirst.

"Does it hurt?" Bjarne asked.

"Does what hurt?" Marcus took a few gulps of water.

"Getting stabbed."

"It depends. Sometimes it happens in battle, and you don't even realize it. But it always hurts later."

"Have you been stabbed many times?"

Marcus chuckled. "More times than I can count," then added, "but nowhere important."

"I want to make my father proud." The lanky young man's eyes were blue, crisp and bright.

Ah, youth. Marcus knew his eyes would never shine like that again. "Of course you will." He nodded toward the others. "Now, go get some food."

Marcus watched Bjarne amble away and scooped another cup of water from the barrel. He drank it down and hung the cup on the side of the barrel. Looking around, he found Holger near the trench they had dug from the waterline to the palisade.

The Northman had his arms crossed as he watched the others fill the trench with wood and kindling.

"Looks impressive." Marcus nodded at the nearby barrel. "What is that?"

"Whale oil." Holger pointed to the trench. "It will burn hotter."

"Won't it set the palisade on fire?" Marcus looked toward the town.

"We soak it in sea water. It won't burn."

Marcus looked at the trench, then toward the water. "What if they attack during the day? They'll see the trench."

"We'll light it earlier." He glanced at Marcus. "They'll attack at night."

"Why do you think that?"

"Even though they outnumber us, attacking a walled town is hard. They will want the cover of darkness."

"Makes sense." The Roman looked around the landing. "You got my spot ready?"

"Yes, I hope it's deep enough. Should be room for two men." His weathered face twisted in concern. "You'll watch out for Bjarne?"

"Yes. I've been working with him for two days." Marcus placed a hand on his shoulder. "He will be fine."

Nodding, Holger started toward a large pot hanging over a firepit. "Let's eat."

Holger was correct. They attacked at night.

A loud horn blast startled Marcus from his slumber. He was lying on a fur blanket near the base of the palisade. As he rolled to his feet, another blast punctuated the night, this time followed by three short blasts. Their lookout had spotted three ships approaching.

Marcus grabbed his sword and buckled it on. He was already wearing his armor and had decided not to use a shield. Bjarne appeared by his side, the whites of his eyes glowing in the pale moonlight.

"It's time." Marcus checked the young man's armor and the straps of his shield. He tightened the latter and patted him on his chest. "Let's go."

The eight other hand-picked men joined them. Holger and a few others followed them to a group of holes. The men dropped inside, kneeling to stay below the ground.

Marcus extended one hand to Holger, and they grasped each other by the wrist. "Good luck, Northman. Don't forget, three quick blasts."

"I'll remember. Try not to die, Roman."

"What fun is that?"

Marcus climbed into the holes and waited for Holger to lay several planks across the top, shutting them in. He heard them lay a canvas across the planks, then cover it with a layer of dirt.

It was pitch dark. Shifting around, Marcus settled down and waited, and he felt Bjarne do the same thing next to him.

It was stifling and smelled of dampness and earth. Marcus closed his eyes and tried to listen beyond their little world. Sweat dripped down his face and neck, trickling beneath the tunic and his armor.

After what seemed like hours, he heard several men yelling.

"Get ready," he whispered as he shifted to his knees.

HAMMER OF GOD

A few moments later, Marcus heard the roar of fire, and soon after, the light from the bright flames slipped through the gaps of the boards. What seemed an eternity later, they heard several short horn blasts.

Marcus pushed the boards aside and crawled from the hole, dirt pouring in around him. He reached down and pulled Bjarne to his feet.

As the others emerged from their holes, Marcus looked around at hell on earth. Thick black smoke billowed everywhere, with a wall of fire as tall as a man, leading from the shore to each wall of the palisade. The sound of battle called to them from beyond the smoke.

Marcus motioned the men forward as he pulled his sword free. He looked over to ensure Bjarne was by his side and started toward the melee. The ten men in his tiny group spread out, about two paces between each man. As they neared the palisade, the cursing and clanking of iron grew louder.

A few steps later, the forms of the attacking Northmen appeared through the smoke. Marcus glanced over at Bjarne, their eyes locking. Nodding, Marcus rushed forward.

It is normal for Northman to yell when they charge, but the success of their plan depended on stealth and confusion, so Marcus had instructed his men to proceed in silence. And so, they did.

Marcus fought with his sword and dagger. He plunged the former into the back of an attacking Northman, spinning away and pulling it free. The Roman was already stabbing another man in the throat with his dagger as the first victim fell to the ground. Out of the corner of his eye, Marcus saw Bjarne stab a taller man, the blade four or five inches into the man's lower back.

Each man secured at least one, if not two, kills before the attackers realized they had been flanked. Marcus was just finishing off his fourth man when the group turned en masse on the ten men.

Although expected, it was the most dangerous part of the plan. Marcus called the men together, and they formed a small half circle shield wall, with Marcus in the rear. Any of the enemy Northmen who attempted to flank the circle encountered the angry blade of the Roman.

One of the nine men in the shield wall went down with a sharp cry. The men standing next to him attempted to close the gap, but that further weakened the line. Marcus felt the tide shifting, and they were moments from collapsing when Holger launched the last phase of the plan.

The town gate flew open, and dozens of warriors poured from the opening, Rognvald in the lead. They crashed into the rear of the Gorm's Northmen, slicing through their vulnerable ranks. Holger and Herlaug were among the new arrivals, the latter searching for his brother.

The Northmen lived up to their fierce reputation. Undaunted by the second surprise attack, they fought back with enviable tenacity. The battle devolved into a series of individual struggles; the air was filled with grunts, groans, and shrieks of pain.

Marcus used his superior speed and strength to incapacitate his enemies. He stayed close to Bjarne, who was holding his own against a more seasoned warrior. He had a wound of some sort on the side of his head, but otherwise seemed unscathed. The odds of victory rose as the size of Gorm's party shrank. A few of the older men who had manned the walls joined the battle, adding to the momentum of the defenders.

As the attackers surrendered, Marcus spun back toward Bjarne. He was fighting an older warrior wielding a battle ax. The younger man was holding his own until he slipped on a patch of bloody grass. He fell to the ground, arms splayed.

HAMMER OF GOD

Marcus dashed forward, but could not stop the Northman from bringing his ax down on Bjarne's left arm, severing his hand above the wrist. As Bjarne screamed in pain, Marcus ran the older Northman through with his blade, then pulled it out as the warrior fell to his knees. Spinning the weapon in his hand, Marcus drove the blade down into his clavicle.

Marcus let go of the sword as the dying man slumped to the ground and rushed to Bjarne's side. The teenager was in shock, his wide eyes staring at his bleeding stump. Marcus pulled his belt from his waist and knelt beside him.

"Hold on." He slipped the belt under his forearm and through the loop. Pulling it tight, he ignored Bjarne's cries of pain. He cinched it tighter until the flow of blood from the wound had stopped. The young man's face was sweaty and pale.

Marcus felt, rather than heard, someone approaching. He looked up in time to see an enemy Northman bearing down on him, sword raised. Lunging forward, Marcus caught him around the waist and drove him backward. The man could not spin his sword to stab Marcus, so he smashed the hilt of his weapon into Marcus's back. Grunting, the Roman ignored the blow and drove the man farther into the ground, where the two rolled around on the dirt and grass.

Marcus used one arm to pin his opponent and stretched for a nearby rock. He wrapped his fingers around the melon sized stone and swung it sideways, catching his enemy above his ear. The man flailed at Marcus, dropping his sword, and trying to gouge the Roman's eyes. Shifting his weight, Marcus struck him again, this time eliciting a loud crack, confirming his skull was fractured. Marcus smashed him two more times until he lay motionless.

Marcus dropped the rock and exhaled, scanning the battlefield. All the fighting had stopped. A few of Gorm's men kneeled on the ground, hands on their heads, surrounded by a dozen of Herlaug's men.

Marcus looked down at his blooded hands, wiped them on his tunic, and stood. Holger appeared out of nowhere and extended a bloody hand toward Marcus. The Northman's weathered face was splattered with blood, mud, and soot. "Glad to see you alive, my friend." He pulled Marcus to his feet.

"You as well." Marcus nodded behind him. "Bjarne is hurt."

Holger looked over the Roman's shoulder and winced. "At least it is not his sword hand."

"True." Marcus took a few steps and pulled his sword from the dead Northman. "Herlaug?"

"He killed Gorm. That is when the others surrendered."

As a shadow descended upon them, Marcus turned and looked up at Rognvald. The giant Northman had a flesh wound on his right shoulder, but otherwise seemed uninjured.

"Good plan," he smiled, "for a fisherman."

"Sailor, not fisherman."

"Aren't they the same thing?"

Holger exhaled and looked over at Marcus.

"Don't get me involved," the Roman said.

"How is he?" Marcus looked down at the young teen, but his question was directed at Holger.

"Drunk. But I'm afraid that won't be enough."

Marcus glanced over at the iron laying in the nearby fire and clenched his jaw. Herlaug was kneeling beside Bjarne, ready to hold him down.

"Open your mouth," Herlaug instructed.

The drunk teen parted his lips, thinking he was about to get more alcohol. Instead, Herlaug placed a rolled-up piece of leather between his teeth.

Marcus knelt on Bjarne's other side and held down his shoulder as the village laeknir cleaned the wound with warm water. Drying it with a cloth, he nodded to Holger, who was standing by the fire. The Northman pulled the iron from the flames, the flat tip a pulsating orange glow.

Marcus used one hand to lift Bjarne's chin toward him. Looking into his eyes, the Roman said, "Don't hold your breath. And bite down as hard as you can."

The sizzle of hot iron on flesh was lost in the heartbreaking screams of the teen. His thin frame tried to squirm away, but a dozen hands held him in place. The stench of burning flesh filled the air as the young lad, thankfully, passed out.

Marcus watched the laeknir apply a salve of boiled honey to the scorched flesh and wrapped a clean cloth around the wound. He laid the arm across the boy's lap and stood.

"He's young." The old man wiped his hands on his tunic. "If he lives a week, he will recover."

"Except he won't have a hand." Holger looked from the laeknir to Marcus and shrugged. "It's true."

"It's his shield hand." Marcus glanced back down at the boy. "He can adapt."

"I guess we will see."

"Now can we go home?"

The Northman chuckled. "No, we cannot cross the sea this time of year. We must remain for the winter."

"One winter." Marcus looked around at the beautiful mountains, his gaze returning to Holger. "How bad can it be?"

EPILOGUE

*The Christian resolution to find the world ugly and
bad has made the world ugly and bad.*
—Friedrich Nietzsche

Spring, 717 A.D.
Metz, Duchy of Austrasia

The sun was setting between a pair of ragged peaks; the shadows extended across the fertile valley below. A soft breeze carried the scent of spring and the promise of warmer days to come. A few scattered clouds flitted across the otherwise empty sky. The chirping of birds echoed from the nearby forest, across the open fields and up to the walls of the fortress.

Marcus took it all in, basking in the warmth. The evening was a stark contrast to the last five months he had spent up north. He had never been so cold, for so long. By the time they had launched their ship to return home, he wondered if his frozen bones would ever recover.

HAMMER OF GOD

"Welcome home."

Marcus turned to find Thomas standing a few feet away. The Roman smiled and took several steps forward, embracing his old friend. "Thank you." The embrace was longer and more intense than usual. Marcus leaned back and looked into his dark brown eyes. "I've missed you."

"And we have missed you." Thomas smirked as he studied Marcus's long beard. "And you have missed the cutting shears."

"This?" Marcus stroked his beard, a habit he had taken up over the winter. "This kept me warm in that frozen wasteland."

"That bad?"

Marcus chuckled. "Worse. They say hell is hotter than an Egyptian desert." He shook his head. "But if hell is as miserable as they say, then it must be cold. Cold like the Northland."

"It sounds terrible. Remind me never to go."

"I was thinking of taking you and the ladies up there later this year." Marcus could not help but smile. "You'll have all winter to convert them to Christianity... and they will have nowhere to run when you start."

Thomas grinned. "I think I'll pass." He tilted his head to the side. "Did you find what you were looking for?"

Marcus nodded. "Yes, Charles will have all the stockfish his men can eat, and more."

"In exchange for?"

"Iron. Good quality iron, not that shit they have up north."

"Seems like a fair trade."

Marcus smirked. "I guess."

"You don't think so?"

Marcus paused and walked toward the edge of the battlements, resting his arms on the cool stone. Thomas joined him and looked out across the field.

"It's inhospitable." Marcus glanced over. "It's beautiful, but they barely survive the winters. The lands are not capable of supporting large numbers, yet they are growing."

"So, they will look for other lands."

"Yes. I'm afraid they will."

"They won't be the first. Men have been migrating forever."

"Not men like this." Marcus placed one elbow on the wall. "They are born fighting the elements. Every day is a struggle for survival. It's like they've spent their entire lives in a forge. Even the weakest among them is stronger than most of the men I know. And now we are giving them better weapons."

"Are you questioning the deal you made?"

"No. I'm questioning what we have done." He shook his head. "We used violence to put Charles in power. And he will continue that violence to secure his kingdom. And we did that to counter Islam."

"As we should." Thomas studied him. "Or should we let Islam sweep across Gaul as well?"

"What's the difference?" Marcus bit his lip. "I've seen hundreds of men in power, and they are all the same. They subjugate. They pillage. They tax. And they do anything they can to stay in power." He looked at Thomas. "We may call it tithes or donations, or whatever else the church wants to call it. It's taxation. We tax the poor and build giant churches, or fund wars. For what?"

"To protect them from Islam. To deliver them to the heavenly father." Thomas squinted back at Marcus. "I thought you believed."

Marcus looked away; his eyes focused on the darkness beyond the wall. "I want to believe."

"I understand." Thomas moved back to the wall. "Faith is uneven. Like the tides. It ebbs and flows."

"Even for you?" Marcus glanced over to his friend.

"Especially for me." Thomas's features grew dark. "The deeper the faith, the deeper the doubt."

Marcus nodded. "It doesn't matter. The Northmen will come, whether or not we give them weapons."

HAMMER OF GOD

"Perhaps we can get them to fight the Saracens." Thomas grinned.

"Perhaps." Marcus shrugged. "But the Northmen are not driven by religion. At least, not yet." He winked at Thomas. "Maybe after next winter."

"That is not happening." Thomas shifted his gaze to the nearby mountains deep in shadows, shadows that seemed to extend across his face. "I know about Allard."

A knot formed in the pit of Marcus's stomach as he leaned on the wall. He had no response.

"I found out a few weeks after you left. Rebecca had been acting strangely, and I couldn't figure out why. Then one night, she started crying. That's when she told me."

"I'm sorry," Marcus whispered. "I should have—"

"No. It was not your place to tell me." Thomas paused, swallowing back the emotions welling up inside. "You did as Rebecca asked, and I respect that." He looked over at Marcus. "I'm sorry I was so hard on you when you attacked the count."

"My previous behavior earned that criticism."

"I wish I could have killed him," Thomas whispered.

"I don't. You don't need that stain on your soul."

Thomas shook his head and, after a long pause, asked, "Did it make you feel better?"

Marcus bit his lower lip, one hand running down his beard. "They say killing doesn't fill the emptiness. That revenge is a fool's errand, leaving you in a darker place than when you started. And, in a way, I agree. That happened when I tried to avenge my family. But that vengeance was indiscriminate." He looked Thomas in the eye. "That is not the case when I killed Allard. I knew no other woman would suffer like Rebecca did. So yes, I felt better."

Thomas nodded and looked back toward the valley beyond. They never spoke of it again.

Marcus tightened the strap on the bag he was securing to his horse. He tied the loose end and turned to pick up another. Isabella had somehow snuck up behind him and handed him the sack.

"Leaving already?"

"Yes, I'm joining Charles on the campaign." He took the sack from her, tied it next to the other, and smiled. "I don't stay in one place often."

"I know." She looked down at her hands and back up at Marcus. "When will you be back?"

"Fall, unless I get myself killed."

She cocked her head to the side and glared at him.

"I know. That's not funny."

"No, it's not." She met his gaze. "You come back a different person."

He stared back at her. She was so beautiful, smart, and witty. Everything a man would want, and he wanted her. He wanted to take her into his arms and kiss her and never let her go. But then he thought about the man he was when he came back after dying. The man riddled with guilt. It was not fair to expect her to live with that man.

"Yes, I do."

"You could not leave. Not fight. You wouldn't get killed." There was hope in her eyes, like a small flame struggling to keep the kindling lit. But the flame faded when she saw his expression. "But that's not who you are."

He looked down at the stable's straw-covered floor and back at her. Tears had formed in her green eyes. He pushed his words past the lump in his throat. "No, it's not."

"Someday." She took a deep breath, seeming to will her tears not to fall. She stepped toward him, her arms open wide. "Be careful."

"I will." He embraced her, the scent of her hair gentle on his mind as he whispered, "I love you. I just don't—"

"I know." She hugged him tighter.

He held on for as long as he could. Then she pulled away, using one hand to wipe away a persistent tear. She forced a smile and started toward the stable door.

He returned his attention to his horse, running one hand down the smooth hair of its neck. "I guess it's you and me."

The horse's head bobbed up and down, one eye staring back at Marcus. He swallowed his regret, pulled himself up into the saddle, and angled his steed toward the door. A light rain was falling, but he did not bother pulling out his cloak. The cool drops were a welcome distraction as he rode toward the fortress gate. As he cleared the opening, he glanced back at the cowled figure standing on the wall above. She lifted one hand. He raised his hand in response and shifted his gaze to the road ahead. It was going to be a long ride.

DEAR READERS

Thank you for reading this Last Roman Prequel. I hope you enjoyed it! If so, please take a few moments to leave a review on Amazon and Goodreads (links on the following page). It may not seem important, but reviews are the absolute lifeblood of independent authors. You don't have to write anything; just tossing me a few stars will suffice (the more, the better). Thirty seconds of your time can help me for a lifetime!

If you have not had the chance to read the other books in the series, now would be a great chance to check them out!

I will continue to release additional prequels and short stories focused on main characters from *The Last Roman* series. Sign up for my newsletter, so you don't miss out!

Thanks for continuing this beautiful friendship,
B.K.

STAY CONNECTED!

Click the **+Follow** button on my Amazon author page.
author.to/bkgreenwood

Email updates: www.bkgreenwood.com

Facebook.com/bkgreenwood

Twitter.com/bkgreenwood70

Instagram.com/bkgreenwood70

PLEASE LEAVE A REVIEW

Just 30 seconds of your time can make all the difference. You might not think it's that important, but reviews are the lifeblood of all independent authors. You don't even have to write anything. Leaving some stars would be enough.

30 seconds of your time can help me for a lifetime! As an independent author, you—the readers—are my greatest strength. Just go to Amazon or Goodreads and drop some stars, or tell everyone how you feel about the book.

Thank you so much for your help with this.
I am honoured to share my worlds with you all.

How to Leave an Amazon Review

- Go to your order detail page
- In the US - Amazon.com/orders
- In the UK - Amazon.co.uk/orders
- Click **Write a product review** button next to your book order.
- Rate the item and write your review then click **Submit.**

ABOUT THE AUTHOR

B.K. Greenwood was born in Derry, New Hampshire, but moved to Chandler, Arizona as a young child. In 2014, he relocated to Austin, Texas, where he now resides with his wife and wolfpack of 3 rescue dogs. When not writing, he enjoys board games, taking the pups on new hikes, and reading.

B.K. loves to travel and has incorporated his experiences into his writing. He reads works of fiction and nonfiction, emphasizing history, adventure, and classics. His passion for history is on display in his series, *The Last Roman*.

Follow his Amazon Author Page:
author.to/bkgreenwood

facebook.com/bkgreenwood

 x.com/bkgreenwood70

 instagram.com/bkgreenwood70

ALSO BY B.K. GREENWOOD

The Last Roman Trilogy
01 - The Last Roman: Exile (2021)

02 - The Last Roman: Abyss (2021)

03 - The Last Roman: Absolution (2022)

The Last Roman Prequels
Hammer of God - A Last Roman Prequel (2023)

The Last Roman Short Stories
Monsoon - A Last Roman Tale (2021)

Hatchet - A Last Roman Tale (2021)

Horns - A Last Roman Tale (2022)

Impale: A Last Roman Tale (TBD)

The Last Roman Novellas
Insurrection - A Last Roman Novella (2023)

You can find all B.K. Greenwood's books at his Amazon Author Page:

author.to/bkgreenwood

Printed in Great Britain
by Amazon

42072640R00149